Once Upon A...
Montana Summer

ONCE UPON A...
Montana
Summer

LISA T. BERGREN

Once Upon a Montana Summer
© 2018 by Lisa T. Bergren

Published by BCG Press
7814 Potomac Drive
Colorado Springs, CO 80920

Printed in the United States of America

ISBN 978-0-9885476-1-2

This is a work of fiction. All characters are products of the author's imagination, and any resemblance to actual persons, living or dead, is coincidental.

Cover design by Timothy J. Bergren
Cover photography by Linda Washburn Roberts and People Images (iStockphoto)

CHAPTER 1

"Miss Stalling!" called a photographer, stepping into her path to make her look up at him.

"Adalyn!" shouted another, trying to get her to turn his way when she ducked her head.

Numerous flashes from several cameras in the dark hallway nearly blinded her.

Adi groaned, lifted her briefcase like a shield and pushed past them as a third took several shots in a row. They'd found her secret passage—the one she took from the parking garage, around the whole length of the building, in order to get to her office via the elevator.

"C'mon!" cried a third. "Give us a flash of that pretty smile! Let us print some pics that will make that jerk regret his decision!"

George, one of the security guards, opened the door at the far end and scowled at the men who followed Adi. "You three!" he bellowed, waving a meaty hand. "Get out of here and leave Ms. Stalling alone! I told you if I found you pesterin' her one more time, I'd call the cops!"

They gave up then, lifting their hands in surrender as they always did. They weren't breaking any laws—trying to get Adi's picture or a few words from her—but neither did they want to be barred from entering the property of Smith & Jessen. Because then, they'd lose a key opportunity to sell a picture to *People* or *Us* or worse, the tabloid papers. Outside, after work, it was even more of a gauntlet. They'd tailed her car all the way home, to the grocery store, the gym...in a very short period of time, the paparazzi had made her a virtual recluse.

She shook her head. How long would it go on? A year ago, when the season of *The One* had ended and Adam gave the final rose to Talia and not Adi—the fan favorite—people had rallied around her. Then when producers convinced her to give it a go as the bachelorette and she'd chosen Connor as "The One"—and he'd immediately proposed—America swooned.

Heck, Adi had swooned too. She'd finally, *finally* found love.

On national television.

Then, three months later, he broke if off. Adi had nodded, stunned, through his cool apologies in the midst of the recap show, describing it as an "unfortunate change of heart."

Shocked, appalled, half the audience practically booed him off-stage. The other half sat in startled silence, perhaps because they secretly hoped that somehow, some way, Connor could be their boyfriend. Or perhaps because they had favored one of the other bachelors for Adi. Who knew?

It was all because of the show, Adi, he'd said afterward, off-stage. *You understand. I got swept up in it all. So were you, right? They got exactly what they were after. Capturing two people falling in love. But it wasn't real, right? It was all just... make believe. A show. A really good show, but more like a mov-*

ie than real life. You're with me on that, right?

Right, she'd mumbled, feeling her head nod, as if it had become disconnected from her body. Disconnected from her heart screaming *wrong, wrong, wrong.*

"America's Sweetheart Shattered," was one of the hundred tabloid headlines that stuck in her mind, because she *had* been shattered. Totally flayed open, Connor's dismissal like a slice across a heart that had barely healed after Adam sent her home six months prior. She had been so sure that Adam was about to get down on one knee and open a gorgeous Tiffany box with the square-cut diamond she'd always wanted. When he broke it off, sent her home, she hadn't shed a single tear she was so shocked. She'd been utterly blindsided. All along, Adi hadn't been able to believe he was drawn to her, *choosing* her, week after week. And then in the end, she couldn't believe that he *hadn't* chosen her.

After all, he'd said the words.

I love you. Adalyn, I think you're the one for me.

Said them. Not once, but twice. A good portion of America had witnessed it with her.

She'd made herself watch the episodes to make sure she remembered it correctly, sobbing through every one, especially those last four, watching the tragedy unfold, edited for max impact. At the same time Adam had been confessing his love to her, he'd also been confessing his love for Talia. And then bemoaning the "mess he was making" to the show's host, Jeremy Ferris. Seeking advice from his parents about falling in love with two women at the same time, asking who they favored more...but the producers never let the audience see their answer. Had it been them who had turned him against her?

But then abruptly, it hadn't mattered.

As *The One's* next bachelorette, it was *her* turn to be in control. Her turn to weed through bachelors and send them packing until she was down to five or six serious contenders. Time and again, she just couldn't seem to escape handsome, charismatic Connor O'Malley.

Oh, Connor. Even the thought of him still made her heart heavy with loss. After Adam had refused her, she really doubted that love would come her way, even in the midst of twenty-four handsome, intriguing bachelors all focused on winning her heart. But from the beginning, it was Connor who drew her. He seemed to have it all. Charm. Passion. Exuberant energy that was contagious. Joy. A respect for her stance of not having sex before marriage—especially as a part of a *show*—spending all night with her talking and cuddling, never pressuring her for more. Even a measure of faith. "As brutal as it was, Adi," he'd said tenderly, "God clearly wanted Adam to break your heart." She could still see him there, holding her hand against his broad chest as he stared down at her. "Because you were meant for *me.*"

She probably watched that particular scene on the show fifty times, wanting to know if she had dreamed it. After all, he said it hadn't been real. But it sure *looked* real in that moment.

He'd won her. Proposed on that final, beautiful episode— shot in idyllic Bali.

And then on the recap show he seemed to spontaneously decide that it was over, famously breaking their engagement…in front of 9.5 million enthralled viewers.

Never had a bachelorette with her own show so famously lost at love.

"Stalling Stalled Out," read one of the headlines. "The Ice Princess Forever Alone," read another. "Sex Could Have Saved Stalling" was yet another—a direct quote from one of the bachelors who hadn't been as patient as Connor.

Adi sighed and leaned her head against the elevator wall, blessedly alone for a moment as she was lifted to the fifteenth floor. Adam had made her believe it, that she was going to be the last girl with a rose...and a ring. Connor had made her believe it, that this was her time, her second chance at love. She'd fallen in love with both, hard. And now, now she just couldn't see how she was going to pick herself up again. All of America seemed desperate to hear that she was in love again, finding her own happily-ever-after. That's why the paparazzi still followed her. They even printed pictures of her with male colleagues with captions like "Third Time's a Charm?"

But honestly?

Honestly?

Adi didn't know if she would ever be whole, in love, or happy again.

Maybe I'll be single for life.

She'd had to do the required post-show promotions. The "after the final rose" show with all the women that Adam had rejected—in which she remained mostly silent while the others bickered and complained and whined, and managed to only dab her eyes once as she answered direct, probing questions from Jeremy Ferris, with the most minimal of responses.

By the time she did that same show with Connor, she knew things weren't the best between them. They'd begun to bicker and they couldn't seem to recapture any of the magic that had been so intense while they were filming. But she'd supposed it was a transition time. Hadn't other couples who'd made it counseled them, telling them to expect just that? Apparently Connor wasn't as convinced it was a stage, because when they were once again on stage, he chose that moment to end their engagement.

In front of all those viewers.

Horrified, she shut down.

She refused to go on "The Late Show" that night and then the "Today" show the next morning. After all, she'd already done that after Adam, forcing a smile and shrugging. Telling America what she felt—she'd been foolish, believing him. Trusting him. Couldn't they assume she felt the same with Connor? Did they really have to see her, in all her abject humiliation, in full freefall? She'd risked a lawsuit, refusing to appear. Only America's collective commiseration with Adi— and their wrath toward Connor—seemed to buy her some grace with the producers and her boss.

By contractual agreement, Adalyn couldn't ever state she wished she'd never been on the show. But that was what she felt, and what she hoped every viewer surmised. *Let it be a warning to you, girlfriends. Never, ever, ever risk your heart like I did.*

Adalyn had graduated summa cum laude from college. But in life? She felt like a complete idiot. A loser among losers.

The elevator reached her floor, eased to a stop and dinged as the door opened. *Pretend to be okay, Adi*, she told herself. *You've got this.* She lifted her chin, pulled back her shoulders and strode down the hallway, greeting the receptionist, Gracie, by name before turning left and walking toward her cubicle. But her boss, Rhett Jessen, rapped on the glass wall of his office as she passed by, waving her in, even as he continued his conversation via wireless headset and paced.

She peeked in, making sure he really meant for her to enter, and, when he gestured to the seat in front of his desk, she obediently sat down. His glass door whirred shut, the glass a thick grade on wide, brushed nickel hinges. She crossed her legs and tried not to fidget, waiting for him to finish his conversation.

"Good morning, Adalyn," he said as soon as he hung up.

He moved around his desk to sit down in a sleek metal chair that looked cool, but not all that comfortable.

"Good morning, Rhett," she returned, forcing a bright smile.

He leaned back in his chair and crossed one foot over the opposite knee. As usual, he looked like he'd just stepped out of a fashion magazine, all the way from the top of his perfectly trimmed, blond hair down to his four-hundred dollar shoes. He wore his shirt unbuttoned at the top, revealing tanned skin. *From tennis? Or a tanning booth?* Adi wondered idly, trying to get her mind off of why he had called her into his office.

Rhett rested his elbows on the arms of his chair. "Adalyn, I hear that the paparazzi gave you a hard time again this morning."

She sighed. "They found that east walkway I've been taking from the garage to the elevators. Security chased them out."

Rhett frowned. "This has all been much harder on you than I could've imagined," he said.

Was that all the apology she was going to get? Sure, she'd caught a few of the previous seasons of *The One*, but she'd never thought about applying to go on the show. But the network was a client of her marketing firm, and one day a producer had caught sight of her walking by. They'd called her in and the producer had chatted her up, encouraging her to apply. "Even if you don't find love," he'd laughed, "you'd have the inside scoop for our account."

What choice had she really had? Especially after her boss encouraged her to follow through? All along, Adi fought the desire to lay the blame entirely on Rhett Jessen's shoulders for her painful losses. Only the idea that he clearly felt remorseful kept her coming to work every day. He'd remember, surely, what she had sacrificed. In time, maybe that would pay off, with a glass-walled office of her own.

Once I'm not America's most famous failure at love. She could make it, she thought.

"I never imagined," Rhett said, rising and going to the window, then looking back over his shoulder with his arms crossed, "that it would cost you so much. You have to believe me, Adalyn." He eased back toward her and perched on the edge of his desk, casting her a fatherly, concerned look, though he was only about forty-five to her twenty-four.

"I believe you," she said. *Some,* she thought.

"I thought it'd be an adventure for you," he said, waving his hand. "A chance to see some exotic places. Flirt. Play. I didn't expect…Well, I didn't expect you'd—Adalyn, I never thought you'd get your heart broken. Twice." A tinge of red moved up his jaw and cheek.

"It's okay, Rhett. Everyone gets their heart broken sooner or later, right?" *Most people just don't do it on national TV. Twice.*

"Right," he said eagerly, seizing the out she'd offered. "And you're through the worst of it, thank God. It won't take long until the paparazzi ease up too. They'll move on to the next season's contestants before long."

"Yes," she said, but inwardly she was calculating. *Another three or four months before the next season begins to air.*

She could make it. She thought.

He cleared his throat. "Adalyn, the partners and I have discussed this. We think you should take a leave of absence. Paid, of course. We feel responsible for this…discomfort in your life."

She blinked at him. Discomfort? Leave of absence?

"*I* feel responsible," he said.

But there was something in his tone that told her. The way he shifted in his seat. Her presence made the partners uncomfortable. Guilty.

"But Rhett," she said, mind whirring, "I've already been gone so long to tape the shows and all the follow-up publicity. I need to get back into work. Get back into the swing of things, and my mind off of all that's happened. Please. I need this, Rhett." She blinked back tears she refused to allow. "I *need* to be here. It's a bit of normalcy when my whole world seems to have gone crazy."

The muscles in his jaw clenched, and he took a deep breath. "Here's the thing, Adalyn. I've suggested that we put you on several accounts, but each of those account managers have respectfully asked that we not include you. They all feel like you'd be a...distraction. At the moment, you're more of a curiosity for clients, rather than an asset. I won't compromise your professional dignity in that way."

No. This isn't happening. This can't be happening. After all she'd wagered and lost, now her job was in jeopardy too? When Rhett had casually mentioned a chance at an account manager position as late as last year?

"Rhett," she said, eyes shifting madly back and forth, trying to figure out a solution, "I-I need this job. You're not firing me, are you?"

"No, no!" He lifted his hands. "We want you here. In time I plan on helping you figure out how we might redeem some of the hard-won knowledge you gained on *The One.* Put you in charge of that account at some point—wouldn't that make sense? You'll be back in the saddle after a break, Adalyn. I know you will. But I just think some time away, time to let this all settle down and fade, would be a good thing."

Fade. As if memories of Adam and Connor, their kisses—their sweet, silky promises—would fade from the sharp, jagged images they were now. As if she could forget her humiliation. As if she could forget her heart shattering into a hundred different pieces.

"Isn't there someplace you could go?" Rhett asked, rubbing his cheek with long, manicured fingers. "Someplace where the paparazzi can't find you for a while?"

Someplace where Smith & Jessen would be out of the limelight too, she translated.

Montana, she thought, then quickly pushed it away.

She wasn't a coward. She wouldn't run away from this. She had a job, a future, and sure, it might be uncomfortable for all of them, but she would make them find their way forward, *with* her. They owed her that, at least.

"Rhett, you've already allowed me paid leave to be a part of the show and to see through the publicity requirements. I'm done with that now. I've done all that you—and most of what the producers—have asked of me. Now I'm asking you to keep me on here. Give me something to do that will occupy my mind. Help me by keeping me busy. In the background, if necessary, but busy. As in eighty-hours-a-week busy. It's—It's what I need. Please?" She hated that her voice cracked on that word.

Rhett took a deep breath. His jaw muscles clenched, but he wouldn't meet her eyes. He walked back around the glass desk to his chair. He sat down and sighed heavily, steepling his fingers before him. "Look. It's paid time off. Who in their right mind would turn that down?" He huffed a laugh and lifted his hands. When she didn't respond, he said, "I'm afraid this is non-negotiable, Adi. Talk to Mary. She's been covering your calls and will continue to do so. Email her anything she and the account managers need to know about. Wrap things up today, collect anything you can't live without and go home tonight. Rest. Recover from all this…And then we'll see you in mid-September. We'll pick up where we left off. Okay?"

"Okay," she forced herself to say. "Thank you." But as she

left his office, her mind was crying, *Why did I say thank you? This is the last thing I wanted. The very last thing.*

CHAPTER 2

At the end of the day she numbly walked into Mary's office.

The middle-aged woman frowned at seeing her face and came around the desk and shut the door. "Goodness," she said, taking her elbow. "You look awful, Adi."

"Thanks," Adi said with a sardonic smile.

"What's up?" Mary asked.

"More like what's down," she said. "I just got back to work and now Rhett wants me to take another leave of absence. Until September!"

Mary's eyebrows lifted and she pursed her lips. "Might not that be good, Adi? A little rest after all this mess?"

"Maybe," Adalyn said, shaking her head. "I just can't see it. I really was looking forward to being back to work. Putting my mind on other things, you know?"

"I get it. But if you want to trade, let me know," Mary quipped. "I wouldn't mind a long summer vacation. Sunshine and long walks. Seeing someplace new. Think about all you could do."

"Maybe," Adalyn said again, inwardly not agreeing at all.

She'd only been back to work for five days! Couldn't they just give it another week or two?

"Listen, it's been a crazy week. But I just ran through the phony email and phone extension voicemail we set up for you to ditch the paparazzi," she said, moving to a stack of notes. Adalyn blinked. They'd set up phony phone extensions and an email? But then that made sense. They probably were bombarded.

"Do you know a Jonah Perry?" Mary asked.

Adalyn shook her head.

"Nicholas Ruvacaba? Lucas Borland? Riley Knapp? Jonathan Dangle? Trevor Solk? Cole Turner? Kyle Bygness?"

"No."

"Yeah," she said smugly. "They tried to make it sound like they were your friends. Probably paparazzi. Or men convinced they're your true special guy."

"Probably." She'd already received hundreds of "fan" letters from men who swore they were ready to propose themselves. A lot of them began, *Dear Adi, this might sound crazy...*

Mary moved those messages aside. "Oh, what about Leila Ragland? Or here—this Chase Rollins? He's called every day for a week."

Adalyn blinked and sucked in her breath. She reached out her hand for the message. "Chase? He's an old friend. I wonder what he wants?"

Mary handed her the slips. "Oh, Adi. I'm sorry," she said, concern lining her face. "He said something about your grandfather."

"Gramps?" Adalyn said, her heart lurching. "What? What did he say?"

"He said your grandfather's been in poor health. But Adi, if you had heard what those others said...some mentioned your mother. Others your sister or brother—and I know you don't have either of those. These vultures will say anything to get to you."

"It's all right," she muttered. "I'll call Chase as soon as I get home."

"Don't worry about a thing," Mary said, coming around the desk. "Call me once in a while and I'll update you on how things are going. Or just if you need a friend, okay? I hope your grandfather is okay."

"Me too," Adalyn said, accepting the older woman's motherly hug.

She went to her cubicle, looked around and decided there was nothing there she would miss for a few months. She said a brief goodbye to a few buddies, grabbed her purse and hurried down the hall.

She took a deep breath, realizing she'd been holding it, when the doors opened and there were no photographers in sight. "Hey! See that, Roger?" she said to the evening security guard. "It's over. I must already be all washed up on the tabloid front."

"Yeah," he said with a grunt. "Maybe they've gone back to their Kardashian beat."

"Let's hope so," she said, walking now more confidently, shrugging off the urge to crouch down and make sure she could dart between cars if anyone showed up, armed with a camera. But her harassers appeared to be absent.

"Where's your car?" Roger asked, huffing a little. "I'll walk ya out." He was a good thirty pounds overweight and spent most of his day behind the central security desk or in the golf cart they used to patrol the building and the parking garage.

"Just up here, and over a row," she said.

They made their way between cars, then over. And that's when she saw them. A line of red rose petals, some obviously crushed beneath the tires of departing cars and scattered, but the trail still visible. She could smell them then, that sickly, rich scent that she had once associated with love, with favor, and now only knew as rejection and pain. Roger paused and looked at her, his hands on his belt.

She steeled herself and moved toward her car. There were more and more petals the closer they got, some even strewn across the hood. And in the handle of her battered, ten-year-old Subaru door, was a perfect, long-stemmed red rose.

Bile rose in her throat and she looked around in horror. *Was this some sick joke?*

Roger raised his right hand to her as he bent to speak into his radio, worn at the shoulder. "We've got a situation here in Row F of the parking garage," he said.

"No, no," she said, waving at him and forcing a smile. What was he going to report? A *flower* situation? That hardly sounded menacing. "It's okay, Rog." She pulled the rose from her handle and flung it backward, not caring where it landed. "Probably someone in the office playing a prank on me. Or just some weirdo fan of the show."

"Some weirdo who has figured out where you work," Roger grunted, still looking about from under his heavy, fleshy eyelids in suspicion, hand on the holster of his gun. She saw, with some alarm, that he'd unsnapped it. He pulled out a flashlight to shine it in the back seat of her Subie, then the cargo area, and at last the front seat. She stifled her giggle over his *CSI*-esque moves, which she deemed far too dramatic for this event. But she knew the security guards lived for this sort of thing.

"All clear," he said.

"Thanks, Roger. It's just another day of being 'America's Sucker-Punched Sweetheart.'" That was another headline that had stuck with her. She'd read too many before she swore off reading anything, from then on avoiding every newsstand in stores or on the sidewalks, to say nothing of the Internet.

"You sure you're okay, Miss Stalling?" he asked.

"I'm fine," she said, pulling out her keys. She frowned when she realized her hand was trembling so much that she couldn't manage to push the unlock button on her key fob.

Roger gently took it from her and unlocked the doors. "Hey," he said kindly, "my shift is about done. Maybe I can call the missus and tell her I'm going to drive you home... come back in the morning to pick you up? That is, if you don't mind that I drive your car. Or we could take—"

"No. Thanks, but no," Adalyn said. "Go home to your family. Your dinner's probably ready soon. And no one has ever been menaced by roses, right? It's just some crazy fan. Someone who thinks they know me. TV has a weird way of doing that."

He huffed a laugh. "Sure, sure." His round face quickly returned to consternation though. "But sometimes those who fancy themselves in love...Are you certain, Miss Stalling? Really, it's no trouble to—"

"I'm sure. I'll see you soon." She managed to press the big start button, and carefully fastened her seatbelt and locked her doors—knowing Roger would find some comfort in that. She forced a cheery wave, switched into drive and eased out of her assigned parking spot.

Adalyn glanced at him once in her rearview mirror, standing there in the middle of the garage, watching her go. He meant well, but she felt more secure on her own, behind the wheel, and the more distance she got from those cursed rose petals, the better she felt. If she never saw a rose again in her life, that would be fine with her.

Twenty minutes later, she was pulling into her ten-story apartment building, happy to not see anybody lurking about on the sidewalks. Due to security restrictions, the paparazzi hadn't ever made it inside her apartment building, blocked from entering the front lobby or garage without a code. Given that she could drive right in, they'd blessedly given up on finding her at home or catching anything other than boring drive-by shots through her dim windows. Her morning runs and gym visits were over for now, of course. She'd taken up web-led workouts in her apartment, where no one could see her—or take pictures of her sweating. Her groceries were delivered, so she didn't have to go to the store either. Someday, she would return to Orange Theory and Trader Joe's. Church, on three-out-of-four Sundays.

But until all of *The One* chaos had blown over, she'd made peace with being a total recluse. In comparison, she'd make J.D. Salinger look like the mayor on Main. *Just let them try to find me. I'm only going to go to work and come home, day in, day out. The most boring media target ever. Until all this fades, as Rhett would say...*

The elevator dinged and she stepped into the carpeted hallway of the sixth floor.

And stopped abruptly.

Because strewn all the way down the hall, all the way to her apartment, were rose petals.

And woven through the handle of her door was a perfect, long-stemmed, red rose.

CHAPTER 3

Adalyn was on her knees when she became aware that her cell was ringing.

"He-hello," she said numbly, still staring down the hallway, the overly-sweet scent of rose petals wafting up her nose.

"Miss Stalling, this is Nathan in security, downstairs. We have a Mr. Chase Rollins at the front desk for you. Do you know him?"

She paused a moment, trying to make his words make sense. *Chase? Here?*

She shook her head, relieved at the strange thought of a friend by her side. "He showed you a picture ID, Nathan?"

"Yes, ma'am. Driver's license says Columbia Falls, MT. You know him?"

"Yes!" She caught herself, feeling the flush of heat at her neck. "I-I know him. Let him come up, please. I'll wait by the elevator. Oh, Nathan?" she said, "can you check your camera footage? Someone's strewn rose petals down the sixth floor hall to my door."

She heard the security guard's muffled voice as he directed Chase to the elevators. "Now, what's that you said, Miss? Something about rose petals?"

"Yes, all down my hallway."

"Some Romeo in your life, then? Someone in the building with a code?"

"I...I don't know." Adalyn staggered to her feet and leaned against the wall, still staring along the length of the hallway, a chill running down her neck. What if the guy was still around? In her apartment? For the first time it registered. *If he got to this floor, he could still be here.* Nervously, she glanced over her shoulder, the hair on the back of her neck rising.

"Do you have a camera on my floor hallway, Nathan?"

"Sure do."

"Can you see me?"

"Yes."

"Can you keep an eye on me until Chase gets up here and we go into my apartment?"

"Yes. Miss. Is there someone's code you want me to cancel? I take it that those flowers aren't welcome?"

The guy was pretty new. Clearly, he was one of the few people in her building who hadn't yet heard who she was. Or ever heard about the show and their signature flower.

"I never give out my code," she said, her voice sounding pinched. She hung up on him, just as the elevator dinged and Chase stepped out.

"Chase!" She practically flung herself into his arms. It had been years since she'd seen her childhood friend, but she didn't care. "I'm so glad you're here!" After a moment's hesitation, she felt him wrap his big arms around her, his broad hands warm on her back.

"Adi girl, it's been too long," he said. "I've been trying to get ahold of you, but you changed your number..."

"Three times," she said, moving away from his welcome warmth. "I'm sorry. Only the security guards and a few people at the office have my most recent cell number these days. And I just found out an hour ago that you'd been trying to reach me. Gramps? How is he?"

"He's been better, Adi. When I couldn't reach you, I thought I'd better come. But maybe we can talk about it in your apartment?"

"Oh, sure." But when she took a step toward it, she remembered the petals. She closed her eyes and rubbed them, not caring if she smeared her makeup. She was tired, so tired.

Hands on his hips, he looked down the hallway. "So, uhh...since you were on *The One*, is this how you're welcomed home every day?" he tried to joke.

She shook her head, not able to muster a trace of a smile, despite her best intentions. "Nope. This is new. I appear to have picked up a stalker. First, in my parking garage at work, which wasn't a huge surprise. But this...this is. As you've seen, it's not exactly easy to get in this building."

Chase's smile faded and his eyes sidled down the hall and back to her. "Think whoever did it might be inside your apartment?" He was as calm as he'd ever been, even when he'd spied a grizzly bear in Glacier on a hike. Wary, but confident. Cautious, but secure. He was big now. A man. When they'd last parted—*What? Six, seven years ago?*—he'd been but a college senior.

"Nah," she said, remembering herself. She was no teen, hiding in his shadow as they explored the woods. She was a marketing executive. A celebrity—be it a defamed one, of sorts. She moved down the hall in front of him, pulling out her key, and then ripping the rose from the handle, again tossing it behind her. "There's no way he could get in."

She tried to get her mind on a different subject than a potential stalker in her apartment. "Chase, I can't believe you'd come all this way. Is Gramps really okay?"

"I need to tell you about him, Adi," he said. "He's okay. But not the best."

Her heart seemed to halt, then pounded painfully.

Gramps. She hadn't spoken to him in months. Not since the day that Adam broke her heart. That day she had called him, a total mess, and he'd done his best to console her over the phone. But then not again in the months since. Not even answering his phone messages, ignoring him as she'd done her parents and every other person in her life, seemingly lost in *The One's* vortex.

"Adi, let's go inside," Chase said, taking the key from her hand and unlocking the door. "I'll tell you everything once you can sit down. You're looking a little pale."

She swallowed hard, feeling more confident now with her old friend at her side. She didn't want to hear what he'd come to tell her. Dreaded it, really. But with him, here, she felt more secure, more *herself*, than she had in months. Like she just might be able to handle more bad news.

The sweet fumes of crushed rose petals rose from beneath their feet. She did her best to ignore it, as he turned the key in the lock and shoved open the sleek door. It was with some relief that she saw that no more rose petals extended inside her apartment. Whoever it was had found a stopping point, at least there, at her threshold.

"Come in," she said to Chase, who looked down the hall again, scanning every inch. As if he expected her stalker to appear. A shiver of fear ran down her back and panic made her heart pause, then pound. She practically hauled him inward, slammed the door and rammed the deadbolt into place, slightly panting as she leaned her hand against it.

She could feel his eyes on her before she turned.

"Adi."

She forced herself to turn, feeling the first tinges of embarrassment.

"You're scared. I don't think I've ever seen Adalyn Stalling scared."

"Well, I'm...." What? Words seemed to fail her. "I'm uhh..." *I'm freaked out. Exhausted. So tired of attention. Of any form. And now this?*

She forced herself to move past him, flipping on lights. Her apartment was modern, clean. All simple lines and light colors over spotless floors. Realizing that her knees were shaking, she fell onto a white leather chair with no arms and leaned her head back against the rounded top. She closed her eyes for a moment as he wandered about, through the kitchen, the dining room, glancing into her half-bathroom—cautiously moving open the door then looking behind it—and then partway down the hall toward her room. Searching for an intruder.

"Chase, tell me about my grandfather." *Tell me anything. Make me forget about this weirdo with a rose fetish.*

Chase's intent hazel eyes tore from the direction of her bedroom and back to her. "Of course. Right." He came to her and sat down on the footrest in front of her, his arms on his knees. "Adi, Gene isn't faring very well. About two weeks ago—"

"Two weeks?" she said, sitting upright. She'd changed her number again, about then. Dropped off of all social media months ago, when her numbers blew up because of all the fans. "Gramps..." She reached out and grabbed his hand. "What? What is it?"

"He's okay, Adi. He's okay, for now." He took her hand in both of his, nothing but compassion and understanding of their mutual love for the older man in his expression or movement. His hands were so *warm*. "Gene had a massive heart attack. He's out of the hospital now. But Adi," he said, his eyes suddenly wet with tears, "the doc doesn't think he has long. He's on tenuous ground. I tried calling you at work—but the receptionist basically hung up on me. And then all I got was that extension with some other woman's voice answering for you."

She gave him a miserable look. "I'm so sorry. You'd be amazed at the stories some people come up with, trying to get to me. My boss figured that if someone didn't already know my extension, they didn't need to speak to me yet. You know, after all that's come down lately."

"Sure," he said, compassion in his eyes. "But since I couldn't get ahold of you by phone or email, I thought I'd better come. I knew you'd want to know about him. And he... Well, Adi, he really needs to hear from you."

"Thank you so much," she said, wrapping her other hand around his two larger ones, feeling so guilty for her absence, her ignorance of those she loved most. "These last months... Ever since I went on the show...I haven't been good about calling him. Anyone, really. And it's been..." She gestured helplessly to the hallway.

"A little Hollywood-crazy, eh?" he said, casting her his crooked grin.

"A little," she admitted wanly.

"Can you get away? Come to Glacier, even for a bit? Come see him? Seeing you would do him good."

"Oh, I..." Why did she hold back? What was she supposed to do for three months here? "Well, maybe."

"Tea. I need to make you some tea. Does that sound good? Gramps always said that tea helped a soul think. Lemon Zinger, in particular. Got any?"

"I think so," she said numbly.

She couldn't make herself rise, but listened to him fumble through her cupboards, waited, even as she heard the kettle whistle. Felt like she was in a dream. *Chase, here? In Chicago? The rose petals...Gramps?*

Chase sat down in front of her again and thrust a steaming mug into her hands. She closed her eyes and inhaled the scent of lemon and spice and sweet fruit.

"So," Chase said. "Tell me about the roses. Could it be a boyfriend?"

"I wish," she said. "I mean, I'm not in *any* kind of mental place for a boyfriend," she rushed on. "But that? Out there? That's a stalker," she finished in a whisper. "You saw that you couldn't just ride on up the elevator. And security—there's nothing that would tell the average Joe which apartment I'm in. Even our post boxes are coded. Our security code for walk-ups wouldn't tell him. It's all very purposeful. And somehow..." Her voice faded.

"Somehow, this guy blew through all security measures." He stared at her, the muscles in his jaw flexing. *When had he gotten man-jaw muscles?* "Where else?" he asked gruffly.

"Just at work," she admitted, "but that's not so hard. It doesn't take a super-sleuth to figure out where a girl named Adalyn Stalling might be working as a marketing exec, even in a city as big as Chicago." She worked for a marketing firm. Press releases were their bread and butter, even in regard to their own employees.

"Does your firm keep them away from you?"

"Pretty well," she said. "The paparazzi still stalk the parking garage."

"How do you know this guy was at your work?"

"More rose petals, in the parking garage. And a rose, on my Subie."

"Today?"

"Today."

"Could it have been one of the paparazzi? Looking for a particularly evocative shot?" he asked.

"Could've," she admitted. "But when I left, there were no photographers." She shook her head. "It was probably some jerk in the office thinking he was funny."

Clearly unconvinced, Chase frowned and rose, fists clenching and unclenching. Then he moved quietly back to the hall. Took hold of a heavy pewter candlestick of her grandmother's and walked to her bedroom, the only place he hadn't searched.

Adalyn forced herself to take a sip of tea. Then another. Waited, while he clearly searched every square foot of her bedroom and bathroom.

"Adi?" he called gently.

She waited a second, then made herself say, "Yes?"

"Can you come here, please?"

She rose, feeling like she had when she entered the set of *The One* again. Herself, and yet not herself. As if she was an actor playing herself.

She strode down the hall and paused in the doorway. He was there in front of her. Blocking her view. On purpose? He turned and took hold of her arms. She looked up into his face—that face she'd once crushed so hard on, when they were kids. "Chase? What is it?"

He closed his eyes and then lifted one hand to run through his hair. "Is there anywhere you can go tonight, Adi? A friend's? Or a hotel—"

But she was already pushing past him.

Standing, mouth agape, sucking in a breath.

Because then she saw it.

Her queen bed, with the crisp Egyptian sheets and over-ly-stuffed duvet turned down, as if to welcome her.

And a single, long-stemmed red rose peeking up from beneath the sheets, resting atop her perfectly plumped pillow.

Her knees gave way and she sank, but Chase caught her.

He helped her walk on wobbly knees to the living room, then carefully propped open the front door as he dialed 911. Quietly, he reported the emergency and within minutes the apartment building's wide-eyed security force of three had arrived, looking as secretly excited over the opportunity as they were concerned over her safety. They hovered in the hallway, pacing back and forth to her bedroom, quietly conferring as they waited for the police to arrive.

"Adi," Chase said, covering her with an afghan that had barely been used; she'd bought it right before she left for the show's taping. "Can you take a leave of absence? I think..." He paused and ran a hand through his brown hair again before perching on the edge of her stiff, modern sofa and looking at her. "I think you ought to get out of here for a while. Come away. You know," he said, lowering his voice, "to our place. To where the paparazzi and guys like this weird dude who've been watching the show are not likely to find you. You never mentioned it."

Never mentioned it, he said. As if he'd seen every episode. She was half-grateful, half-horrified at the thought of it. Chase had watched it? But he was right. Never had she told her prospective bachelors where exactly she'd spent her summers, only hinting at treasured months on a lake in the Northwest. The producers had coached them in that, in order to protect some measure of their privacy. For that at least, she was thankful.

"I—I don't know. I mean...I have some time. My boss actually is making me take some time. I've just had so much change lately. To up and leave?" She shook her head.

"But Adi, your Gramps. He needs you. He needs you *now*. And you…" He rubbed the back of his neck and looked around. "You need to not be *here*."

She stared at Chase. He'd just set it out between them. The only thing that might convince her. Gramps. She hadn't seen him since last Christmas, and even then, just for a few days.

"I want to see Gramps, I do. I *need* to see him. But maybe just for a weekend. A long weekend," she quickly amended, seeing him shift in agitation. "To make sure he's on a better track."

"A better track?" Chase growled, rising and pacing. "And what about you? What about you, Adi? Here you are, the spurned bachelorette of *The One*, with a stalker showing up in your *apartment*?" He spit out the last word. "I've done my share of tracking animals over the years, and from where I sit, I'm thinking you have both an ailing elder in your pack, as well as an enemy on your tail. It's time to hole up somewhere safe."

She stared at him for a long moment, then swallowed. She hated to run, but at the moment, all she felt was…overwhelmed. Frozen.

Chase wrapped his big hands around her shoulders. "Do you have an option? Why not come home for a while? For a couple weeks? Or as long as your boss has given you. Don't you need some time to figure things out?"

Certain phrases stood out to her, then seemed to echo through her mind in a dizzying spin. *Come home. Figure things out.*

She paused. What was it she needed to shake this fog she seemed to be living in? Time? Space? Healing? Gramps?

Maybe all of that. And more.

CHAPTER 4

Chase Rollins watched through the small window as the rising sun cast a pink glow over the jagged Rocky Mountain peaks below the commuter plane, some still covered with a fair amount of snow. Many wouldn't shed their white mantles until June faded into July and that was fine by him. The mountains always had more dimension and interest with some snow on them.

Chase loved each of the seasons for different reasons. Spring, for all the bright, light-green newness it brought with the end of winter's reign. Fall, for the last showy color of the mountainsides—the banner-gold of the Tamaracks, the deep, royal red of the vine maples, the orange-gold of the aspens—all on parade amongst the evergreens. Winter, for her quiet and stark solitude, the soul's rest. But summer's bright clarity…well, summer had forever been associated with fun, happy memories and the hope of new adventures. For a long while, it had meant he'd see Adi again. But that hadn't happened in years.

He glanced down at her, awkwardly asleep against his

shoulder, like she'd been on a hundred different occasions as a kid. It had always been like this for them. Once, anyway. They'd spent the year apart, and every summer, fell back into their easy friendship. Later on, there'd been a budding romance. He'd come close to kissing her ten times or more, that last summer. But never did. He'd always been afraid to ruin what they had.

This. This easy, constant trust. Even after six years apart, here she was. A girl who'd been through heartbreak not once, but twice. A girl who'd been stalked by photographers and now this creep…He took a deep breath and shifted slowly, easing her cheek to a different place on his numb shoulder and gazed down at her with tender feelings making his eyes embarrassingly damp. With him, with *him*, she was at ease. As he'd always been with her.

Even if she might be awkwardly snoring a little, making the bald man in front of them glance back at her in bemusement. Chase raised a brow and quirked his lips in a silent, *Sorry, man. What am I to do about it?*

And truth be told, he wouldn't do a thing. How long had it been since his friend had had a decent night's sleep? She'd accepted all that he'd done—dealing with the cops, booking their red-eye flight to Kalispell, helping her pack a bag—with all the response of a mannequin trained to respond with monosyllabic words.

But when the plane hit an air pocket and jolted, she did too, sitting up straight and glancing around with alarm.

"It's all right, Adi," he said, covering her long, thin fingers with his palm and giving them a squeeze. "We're almost home." He gestured toward the window, deciding distraction was better than commenting on her palpable panic just beneath the surface. As she tentatively leaned closer for a better look, he caught the scent of her floral shampoo, felt the long ends of her deep-sable hair tickle his arm, but he didn't move his eyes from the window. "Pretty, isn't it? With the morning light?"

"So pretty," she sighed, hungrily scanning the peaks as if silently naming each one. There was the vast Bob Marshall Wilderness, where they'd spent a week camping and fishing with his brother, Logan, and her friend, Julie, the summer after her freshman year of college...the last summer she'd returned to the park. The plane banked and they found themselves along the jagged peaks of the Mission Range, then followed along the length of the Flathead Range toward Glacier International Airport. The wide, silvery expanse of the lake glittered beneath them. The peaks of the park were visible in the distance, and perhaps glimpsing them, Adi seemed to remember herself and leaned back into her seat. Contemplating what? Her grandfather? The job she left behind? Connor?

Was it really his business? He and Adi had once been friends, but now? He leaned forward to grab a stick of spearmint gum from his backpack and offered one to Adalyn.

She took the gum, a small smile tugging at her lips. "Spearmint. Even after all this time, you're the only one I know who chooses spearmint over peppermint." She popped it in her mouth and shot him a brief grin.

"I can't be the only one out there who knows what's good," he said, leaning back and folding his arms. "Otherwise the gum companies wouldn't keep making it."

"Maybe," she said. "But they must live in pockets of civilization I don't venture into."

"Like the Flathead," he said, gesturing with his chin to the window.

"I suppose," she said. "Chase," she began, her delicate, brown brows knitting together a bit. How often had he frozen the TV screen to study her expressions like that during episodes of *The One*? It had driven him crazy, watching her go through such stress and trauma. Sure, he knew some of it was made up, produced to bring the audience the greatest amount of emotion possible. But he knew Adi. At least, he had once known her. And what he once knew of her told him that she had given her heart twice, and twice been torn in two.

"Chase?" she said again, looking him over quizzically.

He started, realizing that he had been staring at her and not paying attention to what she was saying. "Sorry." He rubbed his face. "It's been a long night. Come again?"

"I was asking what I should expect from Gramps. You said he was in the hospital, but is home again?"

"Back at the cabins, yes, despite doctor's orders. He's bound and determined to open on time."

She shook her head and it was her turn to sigh. "He's never missed a season in forty-some years. I bet he's hell-bent on not missing this one either."

"Even if it costs him his life," Chase said earnestly. He waited until her chocolate-brown eyes met his. "That's what the doc said, Adi. He's risking his life, continuing to work. The old man said he'd rather meet death working than sitting around on his you-know-what."

"Sounds like Gramps," she said. "Never mind. With me here, he can at least be off most of the day. I'll make sure he behaves and rests. But you know him, Chase. He's not like my mom…bent on traveling the world. Being anywhere *but* Lake McDonald. He's all about the lake, the cabins. Always has been. Always will. To him, the work, the place *is* life." She sat back, seemingly lost in thought.

"For me too," she might've muttered after a moment. But he couldn't be certain.

Nearing the park, the plane banked again and began to

descend over the fields just beginning to really gain some momentum, over the winding Stillwater River, over the suburban neighborhoods that were slowly overtaking what had once been only miles of farmland. The Big Sky secret was out, and while once a lack of commerce had kept the upwardly mobile from moving in, the upwardly mobile—and Internet-connected—had found a way to do so. It was good for the Valley, really, he admitted. The way of progress. But Chase missed the old days. The lack of traffic on Highway 2, the ease of finding a booth at Moose's Saloon…

On the other hand, he was glad they were here. The newbies were passionate about the Flathead, the gateway to Glacier National Park. Keeping Glacier "green." Protecting her waning glaciers. Her animal-life. Much like Chase himself was. It comforted him, the knowledge that he wasn't the only one worried they only had two hundred-and-eighty grizzlies in the park this year, as compared to last year's three hundred. That there were only twenty-five glaciers left in Glacier Park, where once there had been a hundred and fifty.

"It's grown a lot," Adi said, leaning over him to see again.

"It has," he said. "By about ten thousand, probably, since last you were here."

She glanced at him in surprise. "Ten *thousand*?"

"In the greater area," he said. "Not just in Kalispell. Don't worry, though. Lake McDonald is pretty much like you left it. Just with more people coming through."

"Which is good for Gramps and the concession," she said.

"And my brother and sister-in-law," he said. For the last five years, Gene—Adi's grandfather—had been worried about losing his cabin concession. If he didn't keep the cabins up to par and get good responses from visitors, the park had the right to revoke it when it came up for review, come this October. The review spooked every concessionaire in the park, including his brother Logan, who now held the family boat concession next to Gramps's cabins. Logan and his wife, Bea, had made a life on the lake from May to September, resting in October and November, then working as ski instructors at Whitefish Mountain Resort through the winter.

After working in Denali as a wildlife biologist park ranger, Chase felt like he'd won the lottery, winning a coveted position tracking wildlife—and poachers—in Glacier last year. He spent part of each week on the east side of the park, but when he was on the west side, he stayed in his family's historic boathouse-turned-cabin. He knew that he'd be in the park for many years to come. But Adi's grandfather? Well, that was up to God and the people who held the reins of every lodge, motel, restaurant, store, and boat concession in the park. He thought Logan and Bea would be fine. But Gene's cabins… well, they'd been falling into disrepair over the last few years. Logan and he'd tried to help when they could, but it was way more than a Saturday afternoon's work could cover.

He'd let Adi discover that on her own. She was a smart girl, as smart as she was pretty. Prettier than he'd remembered her. When he'd stepped off that elevator, he knew she'd been distracted by the roses, and sure, he had been too. It made his heart pound a little harder that some creep would try and get to her that way. But God in heaven knew how seeing her—seeing her in the flesh after nothing closer than two seasons of *The One* on TV—had almost made his knees tremble. Tremble! That'd never happened before.

He had no idea how Adam and then Connor had been willing to turn away from her. Clearly, they had not seen her as Chase saw her. In watching the show, he'd remembered how he had crushed on her that last summer, always in a quiet rivalry with his brother for her attentions. But in watching her on that show—how she had matured, how she was so classy, so careful with her words, so cautious with her heart until she was sure—even managing to resist the last "Temptation Nights" alone with the three bachelors, insisting on nothing but talk and cuddling—he fell even harder for her.

And when the guys dumped her? He'd wanted to both bash their heads in for hurting her and cheer them on for not taking what he thought—God help him—he *fantasized* might someday be his.

Adalyn's heart.

What are you doing, Rollins? he asked himself for the hundredth time since bundling her up and escorting her to the airport. *You're no better than her stalker, falling in love with her from afar. From a show, for Pete's sake. A show!*

But I've always been in love with her, another voice in his head rallied. *I know the true Adalyn Stalling. Or at least I once knew her...better than any of those guys hoped to.*

Not that she recognized that, of course.

Not that he could tell her.

Because clearly, Adalyn Stalling was one of the walking wounded. And the farthest thing in her mind was love, let alone an old friend's pursuit. So that's what he would be to her, Chase decided. Nothing but a dear friend. Loyal. Constant. Well, as constant as his ranger schedule would allow. He'd watch over her. Tend to her as he might an ailing mother bear...keeping tabs, but not hovering. Giving her room to breathe and rest and heal, in God's good timing.

The plane touched down, braked and taxied to the modest six-gate terminal that only gained its lofty "International" airport moniker because it was but a half-hour flight to the Canadian border. Inside they went down the stairs and into the baggage claim area where Logan awaited them.

"Well, well, well," he said, tipping back his Bobcats baseball hat and grinning down at Adi. "Good to see you again, stranger." He lifted her up in a huge hug.

"Good to see you too," she said with a laugh as he set her down.

Bea hooked a hand through the crook of his arm, not at all jealous. She knew all about Adalyn and "the boys"—as his sister-in-law referred to Chase and him—and their long-standing summer crush on her. But she also was a hundred-percent sure that as soon as Logan met her, his heart had been hers alone. He'd never made it a secret.

"You must be Beatrice," Adi said, stretching out a hand to shake.

"Come here, girl," Bea said, lifting her arms to the taller woman. "I'm a hugger, not a shaker. And anyone who is family to my boys is family to me."

Adi hesitated a second and then gave in. But her resistance surprised Chase. Part of her big-city reserve now? Or residual damage from the heartbreak of the show? As a kid, she'd been all about hugs too.

When they parted, Logan hooked an arm around Bea's shoulders.

"I-I'm sorry I couldn't come to your wedding last summer," Adi said. "I wanted to," she rushed on. "I really did. But I, uh…"

They all knew she'd been on-set filming. Gene had talked on and on about it. Half-worried, half-proud.

"No worries, girl," Bea put in. "I have three picture albums full of photos that I can bore you to death with. My sister and I are hardcore photographers. Not really talented. But for what we lack in talent, we make up with volume."

That made Adi smile. "I can deal with volume."

"We'll get along just fine, then," Bea said with a grin.

"But, uhh, maybe we can wait on the wedding album?" she asked, squinting her eyes and cocking her head. "That's kind of a sore spot for me at the moment. Not your wedding, of course," she rushed on. "Because…you know."

"Oh, I *know*," Bea said. "We all hung out with Gene and saw what an idiot that Adam was. And then Connor?" She let out a snort. "That guy better never come to Montana. Anyone who knows you would like to feed him to the wolves. After your grampa fills him with buckshot. At least that's what he promised."

Adi grinned shyly. "Is it bad of me to kinda want to see that?" she asked. "Not to see Gramps shoot him, of course. Just, you know his face when he found himself at the wrong end of a shotgun?"

"No way, girlie," Bea said. "Not a one of us would mind seeing him pee his pants. That's the least punishment he deserves, treating you like that. But never mind him," she said with a *hmmph*. "This summer will be just what you need to forget his sorry, no-good self."

And just like that, it was all out in the open. Adalyn's heartbreak, as well as their combined, staunch support of her. That was Beatrice's talent, Chase thought. Making everyone she met feel like they were her best friend. Known from the start. And it was a part of making their boat concession so popular last year. Judging from their already-packed calendar, many who had come for a sunrise or sunset cruise—or just to rent canoes or kayaks for the day—planned on returning.

"Half to see my Bea," Logan often said with pride, looking at his petite little wife like he couldn't get enough of her.

"The other half to see my hunky husband," she'd return, her dark eyes glinting.

Their love was sometimes a little much, Chase thought. It was so intense, so mutually passionate, that it made him feel like he was a voyeur in a way. It was like they didn't care who saw they were totally into each other. Kind of like being back in high school, when the kids made out in the hallway. Not that they did that...but they weren't above patting each other on the butt as they passed or reaching in for a quick kiss, regardless of who was in the room.

Adalyn's bag came through on the serpentine track and Chase eased the other strap up on his backpack—his only luggage—and reached for her suitcase.

"I can get it," Adi said, striding up next to him.

There was something in her tone that made him pause, even though every gentlemanly manner his father drilled into him screamed to object. "Sure, Adi," he said, his voice oddly mangled. "Sure," he repeated, clearer that time. As in, *Of course you want to do that, Adalyn. You're a contemporary woman. Strong. Capable. Not needing any man. Got it.*

She lifted the heavy bag from the track and Chase scratched his ear, itching to help. But then she got it to the ground, pulled out the long handle and rolled it back to them. "Shall we?"

"We certainly shall," Bea said, leaping on to Logan's back. "Just as long as this tall drink of water carries me."

He groaned, grunted and then laughed, putting his hands beneath her thighs and settling her a bit more securely on his back. "Too far to the parking lot for you to walk, m'lady?" he asked over his shoulder.

"Far too far," she said dramatically.

Chase rolled his eyes at Adi, whose own brows lifted in surprise. "You'll have to excuse them. Bea was an actress at the Bigfork Summer Playhouse for several summers. She was going to head to New York."

"Until this hunk o' man convinced me to spend my years living a different dream," Bea said, nuzzling Logan's neck.

He laughed and ducked his head. "Not that I mind being Romeo to my Juliet."

Chase shook his head. "Please excuse them. They can't seem to help themselves. Your gramps assures me that they'll settle down after a few years. He says they're just 'randy.'"

Adi grinned. "Randy? I haven't heard that word in a while." Then she glanced back at Logan, who had set Bea down and was trying to tickle her. "But I think it's probably apropos." Her brown eyes followed them for a second longer and then she forced her gaze to the mountains. She took a long, deep breath. "That air," she sighed appreciatively. "That *smell.*"

"Bad? Good?" Chase asked. He took a long breath of his own.

"Good. Really, really good," Adi said.

"What does it smell like?" he asked, reaching for Logan's truck door handle and opening it for her, thinking belatedly that maybe she would've wanted to do that herself.

But she didn't seem to notice. She closed her eyes and breathed in again. "It smells like sun and stone and wheat and earth and….water," she whispered.

She opened her eyes then and with some embarrassment, Chase realized that she'd caught him staring, slightly slack-jawed. His teeth clicked together, so loudly that he wondered if she heard it too.

"You got all that with just one whiff?" he said, adding a little chide to his tone to resume a proper distance.

"Well, maybe *two* whiffs. What does it smell like to *you*?" She nudged him playfully as Bea and Logan finally caught up.

Her nudge heartened him. Chase took a deep breath, hands to his chest, and then reached out his arms, looked around at the mountain-ringed valley, then back to her. "Well *that*, to me, smells like home."

CHAPTER 5

As Logan drove them into the park—the mountains opening up like massive gates to them—Bea kept up a constant banter with "the boys," leaving Adalyn to her own thoughts. The Flathead River rushed out of the park to the left side of the narrow, winding highway, the rapid June snowmelt evident. Chase had been right. This place not only smelled like home, but felt like home too. It was exactly where she needed to be, for more reasons than Gramps's declining health.

But could her stalker really not find her here? Her hometown dates on the show had been back in the Twin Cities, where her parents lived when they weren't on some river cruise in Europe or on a trek to Machu Picchu. Never had she specifically mentioned Montana—only some vague references with Adam that she'd spent some summers in the Northwest. He'd had a love of mountains too. But something beyond the producer's caution—God, maybe?—had told her to not share more than that. So much of her life had been exposed on that show. Contractually, she was required to share a lot. But this place? This place had been one of the few secrets she held back from sharing, even with Connor. She'd told him about it when they got engaged, of course. Begged him to come back with her, when things started falling apart. But thankfully, none of that had been on camera.

On the advice of a friend, she'd gone back on her Facebook and Instagram profiles before the first show released, deleting whole years from her account, as well as anything that would help someone find her. It had pained her to delete all the beautiful pictures of family celebrations, hikes and experiences with friends—like Logan and Chase—but she'd carefully put them in a folder on her computer before eradicating them from her social media stream. Maybe she'd take this summer to print them out and put them in albums, like Bea had been talking about. A real, physical album, rather than something she could find somewhere on her phone or computer.

There was something reassuring about that idea. Those pictures were solid memories of who she had been and who she truly was now, a reminder of her core person, rather than the dejected, lonely, lost TV personality *The One* had made her out to be. "Do you mind if I open my window, Logan?" she asked, since he was driving.

"Sure," he said. "I think it's warm enough."

"Yeah, baby!" Bea called, bringing hers down too. "Bring on Summer!"

Their conversation gave way to the roar of wind and river and the occasional car or truck passing them on the other side of the road. The distinct smell of the water, earthy loam, decaying grass and pine filled Adi's nostrils, even as her skin chilled in the wind. Here, in the deep shadows of the canyon, it was cooler, but she ignored the mild discomfort, resting her chin on her elbow and staring out at the rushing water and the mountains gradually opening to the first, grand expanse of the park, with her towering peaks. Here and there, water-falls broke free of cliffs and cascaded down canyons carved by centuries of such runoff. Birch and aspen swayed in a light breeze, their early leaves a vibrant green against their piney neighbors. Along the river, a bald eagle sailed, searching for a fat trout to pluck for breakfast.

"How's the bald eagle population?" she asked Chase over her shoulder. As a biologist, she knew he'd know. He'd known even when they were kids.

"Stronger than ever," he said, giving her a hopeful smile. When their grandparents were young, bald eagles had been endangered. Their excitement over seeing their population gradually increase had been contagious for Adi, Chase and Logan.

She looked out and saw a nest then, the mother tucking eaglets back into place, only the very top of their fuzzy heads visible. Another sailed in a circle, high above. Last year in Chicago, it had become a social media phenomenon when a bald eagle had chosen a high-rise corner to build her nest and bring three eaglets into the world. People loved the surprise of seeing something so wild make her home in a place so urban.

But it was so much better seeing them here, Adalyn thought. *Kinda like me. So much better for me to be here than on some TV show or on social media. So much better...*

Logan slowed down as they reached the turn-off for West Glacier and Adi's heart sped up. She hadn't known how much she missed this place. Why had she been gone so long? Sure, vacation was short. Her two weeks' allowance from Smith & Jessen had been eaten up by some girlfriend trips to Paris and Rome—along with holidays with her parents—and in the last year by *The One*. But as fun as those cities had been, and as important as it was to spend a Christmas or Easter with her folks when they happened to be in the States, it was here that Adi recognized she longed to be most.

They passed the welcome center, the ranger station, old diner and through the small village of Apgar, then down the winding road to the quiet corner of the lake that had always felt like hers and hers alone. Logan pulled up in the parking lot that was between the Lake McDonald Boat Launch and the Kreature Komforts cabin complex. Hearing their truck, Gramps came to the old screen door and peered out, then grinned and opened it on creaking hinges. Stiff-legged, he climbed down the three stone steps and lumbered toward her, still her Gramps, but looking impossibly aged since she saw him last Christmas in Chicago.

He welcomed her into his arms, and in holding him, Adalyn discovered he'd lost a great deal of weight. His clothes were hanging on him. Was the man eating anything?

"Adi, Adi," he said, squeezing the breath out of her. "It is so good to see you, sweetheart."

"It's good to be seen," she said, leaning back and gazing into his eyes, which now held the glaze of cataracts and were ringed by new lines. "I hear you haven't been in the best of health." At O'Hare, Chase had told her that the doctor had mentioned a couple of minor TIAs, as well as warnings of another stroke or heart attack to come. On top of that, he was malnourished and dehydrated. *He needs rest and consistent care*, the doctor had said.

"Ach," he said, waving her words away and then patting his chest with both hands. "As healthy as an old ox, despite what they say."

Chase shot her a look over the old man's shoulder and crossed his arms. "Now you're going to have to be honest with her, Gene. I didn't bring her all this way to fill her head with big fish stories."

"There'll be time enough to tell me all about it," Adalyn said, looping her arm through her grandfather's. "Shall we go in for a cup of hot chocolate? I got a little chilled on the ride."

"Did you not have the presence of mind to keep my granddaughter warm in that truck, boy?" Gramps chided Chase.

"Hey, it was Logan driving and your girl who wanted the windows open!" he returned, only mildly defensive.

"I wanted to smell it, Gramps," she said, shortening her stride to match her grandfather's new, shuffling gait. "It's been too long since I smelled Montana."

"Too long since you smelled her or saw her or heard her," he groused. "Too long by far. I don't understand it, Adi. How you and your mother could stay away so long."

In his words she heard a measure of hurt and longing, as well as true bewilderment.

"I don't know either, Gramps. I'm sorry for that. Life… well, life gets distracting."

"So I hear, so I hear." He waved away her hand when she reached for the door handle, insisting on opening it for her. "Go on, now."

It was then that she noticed that Chase had carried her bag behind her. "I'll just put this in right here," he said, "and give you two some time to catch up over that hot chocolate and some lunch."

"Thanks, Chase," she said. "For everything. I…well, thanks for everything," she said again, unsure of all she was feeling, let alone how to put it into words.

"Sure, sure, Adi," he said. He paused by the door, hands on narrow hips. There in the doorway, silhouetted by the warm morning sun on the mountainside behind him, she noticed how fine he'd turned out. It was like she hadn't seen him, really seen him, when he discovered her in full-panic mode in her apartment hallway. But now she saw him. Boy, all at once did she see him. Square jaw, wide shoulders, long legs. He had some inches on her, and she was kind of tall. But it was his eyes—those warm, intriguing, hazel eyes—that had always captured her attention. They were keen, taking in every detail, but never too intense, as if they carried the light of his demeanor too.

"Adalyn?" he asked, squinting those pretty eyes and cocking his head. "You okay?"

"What?" she asked, shaking her head. "Oh! Yes, yes." She felt the heat of a blush climbing her neck, her cheeks. "It's all been…just a lot, you know?"

He stepped closer. "I know," he said lowly, so Gramps couldn't hear. "But Adi girl, you can rest here. Recuperate, along with your grandfather. He can let his body heal; you can let your heart do the same."

She nodded quickly, hoping he didn't see the quick tears in her eyes. What was it about the kindness of a friend that allowed grief to surface so fast? It always took her by surprise. "Thanks, Chase. For all you did. Coming out to get me when you couldn't get ahold of me." *For getting me to leave when a stalker was closing in.* She shivered, remembering the rose in her bed. What would she have done if he hadn't arrived? What might the next day have brought?

He reached out and laid a hand on her shoulder. "Seriously, Adi. You look a little…pale. Are you okay?"

"Yes, yes," she said, forcing a bright tone and easing away. She turned to her grandfather. "Gramps, you want me to make you some lunch?"

"Lunch?" he asked, sitting in a decrepit old recliner by the window. "I mostly eat my big breakfast and then wait until I can heat a can of soup, come dinner."

"Which is why you've lost so much weight, I wager,"

Chase said. "You listen to your granddaughter, Gene," he called. "Eat and drink everything she gives you. Rest when she tells you to. You'll be back to yourself in no time."

"Well, maybe," Gramps semi-promised, giving him an apologetic smile. "Appetite's not what it once was."

"Maybe with a little more company, it will return," Adi said. "I always find food tastes better when I'm with someone else than when I'm alone."

"Amen to that," Chase said. He paused again. "Would you mind if I came around tonight after supper? Maybe we could catch up a little?"

"I'd like that," she said. "Meet at the dock, about eight o'clock?" She glanced back at Gramps. He looked like he was already ready to doze. Surely he'd be asleep by seven. Some time on the end of the dock with Chase might be nice. For old time's sake. But then her stomach twisted at the thought of such intimacy. "Invite Logan and Bea," she added hurriedly.

"Sure," he said amiably. "They'd like that. See you later." He gave her an adorable little wink and shoved out through the squeaky screen door.

The oil can has to be around here somewhere, she thought. How many other repairs would need to be made in order to get ready for guests, due to start coming in a couple of weeks? *But first, lunch.* Her stomach was rumbling and feeding her grandfather every few hours had to be a part of the plan. "What do you have to eat around here, Gramps?"

"Well, you could make toasted cheese sandwiches," he said. "I usually have bread and cheese. Maybe even a can of tomato soup in the cupboard." He took off his glasses and rubbed his eyes tiredly, as if even the thought of it wearied him.

"You just take a little snooze," Adi said. "I'll take stock of what you have. Maybe a run to the grocery store in Kalispell will be in order?"

"Maybe," he said.

Tomorrow, she thought. Tomorrow she'd make the drive in. Today, all she wanted to do was make-do while she took stock, not only of the kitchen, but the whole cabin, as well as all the guest cabins. And of Gramps himself.

He set his glasses on the side table and closed his eyes, beginning to nod off even as she watched him from the pass-through in the kitchen. The cabin was old—vintage national park, circa 1940s—but it was relatively clean. To her, it looked like Mrs. Larson still came around once a week to clean. Gramps had never been one to see dust or grime; after Grams died, Mom had seen Mrs. Larson hired. Happily, she still seemed to be in the picture.

She opened cupboard after cupboard. A jar of pickles. A bottle of mustard. In the fridge, she found the promised bread—with but two heels and a lone dried slice left—and a half-pack of Velveeta, but little else. No tomato soup, as mentioned. Not even some butter for Gramps's toasted cheese. Was Velveeta fatty enough to carry the day without it? She supposed so. *Maybe I'll have to take his truck and go to town today after all*, she thought tiredly as she opened the freezer to find nothing but two old, grape popsicles, half-melted and stuck to the freezer floor. *Victims of a power failure at some point.*

She stretched out her palms on the counter and peered through the pass-through at her grandfather. How long had it been this bad? What had happened to her vibrant Gramps, always ready to flip burgers or a "dog" on the grill for not only himself but Chase and Logan too? He'd routinely gone to Kalispell every Tuesday to shop for the week. When did that stop? Last month? Or last year?

A flash of guilt shot through her. What kind of granddaughter was she? Off gallivanting with eligible bachelors in Spain, Greece and Thailand, while her grandfather was here, slowly deteriorating? And what about Mom and Dad? Why hadn't they come to Montana to check on him?

She straightened and rubbed her face, looking to the old ceiling tiles above. *I've been as selfish as my mother*, she admitted to herself. "Help me, God," she whispered. "Help me to get Gramps back on his feet again, even as you help me too."

With that, she took to finding the old cast iron pan, settled some cheese atop the old bread, and made it extra thick to make up for the lack of fat on the outside. She set it on low heat and then rummaged through more cupboards, finding a few packets of hot chocolate. She put a kettle of water on the stove, and as she waited for the sandwiches to toast—hers open-faced due to lack of bread—and the kettle to whistle, she gazed out a dirty window to the lake. Yes, there would be plenty here to keep her busy. *As your heart heals*, Chase had said. Or something like that.

It was an odd feeling. The sense of being home and yet a bit of a foreigner at the same time. But she liked the growing sense of urgency, purpose she felt gathering in her mind and heart. At Smith & Jessen last week, she felt like the partners had just been feeding her minor tasks to keep her busy while they figured out what to do with her; here she felt needed in a hundred different directions. Vital. And she knew this was exactly where she was supposed to be for the summer.

How long had it been since she had felt that?

Since before Connor, she decided, running her hand along the rough-hewn beam to her right. Since before Adam, really. No, before she ever sat down with the producers of *The One* for their extensive interviews, including psychological and physical testing. From that day on, she'd felt like she was living someone else's life.

Here, she wasn't Stalled-Out Stalling. She wasn't the most famously rejected girl in America. She was just Adi. The same Adi who'd been here at five and fifteen. Did she remember that girl? Could she recover a bit of her again, after all that had happened? A bit of her hope, her enthusiasm, her gumption?

Adalyn pulled the kettle from the unit before it could truly scream. If Gramps was asleep, she wanted him to continue to do so. When he woke, he could eat. She'd see to that. Peeking at him, she could see his mouth hanging open, emitting a small, choking snore. She'd let him sleep now and be right there waiting for him to wake up. Then and only then, after she'd seen him eat and drink, would she go see the state of the rest of property.

—ᗢᗢ—

Kenneth stared at Adalyn Stalling's apartment, shifting in his car seat for the hundredth time. Where was she? Had she driven out when he ran into the McDonald's to go to the bathroom? No. She never left that early.

Just like she never left work early. But somehow, he'd missed her yesterday, driving home from Smith & Jessen to the apartment building. And now this morning?

His eyes traveled the length of the street, then back to the garage, then up to the sixth floor. The sixth floor where he'd taken his time in her apartment, examining her refrigerator, her cupboards, the contents of every drawer and closet, before carefully slipping that last, perfect rose in her bed. He'd considered staying last night. Introducing himself at last, just as he'd longed to, ever since Adam had sent her home. That night had been his first epiphany; maybe, just maybe, Adam had rejected her because Adalyn was meant for Kenneth.

When Connor broke their engagement and her heart, Kenneth became certain of it. Why else would a man do such a thing unless fate had intervened? The woman was perfect. Smart and sexy, with that olive skin and sculpted legs and hourglass figure. Her hair…well, he couldn't wait to run his hands through those long, shiny brown strands and pull her full lips to meet his. He couldn't wait for those lash-fringed dark eyes—too long centered on men unworthy of her—to stare only at him.

Yes, he had been close last night to staying. But he knew it was probably too soon. He knew how much Connor had hurt her. That she'd need time to heal. It was enough now to remind her that she was still worthy, still so worthy of a good man's love. Someone who would cherish her. Someone who could afford to keep her safe in his home. She'd never have to go out again. Never face the stupid paparazzi who trailed her. He could go and get groceries, anything she needed, and bring it to her. He could go to work and come home to her. She'd be in that pretty little black dress she wore on her next-to-last date with Adam, the one that just skimmed her knees and hugged her curves without being too trashy. He'd ask her to wear that.

She would make him his favorite meal—chicken cordon bleu—and a fresh salad. She'd be barefoot. He liked a woman with her cute little toes showing. He'd make sure she got them painted. A pretty pink, perfect for summer with her finger-nails to match. He'd have a hair stylist come to the apartment. A masseuse too. If only she let him take care of her, he'd take care of everything. Absolutely everything. And in turn, she would take care of him, be his helpmate, the constant companion he'd always longed for.

They needed each other. In time, she'd see that. When

the time was right, he reminded himself. Until that time, he needed to be patient.

But while he waited, he hungered for glimpses of her. That's what got him through each day. The brief glimpses of her at the gym, where he'd watched her via the mirror. Or in the store, where he'd trailed her from a distance down several aisles, watching her choose gluten-free items and fresh fruit. Even at the post office, when he'd dared to get in line behind her, just so he could get the chance to smell her perfume.

Now, after being in her apartment, he knew the name of that perfume. *Daisy Summer.*

He'd gone straight out and purchased a bottle this morning, just so he could spritz it in the air of his apartment and pretend she was right around the corner, waiting for him in that little black dress.

While he waited for her to emerge from her apartment, he riffled through the shopping bag, fished out the box and then opened the lid. The bottle had a molded daisy on the top. Fitting, he thought, for his girl, this perfume. She was so like a daisy, turning one way and then the other to follow her "sun." Well, soon enough, she'd know that she didn't need to keep searching. Soon enough, she'd know her search was over.

Just as his was.

"Now, Adalyn," he said, lifting the bottle to his nose as he stared at the garage. "Just give me a glimpse of you, girl. That's all I need today. To see your pretty face will give me the strength to wait another day and then another. Until you're ready for me. Truly ready. I can wait, sweetheart. I can. But let me *see* you. Let…me…see…you!" With each of those last words he slammed the palm of one hand against the steering wheel.

With some agitation, he ran a hand through his hair

and checked his watch again. 9:30 am. She was really late for work. Or…*Or*. What if she was sick?

Or worse, did she call in sick because his roses had made her remember all she was missing in Adam and Connor? Had he miscalculated? Hurt her, rather than helped her?

The very thought of it made him nauseated. He slammed his hand against the steering wheel, again and again, chanting, "Stupid, stupid, *stupid*" with each bang.

This was why he always messed things up with girls. Never got his timing right.

Should he go up? Go to the doorman, ask him to ring her apartment? Explain?

And if she was sick, he could…

No. The doorman would never allow that. He'd seen plenty of photographers try and worm their way around the man. It was only because he'd managed to see with binoculars one of Adalyn's sixth-floor neighbors punch in the code that he'd been able to get into the building from the back, let alone up to her floor. He'd figured out which apartment was hers—she kept her blinds shut these days, but hadn't at first. A locksmith mold was all he needed to create a key. But after the cops had arrived last night, he had no doubt that even the buffoons in security had reconfigured every floor code come morning, and seen that Adalyn's locks were changed. He wouldn't be getting up there again now, especially if he hoped to remain unseen. Last night, a timely pizza delivery had distracted them as he did his work on the sixth floor. Today, they'd be wiser for it.

So I'll call Smith & Jessen and find out what's up. He pulled out his cell and dialed the number from memory. He'd taken to calling a few times a day, just to hear her name spoken, even if it wasn't her own voice.

Her extension rang and rang and finally switched to

voicemail. But instead of the normal message, it was Adalyn! Her voice! Dazed, he drank in the sound of her voice as if she were speaking directly to him. But then she said something about being gone…He blinked, and blinked again. Had he heard her correctly? *Surely not.* Hurriedly, he tried to dial again, fumbled, and began again.

With trembling hands he listened to her message, concentrating on every word, which was hard because his pounding heart seemed to want to drown out everything else.

"Hello, you've reached Adalyn Stalling's office. Due to personal circumstances, I am on an extended leave of absence from Smith & Jessen. Please press 3 now to be connected to my colleague, Mary Roberts, or 0 to be connected to an operator. Thank you."

He dialed back and listened to the message three times, trying to get his mind around it. She was taking a leave of absence? He looked up at the apartment. He'd not seen her lift the blinds, as she had done without fail, every morning at seven. Even when she'd been off work before. So had she left town? No. It couldn't be.

One way or another, he had to find out.

CHAPTER 6

After Adalyn had managed to get her grandfather to slowly eat half a sandwich and drink half his mug of "chocolate" as he called it before dozing off again, she went into the office and studied the reservation book—something he still kept by hand. He also was only reachable by a land line and kept an old message machine…the kind that used a cassette tape.

"Sheesh, Gramps," Adi said under her breath. "What happens when that old cassette gives out? Where do you even buy a new one?"

She ran a pencil eraser down the pages of the reservation book. Only half the Kreature Komforts cabins were reserved for the summer. Adalyn glanced out the window and tapped her lips with the pencil. Only half? Ever since she could remember, the cabin complex had been solidly booked from July through September. How long had reservations been languishing?

She grabbed his master key from the hook and eased out through the squeaky door to take stock. There were twenty cabins in five circles of four, each circle sharing a campfire pit and barbeque. Across the creek was a group of newer cabins, added twenty years ago. In years past, families would gather together in these campfire circles, making quick friends with their temporary neighbors, sharing stories of hikes and fishing and bear and moose sightings. Now she could see that several screen doors were broken—either screen or hinge— and one was entirely set to the side. Chinking was missing from between the logs of the walls. A few chimneys were in noticeable decay. *Gramps had never let things slide like that,* she thought with concern. Evidence of his declining health?

Had she just missed such details when last she was here? Had it already been in decline and she was too absorbed in college life to notice? Or had all this happened in the last five or six years?

Choosing a cabin on a whim, she opened the door with the master key. It was winter-musty as well as dusty, the mattresses of the two bunk beds up on their side to prevent mold from forming. A mouse skittered across the far corner, making her jump, then shiver. She hated mice. *Hated* them. And now…How many cabins were infested? She knew that once mice got in, they were notoriously hard to get out. Gramps had always been meticulous about setting traps and watching them all winter, and more intensively come spring. She didn't see one trap out. And with missing chinking why bother? If you trapped one, another could just squeeze back on through.

So, chinking is first on the list, she said to herself, making a mental note. *Exterminators next.* Because there was no way—no way—she'd be on her knees, pulling out dead mice from the traps. She shivered again. She might've once been Montana-tough, but now she'd allow her citified self that luxury at least. No curling, creepy mouse tails for her…*Mmm-mm, no.* She'd gladly assign that to another.

Shaking off the thought of dead mice, she moved to the

kitchen. The appliances—a tiny two-burner stove and oven, as well as a fridge—were probably thirty years old. Both had doors open, again to prevent mold from forming. There was a small chance that guests would deem them "rustic" or "charming." As long as they were clean enough and still worked. But looking around, Adalyn had to admit that the whole place needed an overhaul. The floors required refinishing; the lighting could be updated; fresh linens would help a lot.

She went to the doorway and looked out, then back over her shoulder, then toward the lake and woods and mountains again. The location was incredible…with a reboot on design and a marketing campaign, could she make the cabins a tourist highlight, suitable for the grand old park? Excitedly, she moved to the next cabin and then the next, taking stock. The roofs had all been replaced a few years ago, thankfully, in the traditional green asphalt tile that the rangers favored. The stonework of the front steps at each entry seemed solid. The logs that made up the walls looked like they could last another fifty years—they only needed the white chinking fixed. And fixing that would give them a nice, bright lift.

So does Gramps have any money to put toward that work? If they revamped the campground the way she was thinking and garnered good reviews, could they charge double the price for lodging? She knew that her grandparents had always wanted to keep the prices down, encouraging families to come. But good grief, the big lodges charged over three-hundred a night for a room. Couldn't they charge a couple hundred for a cabin that slept four?

"Especially if it felt like affordable luxury," she whispered, tapping her lips with her finger. "A splurge." She stepped down and closed the door behind her, smiling with excitement for the first time since… well, since the day Connor got down on one knee and proposed to her. She blinked away the tears that seemed to always accompany that particular memory—probably because memories of the day he broke off their engagement immediately followed. From such a high point to such a low—

Stop it, Adi, she told herself. *Quit running that film through your mind, over and over again. It's done. It's in the past. It's time to start thinking about your future.*

And her future? Well, for the next three months, it was this place. This place in which her grandparents had invested most of their working years. These sweet cabins on a glorious lake in one of the prettiest parks in the country. Would it not be a good place for her to stake a claim too? To invest a bit of herself? Give back when all she'd ever done was take?

She moved back to Gramps's cabin, eager to find out what he'd think of her ideas. She'd have to tread carefully. This place had always been his baby...would he think she was meddling? Adalyn found him sitting in his worn wing-backed chair by the window, glasses far down on his nose, a carefully folded newspaper in his hand. "Says here," he said, tapping the paper with some disgust, "that there are already so many tourists in the Valley that locals can't get cell coverage."

"Already?" she said, sitting down in the matched chair that had always been Gram's. "It's early in the season for that to be happening."

"I just don't understand it," Gramps said. "Why you young folk would trust cell phones. At least my phone is always usable, no matter how many people come to the park."

"Unless a storm takes it out," Adalyn said dryly.

"Well, sure," he said, waving his hand. "That happens two or three times a year."

"Or six or seven?" she said, giving him a teasing smile.

"Maybe so. But it's always back the next day," he said,

pointing at her. "Mark my words, Adi girl. You'll be using my old phone at some point this summer."

"Oh, I hope so," she said, looking over at the huge, avocado-green clunker that still had the rotary dial. There was something so reassuring in the heft of the handset, the whirr of the dial after each number. "Remember how we used to have a party line? Chase and Logan would get on when I was talking just to bug me."

"*Hmmph*. Those boys didn't have anything over Mrs. Mason," he said, remembering a ranger's wife who'd lived up the road. "She'd listen to everyone's conversation just to pass the night away. It made Alice so angry!"

"Grams never did abide a busybody," Adalyn said, nestling back and putting her feet up on their shared ottoman.

"No, she did not," Gramps said. "Back in those days, all reservations were done by mail. We didn't have the phone calls and whatnot," he said, waving his hand toward his desk in clear irritation. "It was all," he paused to heave a sigh, "so much more civilized."

"Or maybe it just felt that way because Grams took care of all of that?"

"Could be a bit of that," he admitted.

"It's been a lot for you, hasn't it, Gramps? Since Grams passed on?"

"In more ways than one, Adi girl."

"I imagine. This place," she paused to look around, "was always yours, together. Was it hard to stay? After she died? I mean, did you ever think about moving back to Minnesota? Or to Chicago, to be closer to me?"

"It'd be nice to be nearer to family," he said, tilting his head and then shaking it. "But no. Alice convinced me to move to Montana when I was twenty years old. And the day I got here, I knew I'd die here too. Logging was my trade, at first," he said, as if Adi didn't know. Did he think she'd forgotten? "But Alice was smitten with the park. 'Preserve the forest, Gene,' she'd tell me. 'Don't tear it down.'"

Adalyn nodded, happy to share the well-worn memory with him. "And she got the job at the lodge that summer, right?"

"That very summer," he said, leaning his head back and taking off his glasses, wiping them of dirt and lifting them to the waning light. "It wasn't but a couple of years before this place became available. The rest was history," he said with a smile.

"It certainly was," Adalyn said. "Most of your life has been spent here."

"May through September. Then I was off to log, no matter what your grandmother had to say about it. Had to bring home the bacon."

Adalyn nodded. The two had moved to Kalispell and rented a house there, so their kids could go to school. Some years Gramps had gone as far as Oregon to bring home that "bacon," leaving Grams to see to the kids. Was that what had planted such wanderlust in her mother? To see what her father might have seen? Or as some sort of payback? Leaving him as she had been so often left?

But back then, it was just what people did. Made ends meet best they could.

"So the cabins were here from the very start? When you took over the concession?" she asked.

"The cabins were here. The rest was up to us. The name, the sign, the linens. It was your Grams's idea to host games each night, to create a bit of 'community,' she said." He shook his head. "These days it seems people want more of their own space."

"Oh, I don't know," Adalyn said with a smile. "I remember lots of nights, watching people play charades and share stories of the park with strangers. And it was like they were sudden friends."

"Yes, it was," Gramps said with a nod.

"It was magical for me too, Gramps," she said. "All those years I was here for the summer…to spend all that time with Grams and you, and Chase and Logan…" Her voice cracked and she coughed. "Well, that was a gift to me."

"No more than it was a gift to us, Adi girl. You, our only grandchild. What grandparent wouldn't thank God for such time?"

Adalyn smiled. "Maybe grandparents who didn't like their grandchildren sneaking out to watch the Northern Lights?"

"Ach. Any grandparent who wouldn't cheer that child on is a stick in the mud!"

"Or maybe a grandparent who didn't enjoy a child coming in, dripping on the wood floor and nearly hypothermic because she'd been swimming in the lake?"

"It only made you stronger," he said dismissively, thumping his chest. "Swimming in glacial water is good for the blood. Ask any Norseman."

She laughed under her breath. "It certainly makes the blood pump in sheer shock."

"Especially this time of year," he said, lifting a gray brow and casting her a knowing look. Water this cold—recently melted off the glaciers and snows above—was apt to send a body into hypothermia within minutes.

"Do you still dive in?" she asked, regretting it as soon as she said it. Would he consider it a challenge?

"The first of every July, August and September," he said with a firm nod.

"Umm…Does your doctor approve of that plan?"

"Doc doesn't need to know of it. As I said, it's good for the blood. Not so much in June." He brushed a hand over his mouth. "That water is wicked-cold right now."

They fell into a companionable silence for a bit, each remembering cold dives off the dock. How one's muscles contracted in pain, how the lungs seized in shock...

"So, Gramps," Adalyn said. "I had a look around the place. And I see from your reservations book that you're only half-full this season?"

"Yes," he said sadly. "The place isn't what she used to be. And the summer-folk know it."

She smiled over that term. *The summer-folk.* He'd always called tourists that.

"It seems like we need to do some repairs, Gramps," she said. "Maybe consider a marketing overhaul. You've done such a great job, all your life, keeping things up. But maybe... maybe in these last years—"

"Out with it, Adi girl," he said, heaving himself up to toddle over to the window. "You've seen what I've seen. There aren't some repairs to be done. There are a lot of repairs." He turned partially toward her, but did not meet her gaze. "And I...well, I'm not quite as up to the task as I once was." He gazed out to the lake, through the window. "But it doesn't matter much."

She rose and went to stand beside him by the window. "It doesn't matter?"

"Nah," he said. He turned toward her and took her hand in his. "It's good that the Lord saw fit to bring you here this summer, Adi girl. Because this summer will be our last." He turned and lifted an aged hand to the window sill, gazing outward.

"What? What do you mean?"

"Our concession is up," he said, with a clamp of his lips

and lift of his shoulders. He spoke of the rental agreement he had with the park officials for the property. "We renewed twenty years ago. These days, it's up for grabs every ten. I'm thankful we lasted this long." He waved toward the reservation book. "With the park taking fifty per cent of all we make, those bookings won't see us through. And even if they did, they're asking me to present a plan for the next ten years. Plans to 'renew the property,' they say, all 'while respecting our strict codes to protect the environment,'" he quoted, shaking his finger, with some disgust. "What does that even mean, Adi girl? Have I not been 'protecting the environment' every summer I've kept this place in operation?"

He held her shocked gaze for a moment and then toddled back to his chair, sinking wearily into it. Her heart went out to him, even as her mind raced. This place, lost to them forever? It couldn't be. It simply couldn't be. And protecting the environment…given today's ideas on that, the park service might mean everything from keeping people from a bonfire to recycling every single thing they could, to not washing linens or using paper towels.

All of which was way beyond what Gramps could deal with.

She turned and walked over to him, falling to her knees beside him, taking his hand in hers. "Gramps," she said in a whisper. "You said that it was good that the Lord brought me here this summer. Maybe that was for more than a chance to say goodbye. Maybe it was because I might have ideas on how to renew our concession. Because I do, Gramps. Walking around this afternoon, my mind is full of ideas."

"Oh, Adi girl," he said, lifting his other hand to her cheek for but a moment. "I know it pains you to think of letting this place go. As it does me. But you have your life in the big city. I couldn't ask you to give it up. We've had a good run here.

Now maybe it's someone else's turn."

"But what if…Gramps, what if I *wanted* to do it?" It was out before she'd really thought it through. She bit her lip and waited on him to respond.

He stared at her for a long moment. "Then, Adi girl, we'd need to talk some more."

CHAPTER 7

They agreed to resume their conversation come morning. After she'd fed him a granola bar from her purse and eaten a can of peaches for her dinner, she went to the docks to meet her friends.

Logan sat on the end piling and Bea had her arms around him, resting her pert chin on his shoulder. She beamed a smile of welcome. "I hear you three spent most summer evenings out here," she said.

"Can you blame us?" Adalyn asked, sitting down beside Chase on the end of the dock, where she could let her legs dangle above the water. "Though it could be a bit warmer," she added, zipping up her fleece. She noticed that Chase wore his park service jacket. *USNPS*, she mused. His lifelong dream. "That looks good on you," she said to him. "Can you believe you get to wear it? I mean, *here*, in Glacier?"

He'd been a ranger since college graduation. But it had taken him years to make his way back to Glacier. She'd learned that much from Gramps.

"I pinch myself every day," he said with a wink. Then he

looked out to the lake, and Adalyn studied his profile for just a second. She liked the scruff of beard growth. It accentuated his strong jaw line.

"What project do they have you working right now, Chase?" She knew he was a wildlife biologist, with a specialty in grizzlies, which helped him win his position in the park. His long family history at Glacier and knowing a few key people probably hadn't hurt either.

"I'm actually tracking moose right now," he said. "My goal is to tag a few bulls that seem to elude us every year. I can usually spot them with a drone, but by the time I get there in person, they're gone."

"That sounds dangerous," Adalyn said. She knew that more people died from moose attacks than grizzly attacks every year. Tourists mistook them for slow and friendly. They weren't.

"It's as wet as it is dangerous," Bea said. "He has to hike with waders on."

"Well, I don't go out with them on. But they're in my backpack," Chase said. "Better to wear waders than wet pants on the trail home."

"True that," Logan said. "It only takes one rainstorm to make a hiker swear they'll go naked before they wear chafing wet pants again."

"Mmm, naked hiking," Bea said, nuzzling his neck. "Sounds fun."

"Do you always work this side of the park?" Adalyn asked, eyes wide as she steered the conversation back onto a more suitable course.

"No. I'm either on the East side or in the back country three days a week."

"Do you hike in?"

"Most of the time. Sometimes I get a helicopter ride in

and hike out. But I don't like to do that much. It tends to spook the wildlife, which kind of works against me, you know?" He cast her a quick grin.

"Do you get lonely? Spending all those days out there by yourself?"

"Not when Hannah the Super Ranger goes with him," Logan said, with a scoffing laugh.

Adalyn stiffened. Hannah?

"Be nice," Chase said, scowling at his brother.

"Hannah's a little over-excited about her job," Bea said, helping Adalyn catch up. "She's fresh out of school and somehow landed her first gig in Glacier. All the old guys can't figure her—or her luck—out. But she did some sort of grizzly scat study at MSU which gained some attention, so she's scored a position as Chase's part-time assistant."

"She studies their poop?" Adalyn said.

Chase grinned and nodded. "Not just how the rest of us do it, examining for signs of what they eat. She carries a microscope and does some intensive lab work, right there in the field. In May, we discovered a new bacteria in one sow's gut that might be keeping her from bearing any cubs. She looks healthy; we trapped her last year and I put a small camera and beacon on her to make sure everything else is okay for her."

"His very own Griz Cam," Logan said. "If he'd put the footage on the Internet, he'd be as popular as those pregnant giraffe cams."

"Except Giselda isn't getting pregnant," Chase said.

"Giselda?"

"Giselda is what he's named this sow," Logan said.

"Is she getting any action?" Bea asked cheekily.

"Oh, yeah. She's caught more than one fella's eye," Chase said with a slow grin.

"How often does that happen? Infertility among bears?"

Adalyn asked.

"Not as often as it does in humans," Chase said. "But as the park has gotten more popular—more people on the trails—we've been seeing it more often. That's why it's of interest to us. Just as soon as I get these three bull moose tagged, Hannah and I'll head back out to track her. Hannah wants to tranquilize her and draw blood so she can do some further study."

Adalyn nodded. It was interesting, all he had going on. And while it niggled at her, this Hannah-person in his life, she knew she had no right to even feel an ounce of jealousy. After all, she and Chase were just friends. And she hadn't had thoughts of anything more with him since they were kids. Kids! It was just being here, she thought, looking out at the lake, that brought back such silly, remembered emotions. *Remembered*, she reminded herself again. Not current.

Who knew? A guy as handsome as Chase Rollins had to have more than an assigned junior-ranger interested in him. *Better get used to other girls being around, Stalling.* The Rollins boys had always been like catnip. And now Logan was taken.

"Feel like getting out tomorrow?" Chase asked. "I'm supposed to track that first bull moose near Jones Lake."

"Maybe," she said. "Gramps and I have some talking to do. About his health. And about the cabins. Did you guys know the concession was up?"

"Yeah," Logan said, giving her a pensive look. "His is always the year after ours. We went through the wringer last fall."

"It's tough these days, huh?"

"Harder than ever," Bea put in. "We had to have charts and graphs to present to the board. Plans to improve the boat concession. Plans to upgrade the dock and the boats."

Adalyn ran her hand over the newer wood of the planks.

She'd noticed it'd been replaced, even though it was the exact same design.

"And you'd better believe that they checked up on us," Logan said. "Made sure we'd bought what we said we would. Did what we planned."

"How long did they give you?"

"The last of it was due last month." He nodded over at four new canoes on the beach. "Those beauties and a new low emissions engine in the *Maid of McDonald*."

"As well as thirty new life vests," Bea put in.

The *Maid* was the old ferry boat the Rollinses had used forever for their sunset cruises.

"That must've set you back," Adalyn said.

"Try everything we earned all winter," Logan returned, lifting a brow.

"But we'll make it back this summer, and next," Bea said.

Logan nodded. "Business is good. And updating things—well, you know how it goes. Tourists like fresh."

Adalyn heaved a sigh. "And the Kreature Komforts cabins are far from fresh."

Logan scratched his chin. "There's a lot to be done. But it could be grand again. Or...well, you know. Charming. We can go as far as *charming*. Question is, how long is your Gramps game to run it? Or able to? The man should've retired years ago."

"And after this last stint in the hospital," Bea said, eyeing her sadly, "do you really think he should still be doing it at all?"

Adalyn shook her head. "Probably not. I think he's just been carrying it these last few years since Grams died. Maybe hoping Mom or I would come and pick up the slack." She rubbed the back of her neck. "I should've never left him alone this long."

"Ahh, don't be so hard on yourself, Adi," Chase said, resting his fingers for just a moment on her forearm and giving her a tender smile. "You have your own life now in the big city. Not many people can make a living off the summer concessions anymore, in any national park. Maybe…" He shifted and squinted out at the lake. "Maybe it's time for another family to take on the campground? Make their own memories here?"

She frowned. Why did his words agitate her so? He was only speaking the truth. Something like her Gramps had said himself. She had her own life in Chicago. Smith & Jessen might want her gone this summer, but they would never bless her taking five months off a year. And Mom…well, Mom and Dad clearly had other horizons on their hearts to see. Was it simply time to let it go? And yet the thought of that was just, just—

"I could consult," she blurted out. "Become a marketing consultant," she hurried on. "Freelance through the winters, like Bea and Logan go work the ski resorts. Then run the cabins myself."

Logan and Bea were smiling and nodding, taking that idea in, but Chase wasn't. He was still frowning.

"What?" Adalyn asked. "You don't think I could do that?"

"Oh, I think you could do that," he said. "But is it your dream, Adi? Or just your grandfather's? Are you trying to make his dreams your own?"

"Didn't Logan and Bea do that?" she said defensively. "Take your grandparents' dreams for the boat concession and make it their own? And you, finding your own way here in the park?"

"Yeah, but we never really left, Adi. I mean, I went to Alaska. But that was because I was assigned to Denali."

His words stung, even though he'd said it gently.

"A little like I was assigned school and then a demanding

job?" Adalyn shot back.

He lifted his hands in surrender. "I'm just asking, you know? I don't want you to get in too deep because of some misguided sense of loyalty." He eyed the boathouse cabin and then his brother and sister-in-law. "Running these things has to be kind of a calling. Because it's not really a big money maker."

"You can say that again," Bea said, blowing out her cheeks. "And the bonus is that it's a heck of a lot of work. *And*, as much as I love the park," she added, looking around, "we don't see much of it when we reach the heart of the summer. It's a 24-7 gig then."

"C'mon," Logan said. "It's not all we see. We get to go hike at least once a week. Maybe even to town for a movie."

"Yes, but the bottom line is that we are responsible, 24/7," Bea said.

"Yeah, kinda," her husband reluctantly admitted. "But then you get to work with me 24/7," he said, pulling her closer. "That makes up for a lot of it, right?"

"You betcha, handsome," she said, nuzzling his neck again.

Adalyn considered them. Would she really be willing to work so hard, without a partner like they had in each other? Could she be solely committed to this? And yet, wasn't she pretty much solely committed to Smith & Jessen in Chicago? It was a demanding agency. *So demanding that she'd agreed to give up months of her time to film two seasons of* The One... And even before that, she'd worked eighty-hour work weeks, often going into the office on weekends or completing projects at home.

"There's a lot to consider," she admitted. "It would be great if I can ask you a lot of questions in the days to come," she said to Logan and Bea.

"Sure, anything," Logan said. "You know that."

"And you can ask me hard questions too," she said, leaning into Chase's shoulder for a quick nudge. "I give you permission. You can make sure I have my head on straight."

He smiled down at her and then looked quickly out at the lake. "Seems to me I never had to have permission before," he said.

"Well, yeah. Now you do. Walls, you know. Adulthood and everything."

"Gotcha."

"I have a hard question," Logan said, slowly rubbing his thumb across his jeans and biting his lip. "Why'd you go on that crazy show?"

"Logie!" Bea cried, even while Chase scowled over at him.

"What?" he said, lifting his hands. "Pretty girl like you…" he said, turning back to Adalyn. "Why go on a show like that? With a one-in-twenty-five chance at love?"

"Not that he missed a single episode," Bea said, hitting him on the shoulder.

"Hey! I was curious! It was Adi!"

Bea pretended to wring her husband's neck.

Adalyn grinned and shook her head. It was only the thousandth time she'd been asked the question. "No, it's okay. Let the boy live!" She laughed softly. "Really, it was kind of a fascinating experience. I can tell you all about it sometime. But the short answer is that I did the first season upon the request of my agency. The producers of the show are a client of ours. Insider secrets, that kind of thing. That was the initial drive. My bosses and I thought I wouldn't last half as long as I did."

"Half as long," Chase grumbled. "You were one of the final two."

Her breath caught, remembering Adam. How it had so surprised her, how much she felt for him, in so short a time.

And yet now, with distance, realizing how much of it was the intensity of the experience that manufactured some of those feelings...

"I couldn't believe he chose that other girl," Logan said.

"Me either," Bea said. "She had nothing on you that I could see."

Adalyn smiled. It always felt good when people said they were Team Adi. Even if she had lost that particular round.

"But then you went back," Chase said, eyeing her from the side as if he'd questioned it a hundred times.

"I went back," she affirmed with a sigh. "It's kinda hard to describe. But when you're in it, and you come so close to 'winning,'"—she said, using her fingers as quotes—"there's sort of a fever pitch. And when the producers came around, offering me the chance to be in the opposite position, of having twenty-four guys trying to win me..."

"That's kinda hard to say no to," Chase finished for her.

Her heart skipped a beat at the empathy in his tone. But it was his long, searching look—again from the side—that made her quickly look to the mountains. "Yeah," she managed. "It was almost impossible. And my bosses...well, they loved it. They were pretty much golden with those producers."

"Serving you up on a platter not once, but twice," Logan said, frowning.

"Well, it wasn't like that," she said. "Not really."

"Wasn't it?" Chase asked, his brow furrowed now too.

She heaved a sigh and studied the current of the lake, making part of it shimmer while the rest was glass-smooth. What deeper current had convinced her it was worth another run? Or had it entirely been surface-level? She didn't know.

"But, I have to say," Bea said, breaking the tension, "that Connor! He was totally charming. And," she paused to cough, "so sexy."

"Hey!" Logan cried.

"Not any sexier than you, babe," she said. "Just calling a spade a spade."

Logan gave sway with a reluctant nod. "I'm man enough to say the guy had game."

Adalyn grinned, in spite of herself. "He did." She noticed that Chase was again staring out, not smiling with them. "Too bad that all that charm and draw didn't equate to character."

"I'll say," Chase muttered.

"He turned out to be a tool," Bea said. "I swear, I would've done exactly what you did. James was sweet, but he really was kind of simple, right? He didn't have the brains to match yours. So I would've chosen Connor too. But then, when he up and broke off your engagement…Girl, I didn't even know you, but these two made me feel like I did." She waved at the brothers.

"We were a little overly invested," Chase said ruefully.

"Overly invested?" Bea said. "You were thinking about getting out your tranquilizer gun!"

"Yeah, we all had a few conversations about going after that idiot when he broke your heart," Logan said. "With Chase being a tracker and all, we could've put the fear of God in him."

Adalyn laughed under her breath. He joked. They wouldn't ever really go after someone with a gun. But she appreciated the protective sentiment.

"Would you ever do it again?" Chase asked, staring at her intently.

"Again?" she said. "No. Never. Ever."

"Good," he said. "Love is a risk. But it's never best played out on TV. Right?"

"Right," she said slowly. She agreed with him. But why did she feel a little…*slapped* by his question?

He was rising then, offering her a hand. "I have to go," he said. "My alarm's going to be ringing before sun-up tomorrow."

"Ah, well," she said, standing without taking his hand. His stinging words still hung in the air around them. "Guess it's good I'm not going with you then. I'm beat."

He paused, then nodded as he tucked his hands in his jacket pockets. "Maybe another time."

"Maybe," she said, her tone high and tight.

"Well, here's to many more nights, meeting up like this," Bea said brightly, giving her a quick hug. "I'm glad you're here, Adi. And I'll be praying you can make wise decisions about the cabins."

"Thanks," she said, grateful for the smaller woman's adept ways of easing a situation.

"I will too," Logan said, giving her a side hug and kissing the crown of her head. "I, for one, wouldn't mind having you as a forever-summer neighbor. Ask us anything, okay?"

"I will," she said, smiling as the two newlyweds headed down the dock to their cabin, hand in hand.

Then it was just Chase. She clasped her own hands together.

"I, uh," he began, rubbing the back of his neck. "Well, I..."

She dared to look up at him.

His eyes shifted back and forth over hers. Then he licked his lips and said, "Maybe it's just best I say goodnight. I've said too much already, I think."

"Oh, don't worry about it," she said. "It's nothing I haven't heard before, really." They walked down the dock together. At the end, she glanced sideways at him. "Good night, Chase. Thanks again for bringing me back. Gramps..." She shook her head and put her hands on her hips. "If anything had happened to him—I mean, if anything more had happened and I found out weeks later..." She lifted her hand to her forehead. "I would never have forgiven myself. You went above and beyond. Thank you."

"You're welcome." He folded his arms. "Adi, there's one other thing I need to talk to you about tonight."

She tensed. What now?

"That guy, your potential stalker. You're not going to post anything on social media, right? You'll be careful? To keep your whereabouts a secret?"

"Chase Rollins, I'm not an idiot," she said chidingly. "I already went through years of Facebook and Instagram to make sure there wasn't anything in there that would give it away. I'm not about to post it now."

"That's good. It's just that you said you might start marketing this place. And I know most marketing these days involves social media."

She gave him a gentle smile and crossed her own arms. "Don't worry. I don't want Rose Man to find me here any more than you do. He'll give it up after a while. Find someone else to obsess over. Especially now when he discovers I've left Chicago. From what I've read about stalkers, they like proximity."

Chase paused and the muscles in his jaw flexed. She had to admit she kind of liked it. It made him appear...protective. Is that what he felt? "You've been researching stalkers?" he asked.

"Well, you know. As far as Google. And the great Google mind says that stalkers generally like convenient targets. They're lazy, essentially."

She cast him a sly smile and he eased up a bit on the whole manly protector thing. "Good to know," he said, pursing his lips and nodding. "Can I walk you up?"

"Nah," she said, walking backward through the pebbles of the beach, hands tucked in her pockets. "I think I remember how to get there."

"That's good," he allowed. "See you tomorrow, Adi."

"See you tomorrow."

She walked through the rocks and entered the path through the pines, thinking about his mouth as he said *see you tomorrow*. His eyes—with so much going on behind them all the time. What was it about Chase Rollins? Why could he so easily get under her skin, in some odd way?

Maybe because he always had, she reluctantly admitted to herself.

CHAPTER 8

It took three days before Kenneth decided to call Adalyn's "colleague," Mary Roberts, at Smith & Jessen. He straightened his carefully written script before him. He'd rehearsed it several times. With luck, if he played this right, he'd find out where she'd gone.

Kenneth took a sip of water—room-temperature, just how he liked it. But then he realized that he only had a few sips left. He needed the glass three-quarters full before he made this call. He rose, went to the kitchen sink and refilled it, returned to the desk and set it on the coaster. He took several deep breaths, dialed Adalyn's office number, listened to her message, and then dialed the extension for Mary. As it rang again, he leaned forward.

"Mary Roberts," she said, picking up after the third ring.

"Hi, Mary. Listen this is Jeff Balou, of Prosser & Litlow. I have had several conversations with Adalyn and was calling to tell her that we are leaning toward hiring your agency, only to find she is gone?"

"Oh! Yes, well, unfortunately, Adalyn had to take a leave

of absence due to a family emergency and well...never mind. But I am more than happy to help you myself, Mr. Balou."

"I appreciate that, Mary. But I really felt like Adalyn and I hit it off. She understood my firm's goals, our direction. We've spent hours on this already. I'm wondering if we should simply wait for her to return before proceeding. How long will she be gone?"

"She's scheduled for three months' leave, unfortunately," Mary said. "Are you certain I cannot be of assistance? Or perhaps one of our partners—"

"Perhaps. But I really don't feel good about doing that without speaking to Adalyn first. Might I give her a quick call to discuss it?"

"I wish I could make that happen," Mary said. "But Adalyn cannot be disturbed at this time."

"You can't even call her?"

"I am doing my best to not disturb her. Perhaps if you catch me up on your conversations, I can help you move forward, or refer you to another?"

She was good, but Kenneth had prepared for such stonewalling. "Where is she?" he said with a guffaw. "A psych ward? Just what kind of place is Smith & Jessen?"

"Oh, no, no," Mary said with a giggle. "It's nothing like that! Unless, of course, you call time away in the mountains a psych ward," she said confidentially.

"Oh, that's good," he said easily. "I wish I was in the mountains myself. The mountains are good for the soul. Where'd she go? Wyoming? Utah? Montana?"

Mary seemed to remember herself then. "I really cannot say," she said. He could hear her typing now. Pulling up reference documents from Adalyn? "Mr. Balou, which firm did you say you were calling from?"

He didn't bother answering. With a smile, he clicked his

red phone button, ending their connection.

He had all he would get from the woman.

He sat back in his chair, leaning on the rear two legs. *She's in the mountains*, he thought. He figured it was a likely scenario, ever since he learned she was gone. Had she not spoken about her love of the mountains on *The One*, to both Connor and Adam? But she'd been careful about ever mentioning *which* mountains. He'd have to go through the footage one more time on his DVR, which he'd carefully edited down to only scenes in which Adalyn appeared. Had she mentioned the word "park" in association with those mountains? A state park? A national park?

Quickly, he searched for national parks on his smart phone. There were quite a few, out West. Yellowstone. Yosemite. Olympic. Glacier. The Tetons. Kings Canyon. If you were just looking for mountains, there was also the Smoky Mountains. But there was nothing about Adalyn that struck him as Southern. No, his girl was Northern. Right?

He'd taken screenshots and printed out hundreds of pictures of her in every outfit and gorgeous gown she had ever been seen in, with her hair up, or down, or curled. Of her body in profile. Of her in silhouette, against a tropical sunset. Close-ups of her face, of her looking adoringly at one of the men. A three-quarter view of her face, in serious contemplation. One showed her with tears streaming down her face, her brows curved in distress. Another when Connor managed to delight her. He stared at all of these now, plastering an entire wall of his living room. He rose and touched her cheek, her chin. "Where'd you go, Adalyn? Where will I find you? When I do, will you show me your mountains? Show me why you love them so?"

He knew she would. Once he was there, once she saw how much he loved her...had always loved her, she'd recognize him as the one she'd been missing. The reason neither Adam or Connor had worked out.

Because fate had saved Adalyn Stalling for him.

—⟋⟋⟍—

Adalyn tip-toed down the squeaky wood floors of the hallway and carefully shut her grandfather's bedroom door, glad that he was still snoring peacefully. She checked her watch. Had she ever known him to sleep past seven? It was but another indicator of his advancing age, she supposed. Or the aftermath of his heart issues. Such trauma on the body could take it out of you for a while.

She padded over to the calendar, grateful to spot a "Dr. Ellison" in a few weeks at 1:00. As long as she remembered, her grandparents had always scheduled appointments in town at 1:00. After their guests had left and they were sure cleaning would be completed, and before the next round were allowed in at 4:00. *Not that there are more than two cabins rented that day,* she mused, turning to the reservations book and her grandfather's wavering notes written in pencil. *Gotta fix that. ASAP.*

She lifted her chin and stared out the window. Was it really her task? To "fix" this? Was she ready to sign on to run the Kreature Komforts cabins? *Well, if I gave it a new name, it'd help a lot,* she decided. Honestly? She didn't know if this was her thing forever. She just knew that if she didn't put some effort into it and see where it led, she'd regret it. Adalyn couldn't just let it slip away. Not with all the family history tied up here.

She turned to the kitchen and put a pot of water on— Gramps only drank instant coffee, regrettably—but she needed some caffeine in her body STAT. Then she grabbed a pencil that he obviously sharpened with his pocketknife and a scratchpad and began furiously listing all the items she needed in town, beginning with real coffee, filters, and a small pot. She didn't drink coffee all day, but she liked to begin with something good. And she was going to fill his fridge and cupboards with easy, healthy food. She'd feed Gramps three times a day, help him put on some weight. Get him engaged with her plans to revamp a few cabins that she could market as "newly renovated"—they would become her models for the entire complex overhaul to present to the park officials come summer's end when their concession was up for review.

If she decided to do that.

But that would engage his mind too. Satisfied at the thought, she poured steaming water into a mug and then added a spoonful of coffee crystals.

"That smells good," Gramps said, startling her.

She turned and smiled. "Good morning. How do you feel?"

"Right as rain," he said, putting a hand on her shoulder. "Sun's out. My girl is here. And there's coffee on. What else does a man need?"

She smiled. "I'm making a list for town. Want anything special?"

"Nah. Whatever you decide is good with me." He was wearing an ancient flannel shirt, rolled up at the sleeves. It was separating a bit at the shoulder seam.

Needle and thread, she added to her list. Unless she could find Grams's old sewing basket around.

"Want to go with me?" she asked.

"I'd better see if I can make myself useful around here. Fix a couple of doors on the cabins."

"I saw that yesterday. But don't overdo it, okay? Doctor's

orders, right?"

"Right. I'm slow these days, Adi girl. The ticker's not what she used to be," he said, patting his chest.

"So I hear. You have a doctor appointment coming up for follow-up?"

He took a sip of his own coffee and eyed her from the side. "Snooping through my calendar, are you?"

"Hey, I'm just a bored executive. What else am I supposed to do around here but take care of my grampa?"

He pursed his lips and rocked his head back and forth. "I dunno. Surely there's something more fun than *that* for a pretty little thing like you."

She put a hand around his waist and pulled him closer. "There's nothing else I'd rather do this summer, Gramps. I'm glad to be here."

"I'm glad you're here too, Adi girl," he said, putting a hand around her shoulders and squeezing. "More than you know."

"Well, I'd better be off to the store. Unless you were planning on a spoonful of mustard for breakfast."

"I usually walk over to Eddie's for breakfast," he said, talking about the café in Apgar. There were precious few locals in West Glacier. But if you were looking for one of them, it was the place to find them. "Care to join me?"

"I'd love that. Tomorrow, though? Today, I have it in mind to head to town and get back. If I go now, I'll be home by lunchtime."

"Sure, sure."

"Gramps, when you're at the café, can you ask around for someone who does chinking repair? I think that's the first order of business. To repair the chinking on all the cabins. Also, a good exterminator. I think you have a mouse problem."

He shook his head, as if ashamed, then lifted his thumb and middle finger to the side of his forehead. She noticed the age spots on his hands and arms. The thickened knuckles that spoke of arthritis. "I just couldn't keep up with them this year. Decades at this, and there's never been a summer when the mice won. They started pulling ahead last year." He dropped his hand and cast her a helpless look.

"I know, Gramps," she said, putting a hand on his shoulder. "But this is something we can both hand over to others. Let's get the chinking fixed ASAP and then get an exterminator in right after. We'll show those mice who rules Kreature Komforts."

"I'm on it," he said, looking a bit more like the strong, resourceful grandfather she remembered. "Lou will know of someone for the chinking. His son runs a log-home business in Kalispell."

"Great." She turned and picked up her purse, then reached for his keys. "I'll be back in two shakes of a lamb's tail," she said, using one of his favorite expressions.

"Be careful on that highway, Adi girl," he said. "Even this early in the season, there are tourists, you know, with their eyes on the mountains instead of the road."

"Got it."

She shut the screen door behind her and closed her eyes, inhaling a deep breath of high mountain air, redolent with pine. The lake before her was pristine, just a faint ripple on the water, the golden morning light reflecting upon it. As much as she was eager to get to town, the lake pulled her more. She pulled her phone from her pocket, unrolled her headphones from another and flipped to her favorite playlist of instrumentals. Scrolling through, she found "Grace" from a cellist named Nelson, and let it roll.

As it played, she lifted her arms up and stretched, studying each crevice and peak of the mountains that surrounded the lake. The fires had ravaged the west side last year, but as

Gramps always said, it was a natural part of the process. It was sad to see, in a way, but she knew it was good for the health of the forest. *There are some flowers that only bloom after a fire*, she remembered him saying. She felt like she'd been through a couple fires herself. Might there be some seeds in her even now, just beginning to sprout?

She took a long, deep breath in through her nostrils, held it, then let it out through her mouth. For this moment, it felt like the lake was only hers, and it reminded her of a hundred other moments just like it as she grew up along these shores. How she'd missed it. Missed it, without even fully realizing it. *Thanks, Lord*, she prayed silently. *Thanks for bringing me here.*

She glanced up at the cabin. *Thanks for keeping Gramps alive. Help me. Help me to make wise decisions. For him. For this place. For me.*

She looked back to the lake. She'd always felt confident in her decisions. But this last year... Well, this last year had fairly wrecked her. Made her second-guess everything.

Her phone dinged and she saw she had a message. Her heart caught. *Molly. Shoot!*

Hey, where are you? Called the office to see if you wanted to grab lunch and you're on A LEAVE OF ABSENCE? What's up???

Oh, hi, she returned. Molly was her best friend in Chicago. Really her only friend outside of work. They'd met up in a pasta-making class. *I'm so sorry. Had to leave town unexpectedly. Gramps is not doing very well. I needed to come be with him.* She paused, but then decided to leave the whole stalker thing out. That'd be a better thing to tell Molly in person. *Phone date soon?*

Sounds good, came the return. *I'll be hoping for the best for your gramps!*

Adalyn thanked her and then pocketed her phone again as she trudged up to the old Ford truck, thinking about her friend. Her friends at work...well, they were nice. Good for a little gossip in the kitchen or drinks after hours, but none of them were close. Particularly after her stints on the show. After that, she'd steered clear of them, feeling embarrassed about the whole thing. Work friends seeing you ugly-cry and make out with guys and confess intimate feelings on camera? Well that was just...yuck. It had clearly made those who watched the shows—which was pretty much everyone in the office—feel like they knew Adalyn. When they were just work friends for her. *An intimacy disparity*, Molly had called it, and she was dead right.

Which was kinda like all of America. If they'd watched the show, strangers on the street felt comfortable walking up to her and chatting. She'd been an extrovert before. The show had made her a veritable recluse. She knew from other contestants on previous seasons that it'd fade in time. People would look at you in the grocery store and pause, thinking they knew you from somewhere, but not be able to place you. Jess from season five had told her, "It's like being an actor on a hit show, but only for a year, then being replaced. This is a temporary thing." Many of the female alumni of *The One* all managed to find one another over time, forming an odd sort of sorority, offering support online and on the phone.

But given that she'd been so prominent on two seasons, Jess thought it might last a little longer than usual. Ashley, from season seven agreed. "I hate to say it," she'd said one day, "but I think it will take a while for this to all blow over. It's easier for me, in the middle of nowhere, Texas. Harder for you in a big city. Just more people to recognize you, you know?"

Adalyn slammed the creaky, rusty door shut and turned

the key. The engine coughed and roared to life, as trusty as it had always been, despite its poor appearance. As she drove down through the village and turned on to the highway, she found herself thinking that the old lodge on Lake McDonald would be a good location for *The One*. But then she noticed she was gripping the steering wheel with white knuckles. The beauty of the place would play well for television audiences, but she knew she didn't want that production anywhere near this place she loved. This place was for her, and her alone.

Well, me and the three million park visitors this summer, she mused with a smile. *Now to try and lure a few of them to rent Gramps's cabins.*

—⁓—

Chase was just returning from his expedition to Jones Lake when Adi pulled up in the parking lot the two concessions shared. It made his heart lurch a little, seeing her in Gene's old truck, her hair pulled back in a high ponytail, just like she wore it when they were kids.

He approached her with a cautious smile, having berated himself all morning for saying too much last night. He knew she'd been through a lot. It was like she was wounded, and it took little more than a brush past those wounds to make her wince. He was bound and determined not to make her wince again.

His eyes rounded as he took in the bags upon bags in the back of the truck. "Whoa. Did you buy out Costco?"

She grinned as she stepped out of the truck. "And Target and Walmart and Super 1, I think."

"What is all this?" he asked, pulling down the back and reaching for the nearest bags.

"Food, mostly," she said quietly. "I don't know what

Gramps has been eating lately, beyond breakfast at Eddie's. Seeing how skinny he is, I'm thinking maybe that's all he's been eating."

"I wondered about that," Chase returned. "Bea's invited him over, here and there, but he picks at his food. Sometimes old people get depressed and lose their appetite."

"I'm thinking that's it too," she said. "He has a doctor appointment coming up. If he doesn't start to improve on that front, I'll bring it up."

"I'm sure it will get better, with you here," Chase said, following her to the cabin, his arms now heavy with bags.

"I hope so. Did you find your escape-artist moose?"

"I did. One down, two to go."

"Where are the others?"

"One near Hidden Lake. The other by Iceberg."

"Ooo, it's been years since I went to Iceberg. If you need a tagalong that day, let me know."

"Will do," he said with a smile, dumping his bags on the wooden kitchen table and returning with her to the truck. That'd take all day—to drive over to East Glacier and hike the five miles in to Iceberg and then maybe more to find his moose. He had to admit, he didn't mind the idea of spending all day with Adalyn Stalling in one of the prettiest parts of the park.

"I bought brats," Adi said. "Do you and Bea and Logan want to join me and Gramps tonight for dinner on the beach?" She glanced up at the sky, giving him a chance to admire her pert nose, her olive skin. "I think it'll be warm enough."

"I'm game," he said. "I'll ask Bea and Logan."

A park service Jeep drove down the road and pulled in a circle. Hannah.

She rolled down her window, hitched an elbow over the

edge and flashed him a bright smile that dimmed a little when she saw Adi behind him. "Hey, Chase."

"Hey, Hannah. Hannah, this is Adalyn Stalling. Adi, this is Hannah Blackwell."

Adi edged over and offered her hand. "Hi, Hannah. I hear you're Chase's latest partner in bear crime."

"Bear grime is more like it," she said, smiling. "Nice to meet you, Adalyn? Or Adi?"

"My friends call me Adi," she said. "Feel free to do the same. West Glacier is a small place. Hey, I was just inviting Chase and his family to join us for brats. Want to come too?"

Inwardly, Chase cringed. He'd been looking forward to time alone with Adi, Gene and his family. It wasn't that he minded Hannah being around…it was just that—

"That sounds great!" Hannah said. "I love me a good brat."

"Who doesn't, right?"

"What time?"

"About six?"

"I'll be here. Anything I can bring?"

Adi grinned and gestured to the truck bed. "As Chase said, I appear to have bought out Kalispell. Just bring yourself tonight."

"I will. Thanks, Adi. Hey, Chase, the boss wants us to head to Many Glacier in the morning. There's a sow and two cubs that've been edging a little too close to the lodge. We may need to relocate them. Want to leave at seven?"

"Better make it six. Could take some time to track them down."

"Got it. Did you get your moose?"

"Yep. Found him in the bog just west of that old bridge that crosses McDonald Creek."

"Well, good. I'm heading in to the station. See you there?"

"Yeah, I'll clean up, get some lunch, and be over in a bit." She nodded and then drove off.

Chase grabbed the last four bags and followed Adi into the house. "That was nice of you to invite Hannah."

"Hey, whenever I meet someone new who clearly doesn't recognize me from *The One*, they instantly have Potential Friend stamped on their forehead for me. And given that there aren't a whole lot of young women in West Glacier, I figure I need to befriend every one I can."

Chase took that in. He'd really not thought about that before. Meeting so many people who might have seen you on a show. "Hannah doesn't watch TV. She's more into books."

"Good for her," Adi said. "Maybe we'd all be better off if we read more than we watched TV."

"We still can't catch more than a few channels up here," Gramps said, emerging from his room as if just rising from a nap, pulling a suspender up and over his shoulder. "Unless you get one of those new-fangled dish things." He stopped by the table, loaded with bags. "Well, it looks like we have enough here to make it 'til winter," he said, laughing under his breath. He eyed Chase. "Storm coming in that I don't know about?"

"I think your granddaughter doesn't want to have to leave the lake again for a while," Chase allowed. He looked to Adi, already settling cans neatly into the cupboard. She stood up on her tiptoes, and his eyes slid down over her slim waist and the rounded curves of lovely hips and bottom...

Gene cleared his throat and gave him a knowing look, and Chase felt the heat of a blush at being caught. *Good grief, it's like being twenty again...*

"Some things never change," Gene said with a small, knowing smile.

"What doesn't?" Adi said, turning to unload a bag of refrigerated items into the fridge. "Satellite TV? That's changed a lot in the last decade, Gramps. Maybe we should look into getting one. Maybe one for each of the cabins that we re vamp!"

"Oh, no. We're not going to put TVs in those cabins," Gene said, his bushy, gray brows furrowing. "We can re-chink them and you can gussy them up as you see fit, but no TVs," he said, waving a warning finger. "People don't come to the park to watch television. Or they shouldn't."

"Okay, okay," she said, raising her palms. "I agree with you. Mostly. But we should upgrade the Internet connection, at least. It's a selling point."

"So then we'll have kids all staring at their phones rather than throwing rocks in the lake," he grumbled.

Adi rolled her eyes and shared a look with Chase.

"He has a point," Chase said.

"A point if you never want things to change," she said. "But things have already changed. Gramps, did you find out who we can call to fix the chinking?"

"Yeah," he said. "Fella will be out this afternoon to give me an estimate."

"Good. How 'bout the exterminator?"

"I got a name and number. Figured we'd wait to find out about the schedule for chinking before I called him."

Chase smiled. It pleased him to hear Adi tackling some of the needs of the cabin complex. Heaven knew that Gene needed all the help he could get. "What are these?" he asked, turning to a box full of old, black and white pictures.

"Oh, I thought I'd frame them and put them up in the cabins. People like things like that…a sense of history. I need to find more. I just stopped by the thrift store on Main."

"I know where you can find more. I could take you next week."

"You want to come scrounge through hundreds of old pictures?"

With you? he thought. *More than you know.* "I don't mind a good thrift store hunt for things like this." He picked up a picture of a crew working on the Hungry Horse dam. "It's like a glimpse into history."

"Exactly," she said, taking the picture from him and studying it.

"I think Grams has some pictures like that up in the attic too," Gene said, looking over Chase's shoulder.

"Oh, that'd be excellent," Adi said.

"And you're decorating?" Chase asked, gesturing toward the big bags full of plaid comforters.

"One pod of cabins, as soon as it's re-chinked and de-moused," she said. "They will be our 'deluxe' cabins. I'm gunning for some good reviews and some advance publicity on our plans for revamping the cabins. It'll help us win the park officials over at the review. And I think it will help us garner advance reservations for next year if I can post pictures of what they'll all look like, eventually."

Chase rolled back on his heels. "Whoa. Gene, you're going after another ten years at this game?" How was that possible?

"We're thinking about it," Adi said, pulling her arm through the crook of her grandfather's.

He blinked slowly. "So you'd, uhh, come to stay every summer? Run it with him?"

"Oh, I don't know about that," she said, turning back to the photos and picking up another, this one of eight men in a line, all holding massive, freshly caught trout in hand.

His heart sank with a dull thud just as quickly as it had sped up.

"Maybe I'd just come every summer for the opening, help

Gramps get employees in line, see to repairs, that kind of thing. We may not even be awarded another ten years. I just know I can't stand the thought of letting it go without a fight."

"I see," he said. "Well, I'd better go get cleaned up. I think I smell like moose."

"I wondered what that was," she said, teasingly nudging his hip with her own.

He smiled. "Yeah, you'd think with all the time those boys spend in the water, they'd smell a bit more…fresh."

"I dunno," Gene said. "You smell fine to me."

"I'll see you later, Adi. Gene."

"About six, right?" she asked.

"Right." He eased out the door as Adi filled her grandfather in. It warmed him, the sound of their banter as he walked away. Again, it brought him back to a hundred other summer mornings, hearing them. Being with them. It felt right that Adi was back, and he couldn't wait to see her again that night.

Only trouble was, Hannah would be there too.

CHAPTER 9

"The Chinker," as Adi called him, had agreed to begin the very next morning, and would be done in three days. An exterminator was to come right after, and was scheduled for return visits on a regular basis through the summer. The cupboards and fridge were full, and as Adi set a plate full of brats by the barbeque for Gramps to grill, then unfurled her grandmother's old, red-and-white-checkered tablecloth over the picnic table, she smiled in satisfaction. One day in, and she had accomplished a fair amount.

Chase, Logan and Bea rounded the corner of the trail that linked their two properties, with Hannah in tow. The girl had her blond hair down that eve, and it bounced in shiny waves around her shoulders. With a start Adi noticed she was really cute. Without the heavy, square-cut clothes of a ranger, and now in jeans and a slim t-shirt, she saw that she was really, really cute. Her first thought was *Is Chase into her?* And her second was *What do you care if he is? You have no claim on the man.*

Glad for the excuse to turn away, she set the bunch of

wildflowers she held in Grams's old vase. She'd found some early-blooming daisies on the east side of the cabins and picked a handful.

"Oh, daisies," Hannah said, handing her a bottle of wine. "I just love daisies."

"Me too," Adi said, forcing a smile. *Remember, you need every friend you can get.* She shoved away the all-to-familiar feeling of competing for the nearest eligible bachelor. *This isn't an episode of the show, Adi. Shake it off!*

"It'll be even better when the Indian paintbrush blooms," Hannah said. "Aren't those your favorites, Chase?"

"Yeah. I've seen a few in the high country. The bear grass is going to town this year."

"It is," Adi said. She turned and watched as Hannah moved over to greet her grandfather. It was obvious this wasn't their first conversation. She was kind to him, making small talk.

"My favorite's the bluebells," Adi said.

"There's a huge field of those on the way to Iceberg," Chase said. "It's early, but maybe we'll see some when we go."

"I'd love that," Adi said, uncorking the wine.

"Ooo, what's this?" Bea asked. "You two are hiking in to Iceberg?"

"One of those moose I'm trying to tag has been spotted there. I invited Adi to come along."

"You should take a couple of our kayaks," Logan said. "Do your Iceberg gig one day, camp overnight. Then kayak Swiftcurrent, portage over and then do Josephine."

"Oh, I don't know," Adi said quickly. She glanced over her shoulder at Gene. "Being away for more than a day?" she asked quietly.

"We'd be around," Bea said. "We're used to checking in on Gramps, you know. You should jump on the opportunity. In a bit, you'll be hard-pressed to escape Kreature Komforts."

"About that," Adi said conspiratorially to the three of them. "I think the cabins need a new name. Kreature Komforts is a bit..."

"Kitschy?" Bea asked.

"If a bit means a lot," Logan said. "These days, the park likes a more classic approach. Classic, you know, spelled without a K."

Adi laughed under her breath. "Fifty years ago, it was the way to capture a tourist's attention. Now, not so much."

Chase took a sip from his glass. "So what would you call the place?"

"I don't know," she said, pouring herself a glass of wine, and then another for the girls. "Cozy Cabins? Or something classic, like Cottages Upon the Lake? Lake McDonald Cottages?"

"I like the Cottages Upon the Lake," Bea said, arching a brow and using an uppity tone. "But shall your new-and-improved cabins live up to the lofty name?"

"Uhh, maybe. I bought some pseudo-Ralph-Lauren bedding today at Walmart. I think when I'm done with my deluxe model, it could be called a cottage."

"Or is that more New England than the Rocky Mountains?" Chase asked. "Your grandmother always was about the community that formed around the bonfire. What about something like, 'Cabins on the Lake: A Cozy Community'?" he asked, spreading out his hands as if already seeing the sign.

Adi nodded and took a sip of wine. "Or just 'Cabins on the Lake,' and let the rest speak for itself? I could have a sign made in a classic style."

"What's this?" Gramps asked, carrying over a plate full of brats, with Hannah carrying toasted buns and grilled onions behind him. "You kids siding with my granddaughter about renaming the place?"

"It may be time," Logan said, as the older man took hold of his shoulder and carefully hooked a leg over the bench. He fairly collapsed to his seat. Adi made a mental note to find a lawn chair that he could use at the end of the picnic table. It'd be easier for him to negotiate.

"Part of your campaign for the park officials?" he asked Adi, passing the buns and then the brats as the others sat down too.

"Maybe," she said carefully. It wasn't the first time they'd talked about the name, but always before he'd been super defensive.

"Well, I'd say everything has to be on the table. Hard to make a go of things if you feel like your hands are tied," he said. He took a deep breath and looked around the table. "Now, my young friends, let's say grace." He offered one hand to Adi, the other to Chase.

Together, they all linked hands and bowed their heads.

"Father, thanks for this great place, these great kids, and this great food," he said. "Amen." The rest of them echoed his *amen.*

"Rub, dub, dub, thanks for the grub," Logan said, rubbing his hands together in delight as the brats came his way.

Adi remembered the coleslaw then and scrambled up to retrieve it from the fridge. She paused, just inside the screen door, watching Chase grin at Hannah. Something she'd said? She was giggling and licking her lips, and dang, she really did look cute. Did the ranger assigned as Chase's helper have to be as adorable as that? All blond and blue-eyed and...fresh? Couldn't it have been some nerdy, weedy kid?

She checked herself again. *You have no claim on that man, Adalyn Stalling. And this is not some show.* Besides, who was to say that Chase would even be interested? Yes, the man had come to fetch her in Chicago. But he'd have done that for

Gramps, regardless of who his grandchild was. He was that kind of guy.

That kind of guy, she mused, approaching the table. Loyal. Dedicated. The dude who would always go the extra mile for a friend. Not at all like Adam. Or Connor.

They ate their meal, laughing and sharing stories about tourists. Hannah had been part of a team that helped find a five-year-old that had gone missing that afternoon. "We found him against a tree, head on his arms, crying his heart out," she said. "It about broke my heart. And when we returned him to his mom and dad?" She put a hand on her chest. "That was something I'll never forget."

"They're lucky," Gramps said. "There's been a lot of children who've been swept down rivers. This isn't a place to let your kids roam free."

"I don't know, Gramps," Adi said. "You pretty much let me roam free from dawn 'til dusk."

"That's different," he grumbled. "You grew up here. These city folk...they need to take extra care. They don't know the risk. They see this place, and they focus on the *park* part. Not the *wild* part."

"True," Chase said. "I'll just be glad to get through another summer without any moose or bear attacks."

Logan grinned. "How many others across America will say that exact same thing tonight?"

"They would if they thought about it," Chase said. "Last year in Yellowstone a tourist was gored by a buffalo. Because she was trying to feed it."

"Yellowstone seems to attract a very *special* sort of tourist," Bea said. "I'm glad we live in Glacier."

"Here's to that," Logan said, lifting his glass to clink against hers. The others joined in with their own drinks.

"It's a perfect night," Bea said, looking out to the lake. Before them, the mountains reflected perfectly in the mirror of the lake. "A couple of you should take our kayaks and go out for a bit while Logan and I wash up the dishes."

She glanced toward Adalyn, but Hannah squealed and clasped her hands together. "Oh, I've been dying to get out on the water. Would you mind? Chase, come with me!"

"You should," Adi found herself saying. After all, there'd be time enough for her to borrow kayaks from her neighbors…

Chase gave her a funny, contemplative look, then rose. "Let's do it," he said. "Sure you don't need our help too?" he asked Adi. "It all was delicious."

"No, no. Most of the mess was on the grill," Adi said hurriedly. "You guys have fun. I'll catch you tomorrow."

"Actually, we head to East Glacier tomorrow," Hannah said. "We have to see about relocating those overly friendly bears that want to cozy up with campers. We may be gone for a few days."

"Ahh, I see. Well, hope it goes well," Adi said brightly.

"Thanks," Hannah said. "And thanks for the great dinner! See you later, Gene!" With that, she flounced off toward the docks, her golden blonde hair bouncing around her shoulders.

"See you," Gramps said, following Logan and Bea inside the cabin.

Chase paused and bit his lip. "You sure you're okay? Here on your own with Gene?"

"Of course," she said, a bit too forcefully. "Plus, Logan and Bea are right next door. We'll be fine. You go do your bear thing," she said. "We'll be fine."

He nodded once, studying her. "Thanks again for supper."

"You're welcome. See you later," she said casually, corking a half-empty wine bottle and turning toward the cabin. She could hear Bea and Gramps laughing inside. But on the steps she turned to watch Chase walk down the beach. Then to Hannah, shouldering a kayak as if she was semi-pro. So she was all-girl when she wanted to be, and all super-athletic to boot. Why was it that Chase wasn't already in love? Some sort of ranger protocol? No fraternization allowed?

She concentrated on breathing as the two walked down the dock, side by side. Chase set down his kayak and reached for hers, setting it in the water for her.

And why did him being nice to her make Adi's stomach twist?

Because he's being nice to someone other than you, she admitted to herself.

—⁓—

Kenneth had trailed several of Adalyn's coworkers to a Mexican restaurant for Taco Tuesday. But even with margaritas loosening their tongues, there was little said about Adalyn, other than a brief exchange about her stint back and then her abrupt disappearance. There was some chatter about roses found in the garage and on her Subaru. But no one seemed to know where she'd gone, only that she wasn't due back until September.

September, Kenneth thought. September was an impossibly long time away. There was simply no way he could wait for her to return. He needed to find her, and find her now. Something had happened to her. Something bad. Nothing else would have made her leave her job after so long away for the show.

He did far better that Friday night, following Adalyn's friend Molly to a bar after she left work. He took a seat behind their table of six—four women and two guys. After an hour of drinking and eager conversation had passed, someone finally, finally asked the question.

"Hey, Molls," called a girl from down the table. Loudly, to be sure Molly heard. "What's up with your friend, Adi? Is she okay? That last round with Connor…It was brutal!"

"I know, right?" said another excitedly. "I just couldn't believe it when he dumped her."

"On national television," intoned still another. "That's the worst."

Kenneth gripped his highball glass so tightly he thought he might break it. He forced himself to swirl the ice cube around in the glass and take a slow, thoughtful sip, staring at the silent television in the corner set to sports, as if he had not another care in the world.

"She's okay," Molly said. "Adalyn is a great woman. She'll find love someday. Just not on that stupid show."

"Did you ever tell her to not do it?"

"Only a hundred times," Molly said.

"Why'd she do it?"

"Why does anyone?" asked another. "Love. Everybody wants their chance at a fairy tale romance."

"Some just go on to get some publicity," said one of the guys.

"That's true," said the other. "That one dude worked in his marketing tag line so often, everyone was Googling it. Boom, a hundred thousand hits."

"So is she dating?" asked one of the women.

"No," Molly said. "She's not really ready for that. At least I don't think so. We haven't talked for a while."

"But she's back at work?"

"She was, but then her grandfather got sick. She had to go home to Montana to take care of him. She'll be there until fall."

Kenneth smiled and lifted his fingers to the bartender, tapping his glass, silently asking for another. *This calls for a toast...*

"Oh yeah! Didn't she grow up going to Glacier?" asked another. "She talked about that once when we hung out."

Glacier. There it was, at long last. "Make it a double," he said to the bartender, as soon as he came over to pour.

CHAPTER 10

As the chinkers began removing the rotten material from between the logs and replacing it, Adi began trying out logo ideas for A Little Cabin on the Lake—her new working name for Kreature Komforts—and then started to construct a new website, complete with online reservations.

"So you're telling me that folks will be on their computer and reserve a cabin?" Gramps asked, looking over her shoulder. "How will I know who is coming and when?"

"It will all be right here. On the computer," she said, waving at the screen.

"And what will I do when you go back to Chicago?"

Adi took a deep breath. "We'll have to get you a computer."

"Oh, no, no. I'm too old for such newfangled things, Adi. I'll just keep taking reservations on the phone and writing it down. It's worked for fifty years; it will work for what I've got left."

"But that's the thing, Gramps. It isn't working. It may be half the reason you're running half-full this summer. A quarter-full this June. People are used to reserving places online.

If they can't find you on the Internet, they don't know you're here."

"Sure they know we're here," he grumbled. "We have folks who've been coming here for thirty years straight!"

She gave him a doleful look. "Who? The Pickerings? The Smiths? Anybody else?"

"Well, no." He glanced to the window. "The place isn't what it once was. People come, but they don't often return." He cast her a rueful smile. "Maybe it's time to hang up my hat, Adi girl."

She considered that. He looked weary, every one of his seventy-six years. "Maybe. Maybe it is, Gramps. And honestly? I'm not sure I want to put on that hat. But I know that if I'm to have a chance at it, we have to do things like this," she said, waving at her half-built web site. "Because that's what will convince the officials to give us another shot."

"*Hmmph,*" he said. "I'm still not convinced. Can't you just put our phone number on there?" he grumbled. "Have them call to make a reservation?"

"I could," she said. "But I don't want to. Here, they can reserve their own cabin or if necessary, email me." She studied him as he dragged a hand over his face, as if the whole thing exhausted him. She rose, took his hand. "You look tired. Let's go sit on the swing."

With a nod, he followed her out to the porch, and they sat together, looking at the lake. "Want some lemonade?" she asked.

"No thanks," he said. "I think I'll take a little catnap in a bit, here."

Adi had noticed he took his "catnaps" three or four times a day now. Sometimes for an hour at a time.

"Do you really need to change the name of the old place, Adi?"

"We really need to change the name, Gramps. Trust me. Kreature Komforts was cute once. Now, it just screams old."

"*Hmmph*," he grunted again. "Old is not always bad. Look at me!"

"Don't take it personally. Most businesses revamp their image—their logo—every ten years," she said. "Kreature Komforts has lasted five times longer than most."

He sighed. "It's only that it was your Grams who came up with the name. If you could go back in time with me, Adi girl, and see her face the night she came up with it..." He shook his head slowly, reverently, his eyes distant. "Just the memory of it makes me fall in love with her all over again."

"You miss her still," Adi said.

"Every day," he said, taking her hand. He lifted it to his lips, kissed it, then settled it on his thigh, covering it with his other one. "She would've been so proud of you, you being a big city marketing executive and all."

"I miss her too. She was wonderful." Adi could still remember the way her eyes twinkled. How she squeezed her tight, like she never wanted to let her go. How she could do no wrong in her grandmother's eyes.

"Yes, she was. Yes, she was."

"What do you think made your love work all those years?"

He considered that a minute. "Well, this place, for one. Something we built, together. Running it made us work as a team, in more ways than one. We met lots of couples over the years. We'd often say, 'Let's grow to be more like them.' Or we'd say, 'Let's never be like them.' That's the beauty of the people-business. You meet the best and worst. The world, Adi girl, if you pay attention, is an instruction manual on how to live life."

"I always loved how you two said goodnight. The whole, 'Goodnight-handsome-goodnight-beautiful' thing."

He chuckled and ducked his head. "Hard to go to bed angry if you've just been called handsome by the love of your life."

"Is that all it takes?"

"Ahh, no." He considered it a moment. "I think it takes love and respect and a fair amount of grace. Being lucky enough to find someone you like long-term doesn't hurt, either." He turned to look at her then, and squeezed her hand. "Someday, Adi girl, you'll find him. A man who loves and respects you, just as you will love and respect him. Trust me on this. You won't be alone forever. I know it."

She leaned her head on his shoulder. "I don't know. I don't know if love exists anymore. I mean, what you and Grams had."

"Sure you do. Isn't that part of why you went on that show?"

She considered that. "Yeah," she said. "Probably. But after all I went through. With Adam and then Connor...Well, it's kinda destroyed any hope I had in myself to hold a man's heart. Gramps," Adi whispered, "I just can't go through that pain again."

"Life is full of broken eggs, Adi girl. The trick is to figure out how to be a good omelette maker."

She laughed under her breath. "True. I'm just so tired of being on my own. Looking. Always wondering, is this guy the one? Maybe we can go back to arranged marriages? Because I seem to stink at making my own choices."

"I'm game if you are," he said with a smile, which quickly faded. "I'm tired of being single too, Adi girl."

She smiled and squeezed his arm. "So here we are, two lonely hearts. At least we have each other."

"I'm so glad for that," he said, patting her hand. Then, "What about Chase? Would you ever give him a chance?"

"Chase?" she said, straightening, tucking her hands under her thighs. "I don't know. Has he said something to you?"

"Now I may be old," Gramps said, smiling a little, "but it doesn't mean I've lost all sense of things. He hasn't said anything to me. But the way he looks at you..."

"What do you mean?"

"Well Adi, I suppose you know what I mean."

"I don't. Chase and I are friends. We've always been friends." She rose and paced along the porch, wrapping her arms around a post.

"Maybe you want to be friends with benefits?" he asked.

She huffed a laugh. "I don't think that means what you think it means."

"It doesn't mean friends who become boyfriend-girlfriend?"

"No, it means friends who have sex."

His bushy eyebrows raised in alarm and then in agitation, he waved her off. "Never mind that then. You two have pined for each other off and on all your lives. Isn't it time to fish or cut bait?"

She stared at him. "What about Hannah?" she mumbled.

"That girl is cute as a button, but it's not her that Chase stares after."

"Maybe that's because he can stare at her all he wants in the back country without having *her* grandfather making assumptions."

He laughed through his nose and crossed his arms. "Go ahead and ignore it then, Adi girl. I think you know the truth."

She frowned. Chase? Interested in her? Could it be true?

She sat down on the steps and stared at the lake. She knew he'd wanted her to go with him on the kayaks last night, before Hannah so eagerly jumped in. She'd sensed him beginning to say a few things, but always cut himself off. Because he was…afraid? Of what? Being her rebound boyfriend?

She rubbed the back of her neck, feeling the familiar tension wrap its band about her. Gramps rose and went to the door.

"What if it ruined our friendship?" she asked him, over her shoulder. "If Chase and I…what if it ended badly? And we couldn't even be friends?"

Gramps soberly considered her. "But what if it didn't?" he asked. Then with that, he slipped into the cabin for his nap, leaving her alone with her thoughts.

—ɯ—

Adi spent the afternoon dragging mattresses out of the first five cabins, airing them out, seeing if she could get another year's use out of them. About half were still decent; half had been burrowed into by mice or become so stained that she couldn't just cover them with a new mattress pad.

It was weirdly hot for a June afternoon and she sweated like crazy as she dragged one mattress after another to the truck bed and loaded them in sideways to haul to the dump. She and Mrs. Larson had cleaned the five newest cabins, preparing them for their first guests of the summer, due that afternoon. Adi could hardly stand it—having people check into Kreature Komforts—now that she had "A Cabin by the Lake" firmly in mind. The logo was done, and a new sign ordered in Kalispell, as well as a removable tarp-sign that said, "Newly Renovated Cabins Available Tonight!" The web site, basic but functional, was ready to go. Just as soon as she had these five "renovated" cabins complete, she'd take it all live. But until she had something she really wanted reviewed on TripAdvisor and elsewhere, she preferred to keep the property under the radar. Better no reviews than bad ones.

Bea, getting back from errands, spied her in the parking lot and helped her drag the eighth mattress into the truck bed, squeezing it in on its side. "I think that's all you'll get in. How many more do you have?"

"Another four," Adi said, panting and wiping her forehead.

"Let's load them in mine," she said.

"Oh, no, Bea. You just got back!"

"Hey, no worries! Logie has things handled down on the dock. Nothing happening but the occasional canoe rental until our first sunset cruise tonight. Let me help you with those last mattresses and then let's head to town. I assume you're picking up new ones down there?"

"Eventually. But right now I need to pick up a floor sander and supplies. Mattresses and linens will be last." She'd tried out her sample comforter in one cabin, and liking it, ordered enough for all five cabins. They'd arrive in a few days. "But could we fill any space left in your truck bed with old stoves? All the appliances need to be dumped too."

"No problem. I'll be right back."

Adi smiled as she returned to the cabins and grabbed hold of another mattress. With luck she could get all five cabin floors sanded tomorrow and a first coat of finish on the next day. New mini-fridges, stoves, microwaves and coffee makers were due to be delivered in a few days, along with an upgraded toilet for each. She'd lay tile on the ratty old laminate counters as soon as she could. The communal showers—well, that was a project that she had convinced Gramps to hire out. There were five stalls for women and five for men. The workmen had gutted them, but had gotten stuck on some plumbing issue. In the meantime, they'd erected two very rustic showers on the other side of the campground, pulling water from the lake for now. She knew they couldn't keep that under wraps for long, but Gramps had assured her the rangers would look the other way for a couple weeks until they got it done. "We've fed a couple of them," he said with a wink.

So much to do, she thought. But it felt good to be busy. Good to feel vital. She'd always loved a project...a really good, challenging project. And this for sure was that.

Bea returned, and together they finished loading mattresses and three of the tiny stoves, which were surprisingly light, though disgusting with grime.

"Oh, ick," Adi said, wiping her hands on her jeans. "That's gotta be decades of grease on the sides of those."

Bea gave her a commiserating look. "Getting rid of those will improve the smell."

"It's gotta."

"It's going to be so cute," Bea said. "I can't wait to see the finished product. I'd love to renovate our little old guest cabin in back. Maybe you can help me do that next year." She faltered a bit. "I mean, if you decide to return."

"If I even have the chance," Adi said. "We'll see how this goes."

Bea shut the truck hatch and looked at her. "Do you want to return, Adi? I mean if you get the concession for another ten? Are you really ready to trade in big city life?"

"I don't know," she said honestly, wiping her forehead with the back of her hand and then resting it on the edge of the truck. "To me, it simply feels like what I should do." She waved back at the five cabins to be renovated. "If nothing else than to give the new owners a glimpse of what the place could be like, with some effort. It's like I have to do it to honor all my Gramps and Grams poured into this place. Honor the legacy, you know? Plus it keeps me busy."

Bea nodded. "That's cool. I like that you're following your heart."

"It's not bad business either. I figure I'm putting about $2000 in each cabin, doing all the work myself. I can earn that back in renting them each out in about a week or two... which I have a better chance at doing if I can advertise them as 'newly renovated.' Last year, Gramps only ran half-full all summer. If that's the case again this year, I can take on a pod of five at a time."

"If you do that," Bea said, "the park officials can only admire you. Why would they say no to your proposal?"

"Oh you know better than I how political that particular gauntlet can be."

"True. But all we had to do was rebuild the dock, buy an engine, add some new life jackets. This...You doing it all in advance. They're bound to be impressed."

"I hope so," she smiled.

—∞—

Chase could hardly get showered fast enough the evening he returned to West Glacier. It'd been three days since he'd seen Adi, and he couldn't wait to get over there. He was tucking in his clean shirt as he came down the stairs from the guest room in the boathouse cabin. Logan, pouring a cup of coffee, watched him.

"Heading out again?"

"Uh, yeah," Chase said casually. "Thought I'd go over and check on Gene."

"Gene," Logan said, deadpan. "You got all cleaned up for Gene."

Chase smiled as he rolled up a sleeve on his flannel. "I've been out in the woods for seventy-two hours, wading streams up to my thighs. Trust me, you'd want me to clean up if it was even just the two of us hanging out tonight."

Logan gave him a thoughtful nod, barely hiding his smile. "Well, tell *Gene* I said hello too. Tomorrow's Sunday. Mike and Joy are starting their summer dock hours. See if Gene—oh, and maybe *Adi* too?—wants to come to church with us. Then we could grab lunch, get back and hike up to the punchbowls in the afternoon? This heat is supposed to keep up and Bea tells me that Adi's been working like a banshee. She could probably use a break."

Chase gave him a smile over his shoulder as he headed out the door. "Maybe," he said. "I'm aiming to invite her on that hike to Iceberg in a few days. Maybe even do that kayak trip Bea suggested. So I don't want to overdo it."

"Bro," Logan said, walking over to him. "That girl has been pursued harder than any woman ever, given her two seasons on *The One*. Maybe this isn't exactly the right time for subtlety? She may not recognize it for what it is."

"For discussion's sake, say I *was* interested. Maybe it'd be a refreshing change."

"Maybe." He patted Chase on the back. "Good luck with that decision. Just don't let this summer be your last missed chance. I hated all those autumns when you moped around, mad at yourself for not making a move."

That was enough. "See ya, bro." Chase let the door swing shut and headed down the path to the cabins. He saw Bea on the dock, helping a couple get into a canoe. There were two others in the distance, out on the water. Up ahead, he saw Gene talking to a couple, giving them directions on how to park on the far side, where the "newer" cabins were. But he knew Adi would be on this side, working on the renovations of that first pod. He rounded the corner and saw her struggling to drag an old fridge out. The screen door had slipped its rock-prop and banged against her.

He hurried over. "Hey, hi. Here, let me help you."

"Oh, Chase!" she said, looking up at him in surprise. "Thanks," she said.

He propped open the door again, setting the rock firmly in place, then took the dolly from her. "Here, let me."

"Thanks," she said, sinking to the shady edge of the cabin. "I'll let you, since that's my fifth one today. They're the hardest. Well, I shouldn't say that. I haven't gotten to the toilets yet."

"Isn't it time to call it a day?" he asked, setting the fridge upright in the clearing and pulling out the dolly.

She peered up at him and then to the sinking sun. "What is it, three, three-thirty?"

"Five." He looked around the pod, littered with two old stoves, five ancient fridges, and old linens. "What are you going to do with all that?"

"The stoves will go to the dump. I found a place in Columbia Falls who will pay me a bit for the fridges. They clean them up and repaint them for the retro-crowd."

"You don't want to put them back in after that?"

"No. I think I'll just go with black mini-fridges that will slide under the counters. It will give renters more workspace. I'm ditching the ovens too. Just going with two burners. Most people don't want more than a microwave and a little fridge space. Their attention is out there," she said, nodding to the lake and mountains.

"Good call," Chase said approvingly.

"I'll add a decent barbeque out here too," Adi said. "Grams would've liked that. People out in the center, barbequing together. Eight Adirondack chairs surrounding the fire pit. They have them on sale down at Costco."

"Your grandmother would be proud, Adi."

"Think so?" She looked up at him, and there was a brief, longing look in her eyes that melted his heart a little. She and her grandparents had always been uncommonly close.

They'd practically raised her every summer.

"Know so. Now what can I do to help, so you can, you know...eat dinner? And sleep?"

"Ah, you don't have to help me."

"I'd like to help, Adi."

"Well," she said, looking him up and down. "You might want to go and change into work clothes if you want to help. Look at me," she said, seeming to remember herself for the first time. "I must look like a disaster."

He smiled. Her white t-shirt had a big, grimy streak, as did her jeans. Her hair was pulled back with a handkerchief, damp tendrils sticking to her neck. But God help him, there was something so dang sexy about her, all dewy with sweat and wearing too-big leather gloves and utterly forgetting how she looked until he showed up... "Nah, you look fine to me," he allowed. "But I will go change. What do we need to do?"

"I'd like to get the last two cabins sanded today," she said tentatively. "It's harder than I thought. The big rental sander does its work on the main part, but you have to use a smaller sander on your hands and knees for the edges. I need to get the first coat of finish on tomorrow. If I do that, I can get coat two on the next day, and move everything back in the day after that and be ready to rent."

"Got it. I'll be right back." He hurried back to the cabin, changed his shirt, and trotted back.

By the time he returned, she had a dust mask on and was whirring away at the floor. He leaned against the doorjamb, arms folded, watching her. Most of America knew her as Adalyn, a girl who was wined and dined on the last season of *The One*. A few had picked up that she was competitive, rolling up her sleeves in the previous round in vying for a date with Adam by running an obstacle course, including wading through a mud pit at the end...and winning. But this, this was truly Adi, he thought. Working hard for her grampa, for herself, for their family legacy, when no one was watching.

Except him. Remembering himself, he reached for a second mask on the ground and then went in, taking the vibrating disc sander from her hands. "You go check on Gene!" he shouted over the noise. "I'll finish up this one."

Grateful, she laid a brief hand on his arm and then turned to go. As he sanded, he thought about her long, slim fingers on his forearm, remembering it as if it hadn't been but a light, momentary touch...but something more.

How was it that such a small thing moved him? And if that got him all riled up, what would it be like to kiss her?

CHAPTER 11

Adi had refused his invitation to church that day, citing a need to start finishing the floors. But when she was finishing up the third cabin floor, Chase, Bea and Logan all showed up at her door in swimsuits, carrying inner tubes. One after another, they tossed them aside.

"Put us to work, girlfriend," Bea said. "Because as soon as we're done with the floors, we're heading up to the punchbowls and you're coming with us."

"I am?"

"You are," Bea said firmly. "God knows there's a ton to do around here. But if you don't stop to appreciate why it's good to be here, you'll run away come autumn and never come back."

"And we don't want that to happen," Chase said, giving her a small smile, taking the finishing pad rod from her hand. "It's been too long since we've seen you last, here in Big Sky country. We don't want it to happen again."

She stared at him a moment. What was that? A bit of flirtation? Every time she thought that's what he was up to, he eased back, making her wonder.

Adi cleared her throat. "Well, okay. Awesome. I'd say a dip in the punchbowls would be divine. Can you two take that pad and tray and gallon of finish to cabin five?" She nodded to the supplies outside the door for Bea and Logan. "Have you put finish on floors before?"

"We did the boathouse cabin last year," Logan said, flashing her a handsome grin. "Trust me. We've got this." They disappeared through the door.

"How 'bout I work on the edges and you do the main part on the fourth one?" Adi asked Chase.

"However you want to divvy it up," he said with a shrug. "Sure your knees couldn't use a rest?"

"Nah, I'm fine," she said. With that, she grabbed Grams's old gardening pad for her knees and set to working on the edge, right beside the log walls. After she was finished with one side, Chase moved in with the bigger pad to do the expanse toward the far side, where she set to work. In an hour, they were done, and peeking in at Bea and Logan, saw they were about twenty minutes from finishing too.

"I'll just go check on Gramps and change," she said to Chase, hooking her thumb over her shoulder.

"Good plan," he said. "You'll want boots and socks on for the hike up. The thorny weeds are thick this year."

"Gotcha," she said. She moved toward Gramps's cabin, smiling. In just a bit, a fresh coat of finish would be on the floor in all five of her tiny cabins. It was satisfying, getting to this stage. How much more satisfying would it be to get to the end? See them all done?

She moved inside and not seeing her grandfather, called out. "Gramps? Gramps?"

"In here," came a faint voice from the bedroom. "Adi?"

Alarmed, she hurried down the hall and into his room.

He was on his knees, struggling to get up. "Gramps!" she cried, racing over. She helped him to his feet and then to the bed. "What happened?"

"I…I got dizzy," he said, putting a shaking hand to his forehead.

She helped him put his feet up too, moving to unlace his boots and slip them off. "Do I need to call 911?"

"No, no," he said. "I just did a little too much this morning. With a bit of rest, I'll be right as rain."

"Are you sure?"

"I'm sure."

"I'll go get you some water." When she returned, she helped him sit up a bit and put another pillow behind his back. He had a little more color now. "Are you sure we shouldn't head to town? Have them check your heart?"

"Absolutely not," he insisted. "I have that appointment with the doc coming up. I'll be fine until then. The last thing you need, Adi girl, is having to haul your old Gramps to town, just to find out he's just old and worn out."

"Well, if you're sure," she said.

"I'm sure," he said forcefully. "Now you go and get back to your work in the cabins. I'm fine, Adi. Truly. I'll just take a little nap now."

She hesitated, biting her lip. "I…Bea and Logan, Chase— they wanted me to go with them to the punchbowls."

"Go, go," he said, waving at her, then folding his hands on his chest. He lifted one heavy lid to peek at her. "This isn't a death pose," he said. "I'll be breathing when you return. I promise."

She half-laughed, half-winced. "You're sure?"

"I'm sure. Go. Have fun. Or I'll get up and work myself into a heart attack so that if you run me to the ER, it will be for something serious."

"You're impossible," she said.

"Impossibly wonderful. Now come and give your Gramps a kiss."

Obediently, she moved over to him and kissed his forehead. "I'll only be away an hour or two."

"Be away three or don't bother to come back."

—ɯ—

Chase couldn't keep his eyes off her. She was in cut-off jeans shorts, with a tankini top and her hair pulled into a fresh pony tail, dangling out the back of her Chicago Bears baseball cap. He knew she'd always been an avid football fan, even though he'd never seen her cheer them on. What would it be like, to attend a game with her? She was one of the few women he knew who could talk game and strategy; he'd witnessed it even in the off-season. And with her hiking socks and boots on…there was just something so enticing about the woman.

But she had returned to them reserved, not as excited and relieved to go to the punchbowls as he'd expected. He turned at a log crossing and offered her his hand. It was a little tricky, given that each of them carried an inner tube. She took his hand and skittered across, but didn't even seem to see it. "You all right, Adi?" he asked as she came to a stop beside him. He reached out to help Bea.

"Yeah, I'm fine," she said. "It's just Gramps. Back at the cabin, I found him half on the floor. He'd collapsed and was having a hard time getting up."

"What? Really?"

"Yeah." She put a hand to her forehead and then dropped it. "I didn't want to come—thought I should run him down to town and the ER, but he refused. Said he had an appointment coming up and refused to go sooner."

"Not many more stubborn than your old Gramps," he said.

"He said if I didn't come out with you," she said, "he'd run around 'til he had a real heart attack, so he wouldn't make me go to town for nothing."

Bea shook her head and put her hands on her hips. "He's one of a kind, that one."

"Yeah, one moment amazing, the next totally aggravating."

"Guess you get to be like that when you get old," Logan said. "Fair warning, Wife," he said to Bea. "I'm totally going to be like him."

"Well then, I will too," she said, sliding an arm around his waist. "Won't we be a pair?"

"I told him I'd only be gone two hours," Adi said, checking her watch. "So if you guys want to stay longer, I'll just head back on my own. I don't want to rush you."

"We're almost there. That will probably be long enough," Chase said, turning to lead the way again. Now, at least, he knew why she was so tense. She was worried about Gene. He'd worried that she'd regretted saying yes to this invitation...perhaps not wanting to spend more time with him.

"Thanks so much for helping me, you guys," Adi said. "It makes me so happy to know there's finish on all five floors! Tomorrow I'll get the second coat on and they'll be done."

"They're going to be so pretty," Bea said.

"I know," Adi said, clapping her hands in excitement. Chase had always loved it when she did that.

Up ahead, they could hear the rush of water and the falls. Climbing more steeply then, they made their way up the side of a rockface, emerging at the top, each panting from the effort.

"Wow," Adi said, slowly gazing from left to right at the panorama that opened before them. From here, they could see most of Lake McDonald, the lodge in the distance, and the mountains that ringed the lake. Beside them a waterfall pounded into the granite, forming a huge bowl, which emptied at the far end into the next below, and then another below. "I'd forgotten how pretty it was up here," she said.

"Last one in buys beer tonight!" Logan called, tossing his ring in the water and taking a shallow dive in. He emerged, whooping, his well-muscled arms and chest covered in goosebumps.

"Yeah, yeah," Bea said, as Chase dived in too. "I'll buy then," she said when they both came up, eagerly making their way back to the bank of the pool. Bea clearly wasn't readily goaded into anything she didn't want to do. "This girl prefers her water at about seventy degrees," she said to Adi, gingerly setting her bum in the center of her ring and bobbing toward the middle.

"What about you, Adi?" Chase said, finding his footing and climbing out.

She abruptly closed her mouth—had she been staring at him?—and swallowed hard, looking back to the lake, to the waterfall, to Bea—anywhere but at him. "Me?" she said. "I umm…No. I think I'll take Bea's route, regardless if it costs me a round of beer or not."

"Speaking of drinks," Logan said. "There're some sodas in my pack, Bro. Set them in the water to chill, eh?"

"On it," he said. He slicked back his hair with one hand and picked his way over to his brother's backpack. Did he feel Adi's eyes on him again? He didn't dare check to see. It'd been a while since they'd been swimming together. Six years. But he wasn't the only man she'd seen with a six-pack. That last season of *The One*…well, he'd decided the producers didn't even interview a man who wasn't spending a couple of hours in the gym every day. He didn't do that. But he knew his miles of hiking every day, the lifting of cages and carrying heavy packs…well, it pretty much had done the same work.

Let her look, he thought smugly. Then more plaintively, *please, let her look. Please let her like what she sees.* He set the sodas in the rocks near the base of the falls and finally dared to look her way as she chatted with Bea, casually taking in her long, slim legs, the pleasing curves of her, the hollow at the base of her neck…

He didn't know what she thought of how he looked these days. But he sure liked what he saw. Taking hold of his tube, he positioned it in the water and then sat down, making the girls shriek as he splashed them a bit. He reminded himself that he'd become used to Adalyn's womanly beauty by watching her on the show. She really hadn't seen him since he was a scrawny college kid. The thought of her on the show made him remember her kissing other men. Adam and that idiot, Connor. Their hands on her lower back, her thigh…He closed his eyes and leaned back, concentrating on the sound of the falls, wishing it could beat out the memories of such intimacies. Intimacies shared, bonds made with men who took her heart and threw it away. Had it made her swear off love forever?

"So what do you think, Adi?" he asked her, before he could lose his nerve. "Once you get this pod of cabins done and open for business, should we make our trek to Iceberg? I gotta get after that bull moose, and in a couple of weeks, the snow should be melted enough to get back there. It's really pretty when there's still a lot of snow on the peaks and the lake is full of icebergs."

"I don't know," she said, her delicate brows knitting together. "I need to see how Gramps is doing. Get through that appointment."

"Understood," he said, as if it was no big thing.

"You really should go, Adi," Logan said. "We'll keep an eye on Gene. Three times a day, if it'll make you feel better about it."

"I'll think about it," she said.

Conversation moved on to the boat launch's summer help. Joy and Mike had moved into the bunkhouse. Their college-aged kids, Sam and Katie, would arrive in a week or so. Together, they'd man the launch from sunrise to sundown each day, garnering a day and a half off each week as they did each summer. "Just enough to get some hiking in," Logan said.

"Or run to town for supplies," put in Bea.

"I don't know how you do it," Adalyn said.

"Look at it," Logan said, gesturing to the valley in front of them. "We live in God's country. Every day is a gift here, whether you're dealing with a tourist or hanging out with family in the punchbowls."

Adi got a little smile on her face. Was it his brother's mention of the gift of living in the park? Or including her in using the term *family*? Either way, Chase was glad he'd said it.

—◊◊—

In East Glacier, at Two Medicine Lodge, Kenneth checked into his room, unpacked his bag—carefully placing every piece of clothing in the drawers or hanging them in a small armoire—and then took a detailed map of the park out of his backpack and spread it out on the desk.

It had taken two days to drive here from Chicago, and given the late hour, he knew he couldn't do more than a cursory search of the area tonight. But he wondered if he could get some initial information by asking a straight-forward question. He exited his room, walked down the creaking wooden steps to the main lobby and approached the front desk. The clerk—a young college student identified as Heidi from Ontario, CA by her nametag—looked up and gave him a bright smile.

"Hi. I just checked in. I was wondering if you have an employee named Adalyn Stalling? She's an old friend. I think she mentioned she was going to work here for the summer."

The girl's eyes grew wide. "Did you say Adalyn *Stalling*?"

"I did."

"That's the name of the last bachelorette on *The One!*"

"Really? Weird," Kenneth said. "I bet that's making her summer interesting. But my friend would never go on that show."

"I wouldn't either," Heidi said. "But it's pretty entertaining." She focused on her computer screen. Clicking on one screen and then another, she searched down the list for Adalyn's name. But then her manager came over and asked what she was doing. "This gentleman is looking for a friend. He thought she might be working here."

"Oh, I'm very sorry, sir," the manager said. "We can't give out that information. Privacy and all. You understand, I'm sure. Perhaps you can reach out to mutual friends to try and get ahold of her?"

"Of course," he said. "It's just that I'm only here for two nights. It'd be a shame if she was just around the corner…Tell you what. Can you do me a favor? If she is on your roster, can you let her know what room I'm in? Ask her to come see me. Tell her it's Ken, from college. We shared an English class."

"Certainly," said the woman, not giving anything away. "I can do that."

"Thank you so much," he said, then turned to go and take a seat in the grand lobby, pausing to pick up a copy of *Montana Living* magazine before sitting where he could surreptitiously watch Heidi. He'd snagged her attention. There weren't many college girls who weren't a fan of *The One*. The show's host was forever interviewing groups of them who religiously watched it together—all a part of the fan base known as "One Nation."

Was it possible? Was Adalyn here, somewhere?

Heidi helped two more guests. Then, in a momentary lull, she glanced his way and turned back to the computer screen. *Thatta girl*, he cheered inwardly.

But as she read down the list, her excited brows lowered. She looked over at her manager, saw that the woman was engaged in another conversation, and then back to Kenneth. She gave a little shake of the head. *No Adalyn on the list.*

He feigned a grateful smile and tipped the edge of the magazine to his forehead in salute, then rose and returned to his room.

Now he studied the map, along with a touristy map of the park, denoting every diner, motel, lodge and campsite in the park, as well as on the outskirts. Right outside of Two Medicine was a whole village. Just because Molly said Adalyn had gone to "Glacier," didn't mean she was in the park proper. He would simply have to methodically check every shop and stop where she might be.

Wasn't that the way of a dedicated lover? Someone who was worth Adalyn's love?

No, she would soon see that he wasn't anything like Adam or Connor. He would never hold her heart in his hands and throw it away.

He would pursue her. Day and night, if he had to.

And when they were together…She'd know that he'd do anything to keep her.

Because that is love, he thought, turning to gaze out the window. *True love.*

CHAPTER 12

It was on the walk back when Bea said it. "Say, Adi, do you check into social media much?"

"Uh, no. Ever since *The One*, I've kinda had to avoid it."

Bea was uncharacteristically silent.

Adi stopped and turned, bumping her inner tube against her friend's. "Why?"

"Uh, maybe you want to check in. At least to say you're alive and well. There seems to be some conspiracy theory that you've been kidnapped or committed suicide or something."

Adi blinked at her. "What?" She lifted a hand to her head and slowly shook it. "Can't they all just forget about me?"

"They can't," Bea said. "You kind of are everybody's kid sister, in a way. I think America is worried about you."

"So they choose to believe I committed suicide?"

"Some are scared you might," Bea said, looking embarrassed. "Maybe it's best to just put their fears to rest?"

Adi heaved a sigh and glanced at the guys. "A girl gets burned and the whole world thinks she's ready to hang up the towel."

"Not the whole world," Chase said.

"Yeah, you've got us," Logan said.

"Okay, then. Most of the world." She glanced at Bea, half irritated with her, half glad she'd brought it up. If Mom caught wind of that when she had wi-fi access again in Borneo, she'd be calling her in the middle of the night. "All right, I'll check in." She turned to walk again.

"But don't say where you are, right?" Chase asked.

"Why not say where she is?" Logan asked. He huffed a laugh. "Could be good for business."

"Absolutely not," Chase said, cutting into his last word.

The four of them circled up.

Logan frowned. Bea's brows arched in concern.

"What? You think the paparazzi will follow you here?" Logan asked. "Would they really be that dedicated?"

Adi looked to Chase, with his clenched jaw. His eyes searched hers. *Tell them?* he silently asked.

It was hers to tell. And hadn't Logan just called her family? She felt the same way about them. They needed to know. So did Gramps. So they could help her keep her secret safe.

"The day Chase came to tell me about Gramps, I seem to have picked up a stalker. Or I guess he'd been stalking me for a while. He just chose that day to make himself known."

"*What?*" Bea and Logan asked together.

"It's okay," she said, lifting her hands. "That was part of the reason I came right away. And for Gramps, of course. But also because it was evident that becoming less…accessible would be a good idea."

"What'd he do? Did he threaten you?" Logan asked, his own jaw muscles now working overtime, the veins at his temples pulsing. Together, he and Chase were formidable.

"Ease up on the he-man protector gig," she said, waving them down. "He didn't threaten me, really. All he did was leave me *flowers*. Roses. In the garage at my firm, but then at my apartment too."

"Which he broke into," Chase said, making a slicing motion with his hand.

"And stole nothing," Adi said, trying to downplay it as much for herself as for them.

"But listen to this," Chase said, turning to Logan. "He left a rose *in her bed*. Does that sound like someone who is harmless?"

Bea shivered. "Creepy."

Adi swallowed hard. She'd not liked to think of that night. Preferred to think of it as a bad dream. "Yeah," she admitted. "It was creepy. So when Chase suggested I come here, escape..."

"You leaped at it," Bea said.

"Wise girl," Logan said. "Except for the fact that Glacier will see close to three million visitors this summer. How long 'til someone recognizes you? Until word gets out?"

"Hopefully never," Adi said, but then she shrugged. "But I only have so much power over that. I'll just keep wearing my hair in a ponytail and my reading glasses on. Skip the makeup. I hardly look like the glamour-girl the producers made me out to be on the show," she said, gesturing down to her wet cut-offs and hiking boots. "Gramps can greet most of the guests, show them to their cabins. He likes that, anyway. Mrs. Larson can see to housekeeping duties. I'll skirt the cabins when they're occupied." She glanced around at her friends. "It will be *fine*."

Chase stared at her. "Does your Gramps still keep that loaded .44 in the kitchen drawer?"

She frowned through a smile. "Chase, I really—"

"Does he still keep it there?" he pressed.

"Y-yes," she said. "But honestly, it won't come to that.

Stalkers like the idea of the people they follow. Most are too scared to ever really approach them."

Bea shivered. "I don't know, Adi. He broke into your apartment." She looked at Logan. "Maybe you should lend her your pistol?"

"All right, enough, you NRA-freaks," Adi said, walking on. "He's behind me! Back in Chicago! Quit talking about it or you'll get me all wigged out again." She flung her free hand up in the air. "I'll take precautions! Be smart. Not blab about where I am on social media. All right?"

They all stared back at her, nodding slowly.

But there was something about the fear at the corners of their eyes that kept Adi on edge all evening.

After supper, she went to the beach, gathered some unique stones, and built what Gramps had always called an "Ebenezer," a small stack of stones commemorating where she'd been and where she was now. *Remember the victories, kiddo,* he'd said. *The accomplishments. How God has blessed you.* She stacked the first few, remembering summers-past right here, on the lake. A few more, remembering college. Then two more, for her two seasons of the show. For Adam. For Connor. After all, they hadn't been all-bad. There was a reason—or ten—she'd fallen for each of them, even if they had broken her heart. And at last, she took a wide, curved stone and set it on top. *For this summer. For who I am now. For who I am becoming,* she thought.

The stack was pretty. Montana lakes always had the prettiest, most varied rocks. Brick-red and maroon, gold and green. Blue. Even some striped with white.

She sat back, pulled out her phone and framed a picture, blurring out the background, focusing on the Ebenezer. Then she sat back, pulled up Instagram, added the photo and typed out a brief message. *Hi, friends. I'm alive and well, just taking some time out to remember where I've been and where I'm going. Don't worry about me...I'll be back around come September!* Then she clicked the "share" button. *There,* she thought. *Now people can quit worrying about me.*

The sound of footsteps on the rocks made her glance backward. Chase. Her heart skipped a beat as he sat down beside her. "Nice Ebenezer," he said.

"Thanks. Remember when Grams used to make those crazy rock sculptures? The ones that looked impossible? She was always able to balance them just so..."

"Yeah. I was always sad in the morning to find them toppled. But she said that was part of the art of them...they were temporary miracles, to be enjoyed for the moment, and that was enough."

Adi thought about that. "I'm glad you remembered her saying that. I'd forgotten."

"It's stuck with me," he said. "I remember it often. Especially when I'm in the back country, you know? Seeing the melting snow or an ice formation that I wished I could bring someone else back to see...but know it'd be different by the time I returned. Or a field of flowers that won't be as bright or as perfect the following day. Or the apex of the autumn gold, when with one windstorm, fall will be over. That's when I remember your Grams saying that."

Adi took that in, moved by his words, as well as the images he had spun in her mind. "It's a special thing you get to do," she said, gesturing toward the mountains. "With 1500 square miles of ranger playground."

He grinned and ducked his head, then peered at her from the side, making her heart skip again. *Gosh, he's so handsome...* "Ranger playground, eh?" he said.

"Well, what would you call it?"

He considered that, squinted and looked around, then shrugged. "I guess it's as good a description as any." He pushed himself up and reached out a hand. "C'mon. Let's try and make a rock stack that would make your Grams proud."

"But I just built that," she said.

"C'mon," he cajoled. "Let me see something *surprising.*"

Intrigued, she took his hand and rose, looking for more stones, suitable for building. She remembered one time that Grams had built an arch. Maybe she'd try that. So she needed somewhat triangular stones. Wedges, of sorts...

"So, Mr. Forest Ranger," she called to him, as he lifted a turquoise rock as big as his hand and set it in a pile. "Why are all these rocks such gorgeous colors?"

"It has to do with the glaciers and layers of rock," he said. "They all have iron in them. Some were exposed to air longer than others. Some were continuously under water. But then you get this..." he said, waving over the crystalline waters as if he were a magician. "The prettiest rocks in the country."

"They really are," she said.

They settled into companionable silence then for a while, continuing to hunt for the right building blocks for what they had in mind, as her grandmother had too, once.

"I head back to East Glacier tomorrow," he said as he worked. "You think you and Gramps will be okay?"

"Us? Oh, yeah. I'll get those floors done tomorrow. By the time you get back, maybe my 'new and improved' pod of cabins will be open for business!"

"That will be cool to see. I like what you're doing with them, Adi. I bet Gene is proud of you too."

"I think so," she said. "But honestly, he doesn't seem to have much energy to be excited about anything."

"He's glad to have you here. I know that."

"I do too," she said. "He's made that clear. It's made me..."

Well, I'm really mad at myself for being away so long."

"Life takes us on different paths. I'm just glad your path came back around," he said, giving her a brief wink. He was using a big boulder in the water as his base. He'd put a small rock on it and was stacking a larger one on top, then a larger one still.

Adi set out her arch stones in order. Then she moved a larger rock closer to a second, just at the water's edge. Like Chase, she liked the idea of water washing around the sculpture. Once they were set out, she began building her arch, setting the narrowest part of each wedge at the bottom.

Seeing what she was doing, he said, "An arch, eh? Very Roman of you."

"Hey, anybody who built what they did must've had their rock science down." She thought about seeing their roads, their aqueducts, on her travels two thousand years later. But for some reason, she didn't bring that up now. For tonight, her focus was on this place. This time. She kept working, feeling the arch of nine stones begin to bend and threaten to falter. "I'm doing this with wedge shapes. But remember Grams's?" Her curved stack failed then, falling into the water. "Ahh!"

"Her arches were rocks of all shapes," Chase said with a smile, adding a fifth stone to his stack, which was growing ever more precarious itself. "She truly was an artist at it."

This time, Adi sat back and thought about it. She didn't lay the rocks out again. "She always said that it had to do with finding the contact point of each rock, really seeing that rock in three dimensions, and figuring out where it needed to be counter-balanced."

"I think it's kind of like magic," Chase said.

With that in mind, she set two rocks together, then gently, carefully shifted a third until it felt right. Sturdy. Almost static. Then a fourth and fifth in the same manner. As the arch grew, it was as if the rocks became one—she still needed to pay attention to each individual building block, but gradually, the mass became its own element. She added another and another, ignoring Chase when she dimly heard his own creation crumble and that distinct sound of sliding stone on stone. She could only focus on her arch, remembering her grandmother and those crazy, glorious sculptures she made each summer. Just for herself and anyone else who might be passing by at the time. Temporary miracles.

Before she knew it, she was placing the very last rock against the far side, carefully, carefully—ever so carefully—edging away her fingers, barely daring to breathe in fear it would fall. But it didn't.

"Chase," she whispered. "Chase," she said again, this time a little louder. Her eyes flicked toward him. He was halfway through his ever-larger stack of stone, but he glanced over at her and his eyes widened.

"You did it!" he cried.

"Shh!" she said, half laughing, half terrorized that even a loud noise would send it toppling.

"Oh, okay," he mouthed. "Well done," he whispered. "You must've inherited your grandmother's skill at creating temporary miracles."

She grinned at him and then back at her arch. The stones were drying out, and they were not nearly as pretty dry as they were wet. She cupped her hand, filled it with water and then dripped it across the arch, watching as the colors emerged. All the same, as lake rocks, and yet so varied, simply because of how long they'd been exposed to water and air. *Kind of like people*, she thought. *So much the same and yet so different, depending on what they'd experienced and been exposed to.*

She glanced over at Chase, biting his lip as he worked to find the right position for the next rock in his precarious stack. There was something right about being here with him, in this place, on this night. Even after their time apart, it was as if all those summers had oxidized their iron in similar fashion, making them companionable. Making them fit together, like these rocks did, at just the right contact point...

Adi shook her head. *Quit it. He's just a friend. One of your oldest friends, Adi. Don't destroy this. Haven't you lost enough this last year without losing a friend too?*

"Adi," he whispered, lifting his hands carefully away. "Look! Look!"

She was grinning, just about to say something, when it toppled. He groaned and flopped to his back, ignoring the sharp rocks that had to be poking him. "Hey," she said, rising and going over to him. She offered him her hand this time. "Don't worry. I saw it before it was gone. And it was *amazing.*"

He turned his head toward her, in the floppy way of the defeated. "Do you really think so?"

She grinned. "I really, really think so."

He took her hand and she heaved him to his feet. They stood there a moment, tantalizingly close, and Adi noticed that he held on to her hand just a second or two longer than was necessary. Seeming to remember himself, he turned to look at her arch again and she followed his gaze. "That really is something, Adi."

"I'd never be able to replicate it," she said.

"That's a cool part of it though, right? The temporary miracle?"

"Yeah. I guess so."

He stretched and took a deep breath. "It's going to be a good summer, Adi girl. I can feel it in my bones."

"Oh yeah?" she said, tilting her head up toward him as they began the walk back to the cabin.

"Oh, *yeah,*" he said, as if there wasn't a doubt in his mind.

CHAPTER 13

Kenneth had checked into the Many Glacier hotel and spread out his map. He'd carefully colored in areas with red marker that had proven fruitless. He'd asked busboys and maids. Valets and backcountry guides. Kids who worked the boat docks and others who worked in the stables.

Now he'd do the same here.

He unpacked his bag and hung his shirts on the same wooden hangers that he'd used at Two Medicine Lodge, spacing them three inches apart. He liked things precise. Adi liked things in order too. He'd seen that on the show—how she kept her room nice and tidy. Or had there been production assistants who saw to that?

He dismissed the thought immediately. No, his Adalyn would be precise, like him. Keeping things in order. Life was so much better when things were in order. He checked his phone and then his computer, but there was no Internet signal. Perhaps he'd have greater luck downstairs, near the front desk.

Kenneth went down the three flights of stairs and moved

into the spacious central area of the lobby, where log beams crisscrossed and a stone fireplace towered on one side. It was a testimony to the old national parks in their heyday, still a glorious celebration of man embracing nature, complete with various taxidermy marvels—from a giant stuffed grizzly on his hind legs to an elegant elk's head gazing across the expanse, as if eyeing the next meadow, rather than a hunter's deadly shot. Outside, through the windows was a beautiful lake, riffling silver-blue in the breeze, and towering, white-capped mountains, so near you could practically touch them.

He sank into a leather chair and pressed the home button on his phone, relieved to see one bar, at least. *One bar.* This part of Montana truly was the edge of nowhere, it seemed.

It was a notification on Facebook that alerted him first. An alert from One Nation—the fan group of the show—with their logo. He sat up straighter. Two kids sat down on the couch across from him and started bouncing, but he paid them little attention, even though he'd usually be looking for a parent to come and corral them. Right now, all he could do was concentrate as Instagram loaded, ever so slowly…

Finally, there it was. A picture of a stack of rocks, blurred lake—and mountains—behind it. And the words, her words. Precious words, the first he'd heard from her in months, aside from her automated voice mail message.

Hi, friends. I'm alive and well, just taking some time out to remember where I've been and think about where I'm going. Don't worry about me…I'll be back around come September!

He read them over and over. Memorizing them. Fantasizing about her reading them to him. Seeing her lips shape each syllable. *Remember where I've been and think about where I'm going.* What did that mean? He read through the comments that followed, everyone speculating about where she was and what it meant. Was she regretting her foolish decision to be on the show? Where was she thinking about going next? Were they trying to recruit her for a third season?

The thought of it enraged him. Well, he'd put a firm stop to that. There was no way that his Adalyn should risk her heart again. Not when she'd have security with him. No man would ever hurt her again. He'd see to it. He'd hold her and cherish her forever. Once she had a chance to know him, she'd wonder why she ever stopped to look at another.

He scrolled back up to the picture and enlarged it. Water and mountains. A lake. Could it be Swiftcurrent, just outside this very window? Excited, he moved to the door, intent on beginning his surveillance work at once.

—⟋⟍⟍—

By the time Adalyn awoke the next morning, she knew that Chase had departed for the backcountry with Hannah. She turned on her side and ran her hand over her grandmother's old quilt, tracing the stitches she had made. Was her arch gone this morning, toppled by the early morning waves that often washed along Lake McDonald's shore? She remembered that a few of her grandmother's sculptures had lasted for days, but most were gone in hours. There was something therapeutic about the task. Calming. Perhaps she'd make another this evening.

After all, Chase wouldn't be around, and Gramps was given to early bed times these days. She swung her legs over the edge and reached for her thick terrycloth bathrobe and Ugg slippers to ward off the chill of the mountain morning. Then she padded into the kitchen and started coffee—real coffee—that Gramps seemed to prefer now too over his traditional instant.

Shocking, she mused to herself.

As it brewed, Gramps came in, shuffling in that new gait of his. Gramps had never been a shuffler...he'd always been a strider. Once a tall man, perhaps 6'2" in his prime, he'd shrunk to about 5'10', just a couple inches taller than her now. His back was stooped. "Good morning," she said brightly, shoving the comparisons away. "Ready for some coffee?"

"Please," he said.

"How'd you sleep?"

"With my eyes closed," he said, using the well-worn joke of her youth.

"That's a good way to do it," she said, placing his mug on the table in front of him. "Eggs? I'm scrambling them this morning."

"Two, please."

She slipped two pieces of bread in the toaster and went to the fridge for some ham, butter and jam. This was how she was gradually getting Gramps to gain weight—she got him to commit to one thing, then added to it. Three square meals a day were doing him good. In the couple weeks she'd been here, he'd gained a few pounds, at least. And he had more color in his cheeks.

"What do we have on the reservation books today?" she asked, totally knowing, but wanting to engage him. She started a couple of ham steaks frying.

"A couple from Georgia, who were here years ago. A family of four from Helena, and a family of eight from Idaho."

"Eight!" she said, cracking the eggs into a bowl. "That's a lotta kids."

"Yes. I put them in Cabin 19 and 20. I guess they'll figure out who sleeps where. Those big families always do."

"Did you warn them about the temporary shower situation?"

"I tried," he said. "Got ahold of the Georgia couple and

the Idaho family, but not the Helena family."

"Ah well," she said. "We'll just tell them when they get here and hope the discount helps ease any disappointment." She poured the eggs into an old cast iron pan, which she'd oiled with bacon grease. They immediately began bubbling.

"Looks like those boys are making good progress on the renovated stalls," he said.

"Yes! I'm so happy. They think they'll be done tiling in a few days and it will be ready for use a couple days later."

"And your renovated cabins are coming along, girlie," he said, lifting his mug of coffee in silent toast.

"I'm really excited," she said. "I think today I can get the beds back in. Bea is going with me to town to pick up the mattresses and our new sign. Logan said he'd help me hang it tonight. And the plumber will be back to place and connect all five cabins' new toilets either today or tomorrow. Then all we have to do is get the new appliances in, make up the beds, hang some pictures, and we're ready to promote the new pod!"

He shook his head in wonder as she scraped out the eggs and reached for the ham steaks, now nicely browned. The toast, steaming in the cool morning air, popped up then.

"I've got that," Gramps said, rising to butter them. It surprised and pleased her, this bit of evidence of energy in him. Ever since she got here, he'd seemed content to sit and let her wait on him, as if he only had energy to eat, little more.

Adalyn thought about her Instagram post last night and her friends' concern over her stalker. She'd made it appear on Facebook too, knowing those fans were worried as well. She didn't want Gramps to fret about the guy, but was it wise to keep it totally to herself? Besides, she needed him to greet guests, to do her best to stay under the radar, unless he really wasn't up to it. She slid the ham on to their plates, Gramps added the toast, and they both turned to the table.

Gramps took her hand in his and bowed his head. "Father, thank you for bringing my Adi girl here for the summer. I'm so blessed by her companionship and this food. Help us make it a good day. Amen."

"Amen," Adi said, squeezing his hand.

He took a big bite of eggs, but she paused. "Gramps, there's something I need to tell you."

"Oh?" he said, reaching for a napkin to wipe his face. "What's that?"

"Back in Chicago," she said, stabbing some eggs, "right as Chase came to find me, there was…Well, it appeared I had a stalker."

"A stalker!" he said, his bushy gray brows furrowing.

"Don't stress, Gramps," she rushed on. "All he did was leave me some flowers. In the garage at my work and on my car," she said. Seeing the color wash from his face, she left out the part about her apartment. "It was probably some over-enthusiastic fan from the show. And it was good timing for me to come to Montana," she went on. "To let whatever thing that guy has for me die down. But Chase, Bea and Logan—they think it's best that I keep my whereabouts under wraps, as best I can. And given that I've been on the show for a couple of seasons and done all the publicity, I'm kind of recognizable. So, I was wondering…do you think you'd be up for greeting guests every afternoon? Maybe you could take your afternoon nap a little earlier, just to be sure you can be up? I mean, I'll be around but—"

"Adi," he said, covering her hand with his. "I'll see to it. The priority is to keep you safe." He nodded to the rifle above the kitchen door. "Do you remember how to use that? And I have my .44 in the—"

"Oh, it won't come to that, Gramps. No one has ever been

threatened to death by roses." She shoved a forkful of eggs into her mouth. Chewed them without tasting them.

"Still. If that fool went as far as leaving you roses in your work garage, I'd say he's assuming intimacies that only *he* feels. Which might mean the man is unstable." He poked at his eggs but didn't take another bite. "The world is full of crackpots these days, it seems."

"Happily, that crackpot is back in Chicago," Adi said. "And we'll just make sure he stays there. Now eat, eat! I'll be upset if talking about this ruined your breakfast."

Obediently, he took a bite and then absently spooned huckleberry jam onto his plate. But Adi could see that his eyes strayed again to the rifle.

"What do you think, Gramps? After we see if the new cabin pod draws in more guests, do you think we should go ahead and refurbish another pod? I'm kind of liking the task, and as I told the Rollinses, if we're able to consistently rent them out, the investment will pay for itself in a matter of weeks."

"Sure, sure," he said. "But are you certain you're up to it? Why not simply relax? Recuperate? Hike with Chase. Boat with Bea and Logan." He shrugged, chewing slowly. "Soak up the park?"

"I find the work healing in a way. I love seeing the old turned into something new. It gives my days purpose. And I like that I'm helping you."

"If it makes you happy, then sure," he said. "I even have some savings you can use for the next. But why do all of that work, Adi, if we might have to say goodbye at the end of the summer to this old place?"

Her breath caught at his words, the pain that edged his eyes. Pain that mirrored her own. "Because Grams would like it," she said. "And if we decide to stay on…"

"If you decide to stay on," he corrected, taking a slow sip of coffee. "Make no mistake, Adi girl, I can greet guests this summer. But I can't promise I'll be up to it next year. I'll stay and keep you company, if you want, but…"

"What do you mean?" she scoffed. "Look at you! You're gaining weight and you look better. You have some years left in you, old man, don't you think?"

He smiled with her. "You're my medicine, Adi girl. It's good for this old man to have company like you." He raised his mug again. "Brings life back to my old bones. But Adi, I'm almost eighty. This winter…well, this winter I'm thinking about going to your mother's house."

"Because Minnesota is so much warmer?" she asked with a smile.

"Because the winters here can be as lonely as they are cold," he returned.

That shot an arrow of guilt through her. She hadn't called him enough last year, or written, which she knew he particularly loved…she'd blamed it on him, sometimes. For not being online. Not having access to email or text. But it wasn't his fault, really. It was hers. And she'd neglected him. She covered his hand with hers. "Whatever you need to do, Gramps. But even if you wintered with Mom, wouldn't you want to come back here next summer?"

"Yes, if you're here," he said, nodding. "God-willing."

Her eyes lifted to the calendar on the wall behind him. Next week was his appointment. They'd find out then what was happening with his heart. What the doctor had to say about…everything. Until then, she wouldn't worry about next year. She'd just continue to love on him and feed him and make sure he took his naps. That was all she could do.

—〰—

Hannah had been flirting with him their entire trip, he admitted to himself. She'd tucked a fireweed blossom behind her ear and flashed him a grin as she tied her park-service jacket around her slim waist. She was nice enough. Pretty enough, sure. Smart as a whip, as Gene liked to say.

But she wasn't Adalyn. After two days of tracking grizzly sows, taking sample after sample of scat, Chase was ready to head back to Apgar and Adi. Was she done with her renovations on the first pod? Were they renting them yet? Had she built any other rock sculptures?

That last night they'd been together—when she'd helped him up and he'd felt how good her hand felt in his—well, he'd been perilously close to telling her how much he cared for her. How glad he was that she was home. But she wasn't ready for such intimacies, he knew. She was healing, still. Not ready to trust any man, let alone risk one of her oldest friendships for something more.

"Storm looks like it's building," he said, nodding to the east. "And we haven't yet dried out from last night's rain." They'd been deep asleep when the wind had worked loose the Velcro of their tent flaps, and they'd both awakened in soggy sleeping bags. All morning it had misted, finally clearing that afternoon under the mild warmth of the late June sun.

Hannah paused, scooped a sample into a glass vial, plugged it with a plastic stopper and pulled a pen out of her pocket to note the date, time and location they'd picked it up. She glanced up at him. "Something tells me, partner, that even if there wasn't rain closing in, you'd be wanting to head back to Apgar."

He feigned confusion, saying nothing, just reorienting his pack, tightening the waist belt. "Just ready to get back and ditch this camping equipment pack. You've got it easy, Madame Scientist. You carry your scope and supplies. But I wager I have about thirty more pounds with all this camping equipment. Especially now that it's wet."

"Right. That's it. The heavy *pack*." She rose. "Admit it, Rollins. You're falling for Adi."

"What? Adi and I are old friends," he said, taking to the trail again, assuming she'd catch up.

When she did, she said, "Anyone can see you're more than old friends." She paused. "What is it about her, Chase?" She scurried down the path behind him. He knew he was keeping a pace faster than usual, but couldn't seem to stop himself. "I mean, she's nice and all…"

Chase bit his lip, for the first time catching a bit of what this might truly be about. The tiniest edge of jealousy in her tone.

"Is it that you can't resist the idea of winning a girl that twenty-four others couldn't?"

Irritated, he frowned over his shoulder at her. "You don't know what you're talking about, Hannah."

"Don't I? Bea told me that you guys watched every single episode of *The One*." She laughed a little. Nervously? "Don't be embarrassed. I know it's not usually a guy thing. You guys were old friends. It's natural, the curiosity. And you have to admit…that show's a little addicting, right?"

He shook his head and ran a hand through his hair. Fact was, he was a little embarrassed any time someone found out he'd watched so much of that stupid show. What would people think if they'd known he'd gone back and watched every episode *again*? Wasn't that a little stalker-ish? At least he'd fast-forwarded past the make-out sessions. Those, well those, had made him sick to his stomach. But he'd paused at key moments to study Adi's expression. Gone back to listen to her talk with some "friends" from the previous season, reasoning out why some "relationships"—crazily plural—were "growing" while others "didn't seem to be progressing."

If those same girls were back at Lake McDonald Lodge right now, how would Adi describe *their* relationship? Would she even call what she had with Chase a "relationship" at all, given that they had yet to kiss?

At least she hadn't been as free with her kisses as some of the other bachelorettes. Bea had informed him of that. But he'd counted at least ten whom she'd kissed. Had there been others, off camera? *Maybe some were just mediocre kissers, not worthy of air time...*

"Hey," Hannah said, reaching out to tug him to a stop. "Did you hear me?"

"Huh? What?" he said, aware then that he'd been so lost in his own thoughts he hadn't heard a word she'd said. "Sorry." He turned toward her.

She crossed her arms and looked at him. "Man, you have it bad, don't you?"

He paused. "I might," he allowed.

There was a tinge of storm in her blue eyes then. Fleeting, but there. "You going to do something about it?"

"I might," he said again.

She shook her head, looking to the valley below them, all bright June green grasses and alight with wildflowers—white serviceberry bushes, yellow glacier lilies and blue camas. He noticed her arms were still crossed. "What about us, Chase?" she asked, daring to look at him again.

He paused. *Us?* He understood a little crush. Admitted to a little flirting of his own with Hannah. The attentions of a pretty girl were always flattering, but he thought he'd kept it to a minimum. He had to, given all the time they spent together. "Hannah," he began, frowning.

"I mean, I know we're partners and the boss doesn't like it, but we wouldn't be the first rangers to date. And Adi—she's just here for the summer, right? I got the impression that you were looking for something more long-term these days."

He studied her, feeling badly that he was about to cause her pain. "Hannah," he said again, taking a deep breath. "You, my friend, are smart. Cute as a button, as Gene says. And you routinely kick my butt on these trails. I take your interest in me as the highest of compliments. Really. I just…" He looked back to the valley, ran a hand through his hair and settled his ball cap back on, before facing her again.

"Say it," she said softly. "I think you need to say it, Chase, as much as I need to hear it."

"I just have a thing for Adi," he said, leveling a gaze at her. "Always have. Probably always will. No matter what happens this summer."

She was right. He'd needed to say it. Out loud. There was something in uttering the words that made them real. Tangible. He had a thing for Adi. *Chase Rollins is falling for Adalyn Stalling*, he thought, silently testing out more words. *I'm falling for her.*

Hannah sucked in a deep breath through her nostrils, held it, then let it out. "I figured," she said. "But it's a huge bummer for me." She punched him on the shoulder and resumed walking. "Because you are *way* cuter than Henry Jefferson," she said, referring to the sixty-year-old at their station in Apgar.

"I dunno," he said, following after her. "Henry has some fine attributes."

She glanced back at him and smiled, shaking her head. "It's probably best that this," she paused to motion between them, "remains platonic. Anything else might have become distracting."

"As well as against the rules," he said. "Chief would've had you on one side of the park and me on the other faster than we could've blinked." He admitted to himself that that would have made him sad. Hannah was a good partner, and he was curious to see what her research would turn up about his bears and the decreased birth rate of late. Was it due to something beyond the increasing human infiltration of their habitat? Were they ailing from some genetic code gone wrong?

"Still," she said, turning to walk backward. "When that Adi Stalling breaks your heart, I might be willing to risk Chief Haverson's wrath if you are, Rollins. Keep it in mind, anyway." She pushed her blond ponytail back over her shoulder.

He blinked, slowly running over her words as she flounced in a turn and continued down the trail ahead of him.

He thought that so clearly stating what he felt for Adi would've put her pursuit to bed.

But Hannah apparently didn't think anything would come of his crush on Adi Stalling. She was betting that it was simply a summer fling, nothing more.

The question was...Was she right?

CHAPTER 14

Adi reached up, stretching so far, the ladder felt rickety beneath her.

"Careful!" Gramps called.

But then she had it hooked, the top-left corner of their new sign for A Cabin by the Lake, etched in a classy Bookman Old Style font. The sign was stained gray, the lettering painted a bold blue.

"Woo, that sure is pretty!" Gramps called.

"You think so?"

"Know so!"

She moved down the ladder and reached for the plastic banner she'd also picked up in town that morning. "Newly Renovated Cabins Available Tonight!" it said. She hooked it to the bottom of the sign on additional grommets she'd had installed for just such a purpose. If her new pod was full, she'd take it down. And in a few weeks, when the park was at its busiest, she had no doubt it'd be down every night.

She climbed down the rest of the ladder and went to view it with her grandfather. "Oh, yay!" she cried, clapping her hands. "Do you really like it, Gramps?"

"Love it, honey," he said, putting his arm around her shoulders. "Grams would be so proud of you. Between this and those cabins and even your new-fangled website, you're hauling me into the twenty-first century, it seems."

"Somebody had to," she said, nudging him with her hip. "C'mon. Let's see how that pot roast is faring."

"Sounds good."

They were slowly making their way down the drive when a Jeep came up behind them. With a quick glance, Adi burst into a smile. "Chase!" she said, moving around to the passenger side. "Hi, Hannah," she quickly added for the driver.

"Hey, Adi," Hannah said. "Nice new sign."

"Thanks! Just put it up," she said, glancing back at it again. It really did look good against the green of the trees. A hundred times more visible than the old, rotting Kreature Komforts sign five yards behind it.

"See you next week," Hannah said to Chase. "You have the next few days off, right?"

"Yup," he said climbing out and then reaching behind his seat for his pack. He pulled it out, shut the door and gave her a little salute. Hannah waved back and did a U-turn and rumbled off down the road.

"So?" Adi said, as they fell into step together with her grandfather. "Did you solve all the bear fertility problems in the world?"

"Took a stab at it," he allowed. "We think we're going to need to track down about twenty additional sows who didn't produce this spring, tranquilize them and take blood samples though. We need a greater number of samples for Hannah to finish her study."

"Whoa," Adi said. "That sounds a little more challenging than collecting scat."

"A little," he said with a grin down at her. "But it keeps the job interesting."

She looked him over, admitting he looked good, even after a couple days on the trail. The scruff of a brown beard made his square jawline more apparent. For the first time, she noted the gun in his holster, beneath his NPS fleece jacket. "Do you always pack heat when you're out finding bear poop?"

"I do on occasion, but most don't," he said. "Unless they're a law enforcement ranger."

"I thought you rangers were more peaceable sorts."

"We are," he said with a sly smile. "In general. Most are interpretation rangers, helping guests of Glacier connect with the park, answer questions. You know."

"These days they have to be everything," Gramps said. "Peacekeepers. Firefighters. Emergency personnel. Even tracking down drug runners across the border. When you're an hour or two from the closest police station…"

"And poachers," Chase said. "Don't forget the poachers. If I ever find the guy who killed that old bull moose last spring, he'd better hope I don't have my gun with me."

"Really?" Adi said. "I thought poaching was more a *big*-big-game issue. The things that a South African ranger would have to deal with more than you would here in Montana."

"You'd be surprised," Chase said, pulling up as it came time to part—he toward the boathouse and they to their cabin complex. "Tons of deer and elk are killed every year by hunters without tags. It's pretty hard to police. But last year, on the edges of the park, that moose was killed—only his head taken for some jerk's wall—and we found an injured brown bear cub this spring, her mama likely shot."

"That's terrible," Adi said.

"Ahh, it's not all that bad. Those are the exceptions," he

said, giving her a comforting smile. "Keeps us from being complacent, I'll say that for it."

He set down his pack as Gramps made some excuse and shuffled off, leaving them alone. "It's good to see you, Adi."

"It's good to see you too, Chase." She grinned up at him. "Wait until you see my pod of renovated cabins! Can you come over?"

"Just as soon as I clean up," he said.

"Sounds good," she said. "If you want to eat with us, we have a roast in the crockpot."

"I'll be there," he said.

"Awesome. See ya in a bit," she said, turning to go, hands tucked in the back of her jeans pockets.

Feeling his gaze still on her, she glanced back and saw he was still staring her way, as if a bit dazed. "You okay?" she called.

He seemed to startle, flashed her a grin and picked up his pack. "Fine, fine," he said with a wave. "See you in a bit."

—ᴍ—

Kenneth got out his red pen and carefully outlined the areas he had searched and then methodically colored them in with a broad, red Sharpie. Last night he'd broken through the park's security system—which did not take a genius hacker to accomplish—and searched the employee roster. He'd been reasonably sure that given her marketing prowess, that Adalyn was working for one of the main lodges. But she was not listed.

There were only two possibilities. Either she was using an alias or she wasn't working for the park system. Both were problematic. The park was vast—and his clue of her being near a lake did not help. There were over seven hundred of them. However, her picture showed a larger body of water, as far as he could tell, so he would concentrate his search on the larger lakes first. It only made sense.

If she was using an alias, that would make inquiring after her all the more challenging. But wasn't dedication a hallmark of his love? Someday they'd look back at this and laugh, reminiscing at how hard he'd tried to find her. She'd take it as a compliment, he was sure. Like a prince fighting through a vast, dark forest to find his princess.

He finished covering the Swiftcurrent area in red. Adalyn wasn't at the motel, boat launch, campground, diner, store or in the stables. He'd even spent a day in the village right outside the eastern gates of the park, verifying that she wasn't in the small lodge, teepee campground, gas station or restaurant there either. He'd asked about her at each, then hung around through both shifts to make sure she didn't show up, in case she was using a different name.

He traced the Going-to-the-Sun highway with his nail. Next on the list was Saint Mary Lake, then Hidden Lake… then Lake McDonald. If she wasn't near any of those, he'd have to go farther afield. Bowman. Kintla. If he thought about it, any of those more remote lakes would be an even better place for his Adalyn to retreat and recover. It mattered little. He had all summer. And Molly had clearly said Adalyn had gone to Glacier. She was here, somewhere.

It was only a matter of time before he found her.

—⟋⟍⟋—

Chase rose and gathered the plates.

"Oh, leave it," Adi said. "I'll do them later."

"No worries," he said. "If you cook a meal, you shouldn't be on cleanup duty. Those are Rollins rules, anyway." He stacked Gene's plate on top of his and carried all three to the kitchen.

"I think I'll turn in. It's been quite a day," Gene said, rising slowly, as if it pained him.

Chase glanced at the old clock that had hung above the kitchen door as long as he remembered. It was only seven. He shared a knowing glance with Adi. "Sleep well, Gene," he said.

"You watch yourself, young man, with my granddaughter," Gene said, shaking a finger. "I'll be in the next room, you know."

"Gramps," Adi said, rolling her eyes. "You do remember that we're not teenagers anymore, right?"

"*Hmmph*," he said, draining his glass of a last swallow of water, then casting them both a knowing look. "You might be adults now, the both of you. But that doesn't mean I can't keep trying to keep you on the straight and narrow."

"Nothing but straight and narrow planned tonight, Gene," Chase pledged.

"Goodnight, Gramps," Adi said. "Want me to bring you a glass of water?" She nodded toward the door.

He just waved her off as he shuffled out of the kitchen and down the hall.

"Sorry about that," Adi said, reaching for a dish to dry when Chase finished washing it.

"Nothing I'm not used to after being neighbors with him most of my life," he said, casting her a gentle smile. "I have to say, I'm pretty impressed with you. All that work on those renovated cabins and a perfect roast to boot. Is there anything you can't do, Ms. Stalling?"

"Kill mice. Well, I can kill them. I just can't stand the whole process of disposing of them."

"I'll make you a deal. I'll dispose of any dead mice for you every day that you make me a roast like that."

"You were just hungry after a couple days on the trail."

"No, seriously. It was one of the best I've ever had."

"A temporary miracle," she quipped, lifting the pot. "Once all that succulent, juicy, falling-apart deliciousness on a plate. Now gone."

He grinned. "I've thought a lot about our rock sculptures. Want to try it again tonight?"

"Maybe," she said. "But I was thinking about the old rope swing over at your place. Is the rope still good?"

"Could be. We haven't tried it in years. Had to lock it up in a box to keep the kids from it. Liability issues and all, you know."

"*Pffft*," she said. "Liability. I swear, lawsuits have sucked all the fun out of life."

"True that," he said. "Want me to go see if Logan remembers where the key is?"

"Yes. So much," she said with such glee that he swore her eyes fairly sparkled. Then she was shoving him, pushing him away from the sink. "Go! I'm so excited. I'll finish up here, check on Gramps, grab my sweatshirt and meet you there. Okay?"

"Okay, okay," he laughed, thoroughly amused. *Like a kid on Christmas...*

When he got over to the boathouse cabin, he called out, then realized that Bea and Logan were still out on the *Maid of McDonald* sunset cruise. He walked down the hall and opened the storage closet. On one wall was where they kept all the keys. If he remembered right, the lockbox for the swing rope was an old, orange key. *There.*

Feeling as if he'd found a trophy—knowing it would delight Adi—he closed the closet door and took to the high path that led to an inlet on the lake and the giant ponderosa. It was getting late; the pink tinge of twilight covered the sky and he could hear the low, rumbling motor of his brother's boat in the distance, likely returning from their cruise. Knowing them, it wouldn't take Bea and Logan long to find them. But with some luck, he and Adi would have a good half an hour to themselves.

His grandfather had built and hung this swing, fifty years before. The rope probably hadn't been changed for twenty years—and neither he nor Logan were motivated to climb the towering tree to change it—so they'd elected to lock it up. Chase always figured that someday, when he or Logan had kids, they would find a sawyer to climb the ponderosa with his hobnail boots and do it for them. He regretted he hadn't done it sooner, especially now, with Adi interested in trying it out again...

He climbed the stair-stepping tree stumps up to the top one, unlocked the box and pulled the rope free of a nest of spider webs and pine needles, wiping down his hand in distaste. He hated the sensation of spider webs on his skin. Hannah had taken to teasing him mercilessly about it. He freaked out on the trail when he walked through webs.

"It's still here," Adi said, startling him with her sudden appearance below. She was in a bulky MSU Bobcats sweatshirt, her grandfather's favorite. She looked cute in it with her slim jeans and white Converse hightops.

He tore his eyes off of her, then back up the length of the rope. "Yes," he said. "It appears so. Let me just test if first."

"Absolutely not," she said, already climbing up toward him. "This was my idea, Rollins, not yours."

He frowned at her. "C'mon, Stalling," he returned as she climbed atop the stump below him. "I'm just going to make sure it's safe."

"No," she said, reaching his stump, forcing him to take a

step closer to the edge. "Give it here," she said, reaching for the rope.

He easily swung it out of her reach. "What kind of gentleman would I be if I stood by and watched you swing out on this and fall?"

"The kind of gentleman who knows," she said, giving him a firm look, "that I really want to go first. I've been thinking about this for days." She reached for it again, brushing against him. Held his hip then, to lean farther.

He groaned. "You really are stubborn, woman." He brought the rope closer to her hand and shook his head. He didn't want her to fall off the stumps in trying to snag it. They were already a good fifteen feet off the ground. "*Hold on*," he said, looking up and tugging at the rope. It held tight.

"See?" she said. "Plus, it's better that I go first. If you're going to break it with your weight, at least I'll have had my ride first."

"That's harsh," he said with a laugh. "I'm overwhelmed by your concern for my safety."

She smiled and took the rope from his hand. Studied the wooden disk that formed the seat. "No rot. Rope's fine. I'm going for it. Now, you better climb down so I don't knock you over when I swing back."

He huffed a laugh and, holding her hips, maneuvered around her, catching the scent of her honeysuckle shampoo and a hint of lemon lotion, wishing he could stay that close to her forever. He climbed down the remaining stumps, and she climbed up the final two, to the very top, which was about twenty feet high—and a very good reason for the Rollinses to keep the swing locked up, he thought. It was amazing what their parents and grandparents had let them do without a second thought. They'd all fallen off this swing at various stages at least once in their childhood. Now he didn't know if a parent would ever allow it at all…but tons of kids would be enticed by it. Just as they had been.

He looked up at her. The weight of the rope's arc was pulling at her, and she didn't look as confident as she had a moment ago. "Second thoughts?" he called up to her.

Biting her lip, she looked out to the water, took a firmer grip on the rope and then set off. She swung past him, pulling her legs around and settling the seat firmly beneath her bum. She let out a shriek of pure joy as she reached the end, then came *whooshing* back past him, making him laugh in delight with her. With each swing he caught the scent of her again, but it was mingled with the heady scents of pine and sap and water.

And in that moment, Chase thought he'd never smelled anything more perfect. Adi, as part of the lake, the forest. His place. His…girl?

She was slowing now, and as she swung to the end—still a bit over the water—she lifted free of the seat and landed expertly on the beach beside him.

"As good as you remember?" he asked.

"Better," she said. "So much better. Maybe because I haven't done it in years? You try." She handed it over to him.

Again, he looked up the length of the rope and gave it a firm tug. "I have a good thirty pounds on you."

"What? Are you telling me that a big, grizzly-huntin' ranger is scared of a *swing*?"

He lifted a brow at her. "This isn't just any swing."

"No, it's not," she said, flashing him a teasing, saucy grin.

And it was that—an old, familiar, flirtatious grin—a grin he'd never seen her give any of the bachelors she'd kissed on *The One*—that made him turn and climb the stumps. He paused momentarily on the next-to-last one, but knew there was no way he couldn't go to the top…not when Adi had done it already. He climbed all the way, feeling the precarious pull of the rope threatening to upset his balance.

Chase knew that waiting would only make it harder, so with a brief prayer that the rope would hold, he stepped off the towering stump and sailed into space, letting out a hoot of glee just as Adi had. She grinned as he sailed past her, again and again. Then once more he was on the beach, holding the rope. "Want to go again?" he asked, when he found himself jittery in such close proximity to her. She was so beautiful, with her bright smile. He desperately wanted to abandon the swing, take her cheeks in his hands and kiss her. Or drop the swing, grab hold of her waist and pull her against him, bending to claim her lips. What would their first kiss be like? Why hadn't he kissed her long ago?

"Hello," she said, snapping her fingers in front of his face. "Earth to Chase."

He blinked. "Oh. Sorry."

"Where'd you go?" she asked with a curious smile, hooking her hands in her rear pockets. "Chase?" She stepped a little closer to him. Inviting him?

There it was again. Her waist. Handholds calling out for his fingers to wrap around and ease her closer...yes, he'd ease her closer...

He shook his head and laughed, forcing himself to partially turn away from her, breaking the spell. "You done?" He lifted the rope, hoping she hadn't answered him while he'd been distracted with thoughts of kissing her. "Or do you want to go again?"

"Nah. It's never as good the second time," she said. "But maybe tomorrow."

"She might be done, but we're not!" Bea called, emerging down the path.

"We saw you two from the dock!" Logan said. "Glad the

old rope held!"

"No more than we were," Adi said. Was that a slightly sorrowful look on her face? That they had company? But then she was turning to Bea. "You have to try it," she said. "It's one of the best experiences of my life, sailing out over that water..."

Logan came to a stop beside Chase. "If my wife dies, I'm going to have to kill you. You know that, right?" he said. "She's been begging me to unlock it since last summer."

"I know," Chase said. "Sorry." He remembered that now. The bickering about it. The begging. The cajoling. But when Adi had asked, it was as if all that history flew right out of his mind. All he could think about was finding the key and then, seeing her float past, utterly free...well, if she called it one of the best experiences of her life, he was inclined to call it the same.

They hung out until darkness closed in, then left Bea and Logan to lock the rope up again. It was a moonless night and the path was difficult to discern. She stumbled a little before he finally got up the nerve to offer. "Here, take my hand, city dweller."

"Thanks, Ranger Rick," she said, slipping her fingers into his. They were slim and yet strong. He could feel a few calluses—the result of her recent renovation work, no doubt. What would it feel like to hold her hand in Chicago, once the calluses were gone? The thought cast a cold wave over the radiating heat of his body. He'd never go to Chicago. His life was here. In the woods. Were there any woods of note in Illinois? Bears? Certainly no grizzlies...

They reached the parking lot between their properties and given the warm light cast from her grandfather's cabin and the boathouse cabin, she dropped his hand. "Thanks, Chase. Really. That was so fun," she said, swinging her arms and clapping her hands as if nervous.

"It was. Thanks for dinner," he said.

"Sure, sure."

She paused. He paused.

Then he rushed on, "About tomorrow…"

Just as she said, "Well, see ya."

She was the first to recover. "Wait, what? Tomorrow?"

"Yeah," he said, rubbing his hands together, apparently as nervous as she. "I was thinking…you might have a little time, now. Now that your first renovations are done," he rushed on. "And I have a couple days off." He shoved the toe of his boot in the soft layer of pine needles and soil beside the path before daring to look at her again. "What if we did that trip to the East side? Hiked to Iceberg. Camped at Swiftcurrent. Then take the kayaks down the lakes? We'd be back the next day."

He expected her to protest about leaving her grandfather. Or give him another excuse. But instead, she inched closer and looked up at him. "I'd like that, Chase. Best do it now, before the summer's gone, right?"

"Right," he said, grinning down at her. He cocked his head to the side. "Another week and Logan will tell us to buy our own kayaks. The tourists will be thick in a minute or two, here."

"Can't have that," she said. "Not after I just spent a wad on those renovations. A wad I haven't had a chance to recoup." It was her turn to dig her toe into a stack of pine needles. "So… what time do you want to leave? What should I pack?"

"We should leave by seven," he said. "To get over to the other side and do the ten-mile hike will take most of the day. And I might need to do a bit of bushwhacking to see if I can find that bull moose."

"I thought you said you were off," she protested, but he could tell she wasn't really angry at the thought.

"Do you mind?" he asked. "It's kind of a thrill, finding an animal who doesn't want to be found."

"I wouldn't mind," she said.

"Good. Then bring a couple shirts that you can layer, a couple pairs of pants, three pairs of socks and your hiking boots. You know the park. It's always best to be prepared for all sorts of weather. It's supposed to stay in the 70s for the next few days, but up at Iceberg, it will be down around 45."

"Gotcha. What about food?"

"I'll cover that. Just your clothes, and a sleeping bag if Gene has one for you."

"I think he does. See you in the morning," she said, slowly turning away.

Chase had to stop himself from reaching out and catching her hand. Keep her from leaving him. *You'll see her tomorrow. You'll have her all to yourself for two days.* He shoved his hands in his pockets. "Good night, Adi."

"Good night, Chase," she said, slowly shutting the door.

CHAPTER 15

What are you doing, Adalyn? she asked herself, even as she continued shoving clothes to the bottom of her pack. *Why not do this?* came the next question. The same questions, over and over, circling around her heart, pulling her in separate directions. One part of her wanting to protect herself, hide. The other part wanting to figure out what was going on between her and Chase...if there was anything at all.

Part of her hoped there wasn't. That they could just be friends. That he wouldn't make her fall in love with him, hold her heart in his hand, and then crush it, as Adam and Connor had done before him. It would be so much harder, to take such a rejection from him. So much harder if she lost not just a potential love, but her friend too.

When she got to the kitchen, she spied Chase out in the parking lot, his Jeep idling as he waited for her. She began running through all the food that Gramps could eat in her absence, opening cupboards and the fridge, reminding him to be sure to eat three times a day. He finally took her arm and pulled her to the door and opened it. "I've made it seventy-six years and will be alive to see you return," he said. "Go. Have fun. You can make up for lost time by fussing over me double-time when you get back." He glanced out at Chase and then eyed her warily. "Do we need to talk about safe sex?"

Adi choked on a laugh. "What? No, Gramps, we most definitely do not. Did you not see how I held the guys at bay on *The One*?"

"There's a difference between some 'temptation suite' and a tent in God's country." He waggled grizzled brows at her.

She blinked. "Really? You're serious?"

"Really. You're sharing one tent, right?"

"Probably," she said, her voice high and tight. "But not a *sleeping bag*."

"It doesn't take a shared *sleeping bag* to—"

"*Goodbye*, Gramps," she said, leaning in to kiss his leathery-soft cheek. "Quit worrying about me and I'll try my best to not worry about you."

"I'll be fine, Adi girl. Besides, that Bea will likely come over and pester me more than you do."

"Perfect," she said, giving him one last look. He really did look worlds better than when she had arrived. And he was even well enough to be wondering about her sex life, apparently. All in all, his improved pattern of eating square meals and resting often was paying off. And he was right that he wouldn't be alone for long—Bea had texted her, told her she'd check in on him three times a day, "plus a couple sneak peeks when I make sure he doesn't see me," she'd written.

Seeing her emerge, Chase got out of the Jeep and came around to open her door for her. He took her pack, threw it in the back and then shut her door. "Mind if we keep the top down?" he asked. "It's a little cold for it, but—"

"I'd love it. It's the best way to drive the Going-to-the-Sun. Just like the Jammers do," she added, referring to the old, red, topless buses that took tourists across the Divide.

He grinned, and *Gosh*, she thought, *he has a nice smile. That adorable dimple on his left side might kill me with its cuteness.* "There's an old blanket behind your seat to help keep you warm," he said.

"Perfect."

With that, he went around and they waved at Gramps, still in the doorway, and then as they drove through Apgar, waved at old Henry, who was leaving the visitor center. Minutes later, they were on the highway, one of only a few early-bird visitors, heading east. The road was relatively straight for a span, and Adalyn admired the heavy waterfalls on either side, many of which would become trickling streams, come July and August. This was the part of being in the park all summer that she loved most—seeing so many changes as the weeks went by, able to observe and fully absorb what most tourists only glimpsed.

She leaned her head back against the seat, feeling her nose chill in the cool morning air and her hair whip against her forehead, cheek and neck. How blessed she was, to be here, now. To be here with Chase. To be driving in this amazing park...

"Happy?" Chase called, over the wind.

She only smiled, seeing that dimple again, and nodded.

—◊◊◊—

Kenneth wasn't happy at all. He'd checked out of the dumpy little motel above Saint Mary Lake and had noted that there were no reservations available on the west side. Summer traffic was apparently picking up, and he might be forced to go as far as Columbia Falls to find a place to unpack next.

Maybe that wouldn't be all that bad. It was about time to

find a town in which he could launder his clothes and buy some supplies. He'd been thinking about investing in a nice DSLR camera. It'd give him reason to use telephoto lenses, no matter where he was. Which might come in handy, if he had to watch Adalyn for a while before he made his approach.

He'd plan that approach carefully, he'd decided. Study her ways. Her schedule. Figure out what she liked here, in the park. What was important to her. And then he'd do his best to come beside her in those passions. Wasn't that how it was to go for two people destined for each other? He'd come a little her way. She'd come a little his. It'd be perfect.

He pulled over at Logan Pass, aware that it was here that he should hike to Hidden Lake. See if there might be anywhere that Adalyn might be staying. Could she be a docent for the park service? Unlikely, he thought. It would only be a matter of time before she was recognized by someone from One Nation, and the paparazzi descended upon her. More and more, he was certain *that* was what had driven her from Chicago. Not his overtures with the roses. It had been every journalist from *People* to *The Star* that had been his undoing. Sending her fleeing, and forcing this pursuit of his.

No matter. He would find her. And it would all be worth it.

He put his rented Explorer into park, happy to see the lot so empty. He'd make quick work of this little hike, question a few employees at the nature center and be able to fill in this area with red in short order. Adalyn was somewhere on the west side. He knew that now. He could feel it.

Almost there, my sweet Adalyn.

We are only days away from our reunion. Do you know I am here? As I feel you near?

—◊◊◊—

"Want to pull over, Adi?" Chase called, as they neared the exit for the Logan Pass parking lot. "For old time's sake?"

It was here that they had jumped off buses in their youth, to hike the Highline, then hitchhike back to Apgar—racing every year to see if they could beat their record. Here that they had hiked to Hidden Lake, searching for baby goats in Junes-past—what Chase liked to call "woolies" because of their thick, white coats.

"Nah!" she returned. "Big day ahead! Let's get to Swift!"

"Swift" was how some of the locals referred to Swiftcurrent, the glacial lake that glittered in front of Many Glacier Lodge. Chase thought it was the prettiest part of the park. Lake McDonald held his heart—because in many ways, it was home. But Swift was his favorite place to visit—not to mention home to the thickest population of bears nearing tourists in the park. There was a reason that he and Hannah were often over this way. If things kept up as they had in years past, they'd have to relocate a good number of bears who found it much easier to rummage through campground trash cans and tourist tents for food than dig for termites or fish the rivers.

He shoved the thought out of his mind, wanting to concentrate more on Adi, beside him in his Jeep, than what would be next on his ranger task docket.

Chase sneaked a peek at her. Watched as the wind made her jacket billow and her t-shirt cling to her slim form. Her hair flew about, a brown tornado of kinetic energy. Her legs were crossed on the edge of his dash, feet hanging slightly out. But what pleased him most was the utterly content expression on her face, the sense of peace about her that he hadn't felt since her arrival. He'd asked if she was happy. He'd known that she was, even before she answered.

And because he knew that, and she was with *him*, it made

him even happier.

Watch your heart, Rollins, he warned himself again. He'd observed enough wounded animals to know that you never got too close. Not unless they trusted you or were too weary to care. Adi didn't strike him as too wounded or weary any longer. Maybe, just maybe, she was ready to venture into trusting him. But he knew that was tough territory too. Hadn't Connor convinced her to trust him? Only to break her heart two months later? Hadn't Adam talked her into believing him, only to choose another? Hadn't someone she trusted settled her into a limo and sent her away while she dissolved into tears?

"You okay?" she asked, lightly touching his forearm.

Only then did he notice the white-grip he had on the steering wheel, the way his teeth clenched together. He took a deep breath and forced a smile. "Yeah!" he lied. "Fine!" *Only ready to kill your exes,* he thought.

What would Adi have been like if she hadn't gone through what she had? Might they have picked up where they left off? Be farther along by now?

She might not be here at all, came the thought.

And it was true. Adi had come home because of four things: Her boss forcing a leave of absence; her grandfather's failing health; her weariness of being in the spotlight; and her stalker.

So in a way, he had to be thankful. Not that she had gone through what she had gone through—utter heartbreak. Not that she had endured such incredible, invasive public scrutiny—half the country commiserating with her, half of them judging her for losing at love. Not that she had a stalker. But he had to be thankful that regardless of how it had happened, God had found a way to bring her back here, this year. And that he had been ready to be her friend, her confidant and encourager, her protector. Even if that's all it ended up being.

Even if that's all it ends up being, he repeated silently to himself. *First, her friend. Second, her confidant. Third, her protector. Anything beyond that? I'll only count it as a blessing.*

But, please, Lord. May I claim that blessing...

—‍᷍‍᷍‍—

As suspected, Kenneth could find no available accommodations in West Glacier. The lodge and campground were full. Searching the web, he saw that even the nearby Belton Chalet was booked solid. There was nothing for it. He'd have to go to Columbia Falls and regroup. There, he'd found a Motel 6 for $99 a night.

But as he left the lodge, heading toward Columbia Falls, he saw a sign on the road for "A Cabin by the Lake." Better yet, he saw the vinyl sign hanging below it. "Newly Renovated Cabins Available Tonight!"

He'd driven by, but up ahead, he spied a turnabout, pulled over, waited for a camper to lumber by and made a U-turn. In minutes, he was pulling up in the parking lot. He got out, walked over to the charming, old cabin with an OFFICE sign above the door and knocked.

It took a few minutes, but an old man—just yanking up his suspenders as if caught in a nap—came to the door. "May I help you?" he asked, squinting against the afternoon sun.

"I'm looking to rent one of your cabins," Kenneth said. He gestured toward the road. "It looks like you have some availability?"

"Oh, yes, yes," said the man, turning back as if to search for a key, and then remembering himself. He was maybe seventy-five, eighty. It surprised Kenneth, that an elderly man was still in charge of the property. "So, we have older cabins that have not yet been renovated. But there are a few available tonight that are brand-spankin' new," he said, smiling as if he'd just birthed this particular baby himself. "Or at least newly renovated. And we have renovated shower facilities to boot," he said. He paused to take a better look at Kenneth, as if considering whether he was worthy or not.

Kenneth found himself standing up straighter, striving to be found worthy, then chastised himself. There was no one, *no one*, that could make him feel that way any longer. He had the cash this old man needed, right? "May I see the cabin?" he casually asked.

The man paused. "The renovated cabins are double the cost of the old ones. $199 a night."

Kenneth considered that.

"Want to see both?"

"Sure," Kenneth said.

Kenneth followed the old man—walking painfully slow—to the first round of cabins. Outside, two families were already barbequing and talking around a small campfire. He lifted his chin in greeting, but looked away soon after. He wasn't here to make friends. He was here to find Adalyn.

The man, Gene, he learned by others greeting him by name, showed him inside. The cabin had indeed been newly renovated. He immediately picked up the scent of new finish, saw the overly-crisp corners of unused linens. New appliances. Everything was spotless. Two bunkbeds in the bedroom off the kitchen-slash-living space, which was a bit silly for just him. But again, it was all clean and new. And this was the west side. His last stop in the park.

"I'm not sure how long I'll need it for. Can I tentatively reserve it for a month, if necessary?" he asked, turning to Gene.

"A *month*?" Gene said, raising bushy gray brows in surprise. "I suppose so. There's a lot to explore here, sure." He eyed Kenneth. "But few are able to stay so long."

"I'm on a long vacation," he said. He gestured about. "What a great place to get to know Glacier. I have it in mind to pick up a camera. A real camera, you know? And figure out how to use it."

Gene smiled. "Plenty of inspiration around here. And you're a lucky man. I think that after word gets out about what my granddaughter has done here, you won't be the only one interested in staying a month."

"Your granddaughter?" Kenneth asked, bending to look at several artfully-framed, historical photos.

"Yeah, my Adi," said the man, wiping a weary hand over his brow.

Kenneth froze. *Adi?* Had he heard him right? He worked at composing himself. "Adi? Is she about?" he asked, straightening as if he had no care in the world. "I'd like to compliment her on her fine work here. She's done an amazing job. Really amazing. Or you can tell her I said that." *Stop. Stop talking*, he told himself. *You'll alarm the old man.*

But the man seemed more tired than worried. He rubbed arthritic fingers over his forehead. "She'll be back tomorrow night, I think. Seeing that you're staying so long, young man, you'll get a chance to tell Adalyn yourself."

Kenneth had to turn toward the window before his expression betrayed anything to the old man. His hand trembled as he laid it on the sill. Not from fear, but elation. He wanted to dance. To sing! This was Adalyn's grandfather. *Her very own grandfather.*

Adalyn was away, but she lived here.

Here.

And surely fate had ushered him to her very door.

CHAPTER 16

The rangers down at Swiftcurrent had known what they were talking about. In a verdant meadow just short of Iceberg Lake, he spotted him.

"Down," Chase said, waving his hand and whispering to Adi, right behind him.

Without hesitating, she crouched.

He lifted a slow, steady hand, pointing to the moose's thick antlers, rising above the grasses, the grand, old head. "Do you see him?"

He sensed her rising from her haunches, just a bit. "Oh. Chase," she breathed. "He's…magnificent."

He had to agree. The eighteen, maybe twenty-year-old was majestic, with a trophy-worthy rack atop his head that might've weighed forty pounds. Anywhere else, this bull would've been taxidermy-fodder. Here, in the park, he might be golden for what? Four, maybe five more years? "You need to stay within park bounds, buddy," Chase said, slowly pulling the rifle from his back holster, pumping the tranquilizing weapon, finding the moose's flank in his scope and firing.

He was glad there were no other hikers on the popular trail this early in the season. It always upset them to see Chase take down an animal, even if it was for the animal's own good.

They cautiously approached the bull a few minutes later, after he rose, stumbled, tried to rise again and then fell over flat on his flank. "Perfect," Chase pronounced, ushering Adi closer. He quickly fished out his field sample kit from his pack, took a blood sample, made notes about time and date in a log book, examined the moose for any notable injury or issue, tagged the bull's ear with a plastic number 54 and tiny satellite tracking device and then backed away.

"That's the last moose in the park that had avoided tagging," Chase said. "I've been chasing that bad boy for two years!"

"It's kind of terrible, watching him collapse like that," Adalyn said, beside him.

"I understand," he said, leading her a safe distance away, with a large boulder between them. "But it was for his own good." He paused, staring. "Now we can use a drone to check in on him once in a while. Study his habits."

Together, they waited.

And then waited some more.

"He's okay, right?" she said.

"Yep," he said.

A minute passed. Then another. Just when he began to wonder if he had miscalculated the dosage, or the moose had had some sort of adverse reaction to the tranquilizer, the bull seemed to startle, remember where he was and lumber to his feet. He shook himself off—as if he'd been covered in water—and looked about. Seemingly satisfied, he lumbered off.

Adi watched until he disappeared around the corner of the trail. "That all you got?" she asked.

He smiled and grinned down at her. "What? You want a bear?"

"Heck, yeah," she said. "You're the grizzly whisperer, right? Bring on the bears!" She lifted her hands.

"You're only that cavalier because I'm carrying this," he said, gesturing to the can of Counter Assault, the bear spray rangers favored.

"Well, yeah," she said, setting off again on the Ptarmigan Trail, intent on reaching the lake ahead. "Plus I'm in the company of a park ranger who studies bears half the time he's in the wild. Gives a girl some confidence." She glanced back at him. "Have you ever needed to use that spray?"

"Yes," Chase said. "Twice last year. Once the year before that."

"Really? What happened?"

"The first time, I surprised a mama bear with two cubs on the trail to Grinnell. She didn't like that much and came after me. I felt terrible because I got one of the cubs too."

"Oh!" she cried. "But I suppose if it's the difference between getting mauled and some temporary pain..."

"Yeah. I really had no choice. They were okay the next day. I hiked back in with a buddy and checked on them. With binoculars," he added with a smile.

"Good choice. She probably wasn't your greatest fan."

"Probably not. Last June, I came upon a sow in a patch of huckleberries, surprising her. And then a male griz in late August—he was entering hyperphagia and had just taken down a deer. I interrupted his meal, which made him very, very angry."

"How scary," she said, shivering. "What's hyperphagia?"

"It's the time in late summer, early fall when bears take in double their daily calorie intake. Prepping for winter. They get more territorial about their food."

"Hangry, eh?"

"You could say that."

"How close did they get?"

"The spray can shoot thirty-two feet. I'd say the closest any of them got to me was five feet. They're big and bulky. Makes you think they might be slow. But they're terrifyingly fast, when properly motivated."

She shivered again. "Okay, I change my mind. Let's not see a bear today, okay?"

"We'll see," he said.

They crested the last hill and paused, Adi gasping. "Oh my gosh, Chase. I'd forgotten how beautiful it is!" The cirque—a basin of rock. Daisies were just beginning to flower, along with a few of Adi's favorite bluebells, red Indian. The Ptarmigan Wall—an elegantly thin ridge of rock separating the Many Glacier and Belly River valleys dominated the right side. Mount Wilbur and Iceberg Peak completed the surround. And at their base was a turquoise-blue lake, all the bluer because of the contrasting white icebergs that floated atop the water.

Adi smiled and stared reverently upward, even as she continued down the trail to the lake's edge. They were still all alone on the trail, and it felt as if they might be the only two people in the world. He wanted to take her hand. Had begun to reach for it when she crossed her arms and smiled at him, eyes round with wonder. "I don't think there's any other place in the park," she said, waving upward, "where I'm so aware that I'm on the edge of the Continental Divide. Well, maybe on the Highline Trail."

He nodded and crossed his arms too. "It's true." He glanced backward. "And check out those wildflowers." Daisies were just beginning to flower, along with red Indian Paintbrush, False Alphodel and Northern Eyebright. He pointed the last two out. "Those flowers are normally only found in Greenland. They're remnants of the ice age."

She smiled. "Temporary miracles?"

"You could say that. They'll be gone in a month when it gets warmer."

They walked along the lake's edge, watching the icebergs—some spanning fifty feet wide—slowly drift in the gentle breeze. The lake, surrounded as it was by peaks, spent most of the day in shadow, preserving the remains of the winter's snow bank and ice that slowly leeched into the water, delighting tourists all summer long.

"Ready to head back?" Chase asked. "I'll buy you a mediocre burger at the tourist-trap restaurant in Swiftcurrent."

"You sweet-talker, you," she said, casting him a sly smile. "But let's stay another few minutes, okay?"

"Okay," he said, turning to stand beside her.

This time, he didn't pause. He reached for her hand. Held it.

And then he started to grin. Because she didn't pull away.

—⚓—

Kenneth returned to the cabin complex that afternoon. He grabbed six grocery bags from the car, carried them to his cabin, then went back for the remaining six. He set the frozen food in the tiny freezer compartment, put a few beers in the door to chill, then placed the eggs, fruit and vegetables in the fridge. In the cupboard he stored many cans of soup, some pasta and sauce, bread and peanut butter. Satisfied that he had plenty to keep him right here, waiting for Adalyn to get back, he turned to the boxes on the small kitchen table, winged by two old, wooden chairs.

He pulled out the new Nikon, then the long lens. He set the camera battery to charging, and then pulled out new Vortex Diamondback binoculars, as well as a birding manual for Montana. He was only interested in one bird, of course. But if anyone were to see inside his cozy little cabin, they would assume he was pursuing a hobby. He rose, running his hand along the log wall, thinking of Adalyn touching every bit of these walls, these floors.

Touching them was almost like touching her.

He salivated at the thought.

Soon, my Adalyn. Soon. Soon you will be in my arms.

—⚒—

She'd asked for a few more minutes, but now she wished she'd asked for an hour. Because when Chase took her hand, electric waves shot up from their fingers to her elbow to her shoulder and over her neck. She felt the welcome heat of his skin against the chill of the steep mountain valley, the comforting strength of his bones and flesh covering hers. How could something as simple as an innocent touch like this feel so…big?

After a few minutes, she dared to look at him, and he held her gaze.

"Ready?" he asked gently.

"Yeah," she said, a little breathless. What did this mean? Was Gramps right? Was Chase really into her?

He turned and led the way down the path, holding on to her hand all the way to the top of the hill. She felt pulled along in more ways than one. Tethered. Delightfully tethered to this big, strong, totally sexy man who had long been her friend. The man who was holding her hand. Holding it not because she needed help, but because he clearly wanted to.

She thought back to Adam and Connor and the others who had been in such a rush to kiss her on the show. Stake their claim. But right now, after feeling this, Adi thought that if any one of the bachelors had simply held her hand in the right way, in the right place, it would've stood out to her. It was both an innocent yet complete connection at the same time. The tease of touch hinted at so much more to come... making it somehow, some way, sexier than a kiss.

Although I wouldn't mind if he kissed me, she thought.

"What?" he said, glancing back at her on the trail.

"What?" she asked back.

"You're blushing," he said, a slight, curious smile on his full lips.

"What? No," she said, putting a hand to her cheek, her neck. "I just forgot sunscreen."

"Ahh," he said, letting her off the hook, though they'd been in the shadow of the mountains for most of the day.

It was then that she let go of his hand, suddenly feeling too close, too intimate, too soon. It reminded her of how it'd felt with Connor. "C'mon," she said to him, setting off down the trail again. "I suddenly want a really bad burger in my belly."

They reached Swiftcurrent around four o'clock and went to eat at the diner as soon as they arrived. Chase stopped in at the ranger station to make arrangements to camp behind it in a small clearing reserved for staff—the campground was booked solid—and then Chase suggested they head to Many Glacier Lodge to grab a glass of wine and watch the sun set behind the peaks from the deck.

"Sounds perfect," Adi said. "But do you mind if I grab a quick shower? I'm a little bit rank."

"Me too. Meet you back here in half an hour?" he asked.

"Sounds good." She riffled through her pack, pulled out some shampoo, a comb, a camp towel and a pair of flip-flops—as well as clean jeans and a shirt—then padded off down the trail to the campground's communal showers. He pretended to be searching his own pack for supplies when she glanced back at him, but truth be told, he was staring after her like some dumbstruck fool.

What is happening to you, man? he asked himself. He didn't know…or at least, he wasn't willing to admit it yet. But he did have to admit that it felt good. Really good.

When they reunited, both smelling of soap and shampoo, they got into the Jeep and went to the lodge. He grabbed his jacket from the back seat. "Do you want yours?" he asked.

"I think I'll be okay," she said.

They entered the lodge and went to the bar, got their wine and headed out to the row of big Adirondack chairs that lined the rail. "Gotta love one of the prettiest views in Glacier," he said, clinking his glass to hers after they sat down.

"It is," she said, gazing in awe at the lake before them, as well as the mountains they'd been so close to earlier in the day on the right, and the others they'd approach tomorrow on the left.

"I wasn't only talking about the mountains, Adi," he said, daring to meet her eyes.

She smiled. Was that the hint of a blush at her cheeks again? "Why, Chase Rollins," she said. "That's sweet of you to say."

He shrugged. "That's just the truth." He moved his wine glass to his right hand so he could take her hand again in his left. He spread his hand wide and she matched each finger with her own—just slightly shorter than his—and then interlaced her fingers between his, smiling.

After a moment, she said, "So, what is this, Chase? What are we doing?"

"Well, Adi, it appears we're holding hands in one of the

most gorgeous spots in the park."

"It doesn't strike you as new? Since we've never really held hands before today?"

"It most definitely strikes me as new. And I have to say, I really like it. Do you?"

She continued smiling. "I think I do."

"Now, can we just let it be? Not talk about it? I know you're used to dissecting every bit of a relationship on *The One*, but can this be different? This thing with us?"

Her smile faded and she abruptly pulled her hand away. "Sure. Of course. It doesn't have to be at all the same."

Silently, he cursed himself for a fool. *Of all the idiotic things to say...* He missed the feel of her hand in his. And now there was an odd tension between them.

"Is that what you think, all the time? When you're with me? What you saw of me on the show?" she asked, her words fast and clipped.

He paused to wait for another couple to pass them, taking seats at the end of the line. "Not all the time," he said. "But some." He reached up and rubbed his forehead and sighed. "Look, I'm sorry I said anything, Adi. That was stupid of me."

It was her turn to sigh. She took a slow sip of wine. "It's all right, Chase. It has to be hard, to have those images in your head. I know if our roles were reversed, I'd have a hard time with it."

"It's kind of like competing with ghosts," he admitted. "Ghosts who held your heart."

"They did for a time," she admitted. She shook her head. "But not now." She held his gaze. Was she saying...was she saying that he might?

"I have to wonder if I'll ever be free of the show," she said. "It's like a giant squid. Every time I get free of one sticky leg, another seems to grab me."

He held out his hand. "Maybe I can help you? I'm pretty good with a tranquilizer gun."

Hesitating a moment, she finally took his hand again. "A tranquilizer would be good. Or better yet, why not just use your .44 and end that squid for good?"

"If only it was that easy," he said. "I'd do it in a heartbeat. But isn't that like any hard experience? There are shadows or squid legs that stick to us for a good, long while. But eventually they lose their grip." He paused. "I'm willing to wait, Adi. Until they give up. I'm not going anywhere."

She glanced at him then, but said nothing more. And together they watched as the sun—far distant across the Western wall of the Divide—at last sent up rays of peach and golden yellow to the clouds above.

CHAPTER 17

Adi supposed neither of them slept well that night. She tossed and casually turned, all too aware that Chase was only inches away from her. He didn't seem to be doing any better than she. Occasionally, his breathing would slow and become more rhythmic, but then he was turning again. Every time he flipped toward her, she felt like she had to turn away. Every time he rolled away, she turned toward him, eager to give her other aching side a break. It'd been a long while since she had camped out.

And apparently these rangers hadn't bothered to clear their reserved campground of rocks. *Maybe it made them feel more macho to sleep on a bed of rocks*, she thought. Or maybe they were just more used to sleeping in all sorts of conditions. Unlike Adi, who had been sleeping in luxurious hotels around the world of late. Even the guest bed back at Gramps's cabin had a comfort-foam mattress, a remnant of her mother's last visit. "Said she couldn't sleep on that ratty old mattress any longer," Gramps had said, when Adi remarked on it.

But she could hardly say anything to Chase. She didn't

want him to think she was all-princess-and-the-pea. No, a ranger wanted the person they loved to be able to tough it out with them, regardless of where they slept. She was certain of it. And hadn't Hannah spent countless nights out in the backcountry with him? Adi doubted that she complained.

It was with some relief she saw dawn's light warming the eastern wall of their tent, just as Chase was snoring softly. Carefully, she sat up, eased out of her sleeping bag and slipped on her boots. She was fully dressed—the nights were still cold and she hadn't wanted Chase to get the wrong idea. Apparently, neither had he, since he'd kept on his thermal long-sleeve and jeans and socks.

"I don't remember you being an early riser," he said, startling her as she was trying to silently unzip the tent and failing miserably at it.

She glanced back at him. His short hair was adorably mussed, flat on one side, sticking up on the other. He ran his hands through it and rubbed his face, then closed one eye and squinted at her with the other. "You really ready to get up and at 'em?"

She smiled. "Go ahead and sleep a bit longer, if you want to," she said. "I'm just going to go and try and catch a cell signal near the lodge. Check in with Bea about Gramps." She'd be up; they often rented metal fishing boats in the wee hours to fishermen.

He nodded and flopped back to his sleeping bag.

When she was halfway down the road between Swiftcurrent and Many Glacier, she caught her first bar. She turned and climbed down the bank, sitting on a rock beside the lake as messages rolled in.

BEFORE YOU EVEN ASK, Bea had texted, *THE OLD MAN IS FINE. Sleeping like a log. I'll make him eat all his eggs and two pancakes. QUIT WORRYING.*

She smiled, and scrolled to the next, from Mary, back at Smith & Jessen. She was surprised—the office hadn't reached out to her since she left. *Call me as soon as you can.*

Adi checked the time. Back in Chicago, the office had just opened. She took a chance at dialing, hoping her signal would hold, then clicked through to Mary's extension.

"Adalyn!" Mary said, apparently recognizing her phone number. "How are you?"

"I'm well," she said. "Really well."

"You sound good. I'm glad. Listen, I hated to disturb you during your leave, but Mark was wondering where I might find the file for your logo ideas on the Terell account. We couldn't seem to find them on your desktop."

"Oh, I think they're in a sub-folder," Adi said. She waited while Mary went to her computer, then talked her through the tree of folders to find the right one.

"There it is," Mary said, relief evident in her voice. "Thank you so much."

"No problem. Everything else going okay?"

"Oh, yes, fine. We miss you, of course. But we're hanging in."

"I'm glad," Adi said. "Well, don't worry about disturbing me, Mary. Just give me a ring if you need anything else."

"I will." They were in the process of saying goodbye when Mary said, "Oh, hey. I got a weird call from a potential client a couple weeks ago," she said. "A Mr. Balou?"

Adi frowned. "Balou?"

"Something like that. He really wanted to speak to you, and pressed me for your number."

Mentally, she ran through her potential contacts. There was no one with a name close to that. "Probably just one of the paparazzi, looking for a clue to my trail," she said. Or could it be the creep who had left her all those roses? Would he dare to call the office? Play the role of a potential client to figure out where she'd gone? He'd dared to enter her apartment...

Mary hesitated.

"You didn't give him any information, right, Mary?"

"Well, umm...I'm really sorry. He sounded so legit, I think I let it slip that you were unavailable until September. But all I said was that you were somewhere in the mountains," she added hurriedly.

Adi bit her lip. "That's okay," she said. "You didn't mention Montana, right?"

"Oh no. Of course not."

"Well, then, that's okay," she repeated, as much for herself as for Mary. Her heart was beating faster, even remembering that night in her apartment... "There are a ton of mountains out west. One look around and he'd give up," she said with a laugh, looking at the ridge to her right. "I'm a needle in a haystack."

"Good. See that you stay that way. Rest up and come back to us soon, all right?"

"I will. 'Bye, Mary."

They hung up and Adi stayed where she was, staring out at the lake. Talking to Mary, remembering that last, spooky evening in her apartment, made her real life come rushing back in frightful clarity.

"Everything all right?" Chase said, jumping down to a rock above her, then easing on to one beside her.

"Oh, hi. No more sleep, huh?"

"Nah. I'm excited for another day together."

She thought about telling him. But why worry him?

"What could be wrong on a day like this? Let's grab some breakfast and get on to our float and hike. Maybe we can beat most of the tourists," she said, gesturing to the empty lake before them.

"At this hour, Adi girl," he said, rising to offer her his hand. "We'll be alone with the griz and geese."

—⁂—

Using the password for guests—"LittleCabinGuests"—Kenneth logged on to the cabin complex wi-fi, which had a fairly decent signal, considering where they were. He lifted the small framed sign, which Adalyn had clearly designed and had printed. Yet another touch of her in this cabin.

He logged in to Facebook and navigated to the One Nation fan site, scrolling through mindless posts about the men on the show, pausing only on stories related to Adalyn. There were a fair number—most of the fans were curious to know if she was all right and where she had gone. Six had reposted her Instagram picture of her stack of rocks and message, dissecting what she might have meant and polling others to see if anyone recognized where that lake might be. Some had taken shots of pictures of women who looked like Adalyn—but weren't—in places around the world. There was even a hashtag, *#findAdi* that was trending on Twitter.

He smiled in satisfaction. Wouldn't they all be so jealous of him if they knew that he had found her? That he had discovered what she'd been up to these last weeks—refurbishing these cabins? That he had met her grandfather? He knew it was a scoop worth a couple thousand dollars from the news rags. Not that he would sell Adalyn out. No, this information was for him alone.

Only one thing disturbed him. Old Gene intimated she'd been gone a couple of days. Where had she gone? What was she doing? He began pacing, rubbing his hands. It was torture, to come so close to finding her here, only to discover she was absent. What did Gene mean, when he said he *thought* she'd be back sometime tonight? Why hadn't he known the exact time? It had taken everything in him to avoid pressing for more details, but it seemed that the old man was negligent in watching out for his granddaughter's welfare if he didn't know that. Was she out hiking with a friend? Wasn't that part of Survival 101? Conveying clear plans with someone back at home?

Feeling as if he might crawl out of his own skin if he stayed in the tiny cabin any longer, he grabbed his binoculars, slipped the battery and SD card into his new camera, then headed out. If nothing else, he could begin establishing the perimeter of the property. Become accustomed to the routines of others in the cabin complex, as well as her neighbors at the boat launch. He'd begin documenting everything with pictures and logging notes into a small, leather book he carried, just as he had with Adalyn's apartment and office in Chicago. Had that not led him to Molly and the critical detail he needed to find her here?

One didn't win a woman like Adalyn by being sloppy about his work. No, he needed to take meticulous care. The hour was soon upon them. And everything—absolutely everything—had to be in order.

—⁊⁊—

Adi was uncommonly quiet as they paddled down Swiftcurrent Lake, then climbed out, shouldered their crafts, and portaged over to Josephine. They had left their packs by the ranger station in Swiftcurrent, neither of them ready to commit to another night on this side of the park. Chase had wondered if concern over her grandfather was getting the best of her, despite Bea's assurances via text.

"You all right?" he asked, turning back to wait for her. "Is it getting too heavy?"

"Nah," she said, but switched the boat to her other side. "I'm all right."

"You're sure quiet this morning."

"I guess I am."

He turned and continued walking. "What?" he asked over his shoulder. "Did I keep you up snoring last night?"

"Something like that," she said. He glanced back at her but saw she was teasing him.

He nodded. "It's hard, if you haven't camped in a while." Unbidden, a scene from her season with Connor flashed in his mind. A "camp" on a private beach in Bali, complete with private chef and masseuses for them both on their day-date alone. *Awesome,* he thought. *And all you have to offer her, Rollins, is a measly park-service-issue tent on hard ground. No private chef or masseuses in sight.*

Chase shoved away the thought. He knew she wouldn't like it...him, comparing himself to the others. That hadn't been real life. This was real life. Really real life, he laughed to himself as mosquitoes swarmed about them. Here between the lakes, the mosquitoes were always thick. He stopped and set down his kayak and pulled off his small day pack. "Here," he said, "I have some spray."

She set down her own kayak and came over to him, even as she slapped at her neck and then an arm. "They're nasty."

"We'll be clear of them in a bit," he said. He uncapped the bottle and went around to spray her. Obediently, she lifted her arms and he sprayed her neck, shoulders, back and legs. Her legs—man, the girl had some fine legs. Lovely muscles and lines. Some new color on them from their hike yesterday to Iceberg, from the looks of it. He rose and handed her the bottle so she could spray her front, then took the bottle and did his own. Silently, she reached for the bottle and sprayed his back. What was it about such a silly task that felt oddly intimate? Why was it that everything he seemed to do with Adi felt that way? New? Oddly exciting?

You wouldn't feel the same if Logan was spraying you down, he admitted to himself.

She handed him the bottle, but she clearly wasn't thinking the same thoughts he was. Her brow was furrowed, her mouth in a thin line. "Hey," he said, gently hooking his hand through her elbow. "What's up, Adi? Something's worrying you. I can see it on your face."

She looked away and then back at him, sighing. Giving in, it appeared, to telling him. "It's just that I had a call from the office."

"Oh?"

"At the end, Mary told me that someone had called and tried to get details out of her about where I was."

It was Chase's turn to frown. But he held it in check, not wanting to add stress. "She kept it under wraps, though. Right?"

"Mostly. The guy was pretty convincing. She let it slip I was in the mountains somewhere."

"Well, there are a lot of mountains. She could have meant in the US, or in Europe or New Zealand, for that matter. Right?"

She bit her lip. "It's only that on the show...I talked about spending summers in the mountains. Most would assume that was someplace in the US."

"Still," he said, reaching out to run a reassuring hand down her shoulder to her forearm. "There are a heck of a lot of mountains in the States."

She continued to work on her lip. "But I posted a pic on Instagram. Bea said everyone was so worried about me. There were conspiracies that I'd died..."

"Let me see it," he said, putting out a hand.

She reached for her phone, scrolled through to her Instagram and then handed it to him. They had no service out here, but her history was visible. He clicked on her picture—the Ebenezer she'd built—with the blurred out image of Lake McDonald and the mountains behind it. To him, it was readily recognizable. But how many others would be able to do the same? They'd be few and far between.

"I didn't really worry about posting that. Most people probably think I'm on the move, rather than being holed up somewhere."

"But now you're worried that call was from your stalker."

"Well, yeah."

"Easily solved," he said, hauling his boat back to his shoulder. "We find a picture of some beach somewhere and you post that tomorrow. In a week or so, a picture of a desert. Make him think that you *are* on the move, regardless of what Mary said. You were in the mountains. Now you're not."

Relief washed over her face. "Now that's a really good idea, Mr. Rollins."

"Keep me around, Ms. Stalling. I'm full of them," he said.

"I just may do that," she said, shouldering her own boat. "Now tell me we're almost there."

"We're almost there."

"Honest?"

"Well, almost."

CHAPTER 18

Adi tried to settle into the beauty of her surroundings, resting in Chase's idea that she could throw her stalker off her scent by posting false pictures. But she couldn't seem to shake the feeling that she was somehow exposed again. Ever since she had arrived in Montana, she had considered Glacier her shield, her separation from all that had happened, a connection to a part of her life and history she loved best. Here, she wasn't the famously "Spurned Stalling"; she was just Adi. *Adi girl*, as Gramps called her. A nickname she'd noticed Chase had picked up too.

Again and again Chase tried to cajole her into conversation, but she just felt so dang weary that she responded in the briefest way possible. She felt a sudden urgency to return to the west side, to Gramps's cabin. She needed to throw herself into the work of refurbishing the next pod of cabins…*that* was what would distract her from these worries. And if she was there, then she could keep an eye on Gramps. Ever since that call with Mary, she'd been oddly worried about him too.

She eyed the historic, wooden *Morning Eagle* chugging

along the far shore, one of two boats that ferried tourists from the end of Swiftcurrent to the end of Josephine. Chase followed her gaze.

"We could hitch a ride with them," he said. "I'm sensing you want to get back."

She smiled, grateful that he was so in tune with her. "I'm sorry," she said, resting her paddle across the edges of the kayak. "It's not you. Or this place," she said, gesturing about the pristine valley.

"It's him," Chase glowered. Not angry with her, but rather with this unknown man intruding upon them.

"Maybe it was a journalist. Not him at all."

"Maybe," he said. But by his tone, they both thought it was the stalker.

"When we get back, Adi, I want to take you to the shooting range. I assume it's been a while since you've shot a gun?"

This time, she did not protest. She knew that Chase was only around half the week. Gramps was likely to sleep through a home intruder and he wasn't in any physical shape to fight someone off if he did wake. Adi reminded herself that most stalkers just liked to watch. But from what she could tell, few stalkers ever entered their target's home. That had been uncommonly bold. "Okay," she said. "I'll take you up on that offer."

Together, they turned and paddled to the boat launch. Two hours later, they were back at Chase's Jeep, and three hours after that they pulled up in the parking lot between their properties on the other side of the park.

Chase hopped out and came around to help lift her pack from the back. But he didn't hand it to her. "Thanks for coming with me, Adi. It was fun." He gave her a gentle smile. "Well, most of it."

"It was," she said, looking up at him. She felt oddly

shy with him, here where her grandfather might see them through the window.

Seeming to feel none of the same, he pulled her into his arms and gave her a long, tender hug. "It's going to be all right," he said in her ear. "We'll work through this."

She nodded, surprised to find her eyes wet with tears at his choice of words. Somehow it made her feel less lonely, less vulnerable. "You're right," she said, pushing back hair that was falling in her eyes. With the top down, much of her ponytail had worked loose on the ride home. But they'd both welcomed the wind about them, content to be lost in their own thoughts. She lifted her pack. "Will I see you tomorrow?"

"Maybe," he said. He gave her a shy smile and reached for her hand. "But tomorrow is a long ways away. What about tonight, after supper? Down on the dock? Or maybe you need to swing again?"

She smiled back, watching how his thumb rubbed across her fingers. "I'll see how Gramps is faring. If he turns in early, I'll meet you on the beach. Maybe a bonfire tonight?"

"Now that sounds good. You should see how Bea downs s'mores. She's an animal."

Adi laughed and pulled away, lifting her pack. It sounded reassuring to her, to be with Chase, but also Logan and Bea again. "Maybe I can introduce her to the finer points of s'mores with a layer of peanut butter."

"Ugh," Chase said, clutching his chest as if she'd just shot him. "One really should not mess with a classic."

"Unless it's to make it better," she said, resuming a debate they'd had since they were teens.

"We'll see how much class my sister-in-law really has."

"We'll see if she has adventurous taste buds."

"Whatever, Stalling," he said, shouldering his own backpack and backing up toward the trail that led to the boat-house cabin, adorable dimple clearly on display.

—꿰—

Kenneth had been climbing up the hill from the beach when he saw the Jeep roll into the parking lot. He eased behind a giant ponderosa and carefully peeked around the edge to watch them.

It was her.

Really her.

Seeing Adalyn again, after so long apart, threatened to make him forget to breathe.

He watched as she bantered with the tall guy. Stiffened as he took her hand—so familiar! And after that long, lingering hug. Where had they been? Gone for all this time? Had she spent the night with *him*?

When her grandfather had said she was gone, he'd thought she might be camping. But Kenneth had thought she might have found a female friend, her heart far too wounded to take up with some new guy.

Kenneth felt the heat of anger rush up his neck and cheeks. He knew he should turn away, that it wouldn't do for him to be discovered there, so obviously spying upon them. But he couldn't stop himself. Couldn't bear to miss a moment of seeing her. Nor miss the chance of figuring out just who this man was, and what claim he might have on Adalyn's heart.

You cannot have her, he thought. *I will not allow it.*

She cannot bear another heartbreak. Only I am safe for her. It is for me that fate made a way. Me. Fate that brought me here, to her very own resting spot.

Not for you.

He stared at the tall man as he pulled off his NPS ball cap, ran a hand through his thick, brown hair and put it back on again, even as he shouldered his pack and backed away from her, still bantering.

Never had he felt such hatred for another.

At least, not since Adam. Or Connor. It had been pure torture, watching those two with her. And there was no way that he would idly stand by and watch another woo his Adalyn, only to break her heart.

He forced himself to walk down the beach toward his cabin as if he'd never seen the two of them. The other men had gone away. So would this one. He'd see to it.

Because Adalyn Stalling would be his.

One way or another.

—⟋⟍—

Adi had arrived just in time to help Mrs. Larson turn two of her refurbished cabins, because according to Gramps, two families were returning that night to claim them. "Paid in advance," he said. "Didn't want anyone else to swipe them, after they caught a glimpse." He patted her on the back. "Your new pod of cabins appears to be a hit, honey."

"The new sign and name helps too," Mrs. Larson said approvingly. She nodded, making her chin disappear into the chubby folds of her neck. She was flushed and sweaty, obviously rushing to get done.

"That's great," Adi said. "Let's divide and conquer. I'll do Cabin Five, you do Four?"

"I'm so glad you're back," the older woman said, placing a hand to her lower back. "If we're going to turn more cabins this summer, we're going to need to hire some help. I'm not as young as I used to be."

Adi nodded. "I hear you," she said. "I'll put out the word with the Rollinses, see if they know anybody."

"Or I can bring my nephew," she offered. "He just sits around and plays video games. But once he has direction, he's a pretty good worker."

"Tell him he's hired," Adi said. "Bring him tomorrow?"

"I will. His mother will be thrilled."

"No more than we will, if business truly picks up."

She moved to Cabin Five and propped open the door. Gramps hovered there, crossing his arms and leaning against the jamb. "At least you won't have to do Cabin One more than once a week."

"Oh?" she said, confused. She stripped the sheets of one bunk and then the other. The top bunks appeared untouched.

"Yeah. A man checked in yesterday afternoon. Said he planned to stay for a month. Bought a fancy camera and has been messing with it all day on the beach and in the woods."

"A month!" she said. "Well, I guess that's good news. One down, four to go. I want to show the park officials that we booked these solid when we come up for review."

"I don't think it will be hard, Adi girl. They're as pretty as they were the day Grams and I opened. If not prettier. And I hate to admit it, but people really seem to like the new name. We've had ten, maybe eleven people in today, inquiring. Interrupted more than one of my naps."

She grinned. "Well, you go and rest now. If anyone else rolls up, I'll hear them and go talk to them myself." She paused, remembering her plan. "Or I'll send Mrs. Larson."

"You don't have to tell me twice," he said. But he paused at the door. "Did you have fun? Over on the east side?"

"We did," she said.

Gramps smiled at that. "Well, good. You deserved a break. You get to Iceberg?"

"We did! And we found Chase's wiley moose. Tagged him and went on to the lake. Oh, Gramps. I'd forgotten how beautiful it is."

He nodded and looked to the lake. "I'd give my right eyetooth to see it again. Just once." He shook his head. "But those days are over for these old bones."

She shared a sad smile with him. "At least you have the memories."

"There's that. Well, I'll leave you to it and go grab that catnap."

She tossed a hand towel from the bathroom on the stack of linens, then reached in a cupboard to set out a fresh roll of TP. In the cupboard was a brush and toilet cleaner, and a minute later, she had it scrubbed clean, turning to do the sink and mirror. In the kitchen, she emptied the mini-fridge of ketchup and half a pack of cheese; she hated to toss such items. But she knew most guests would prefer to arrive and find it empty. *Maybe I'll keep a bunch of commonly used items for guests*, she thought. *Things like condiments.* That was the thoughtful kind of detail that she knew helped garner good reviews.

And Gramps will eat this cheese, she thought. He favored the fake version for his grilled cheese sandwiches, while Adi preferred classic cheddar.

She bundled up the linens and carried them out the door toward the central laundry room. It was then that she saw the man coming her way, looking down at the control panel of his DSLR. He looked up, spied her and smiled. "Hey," he said.

"Hi," she said. "Are you the new guest in Cabin One?"

"I am. Kenneth Obering," he said, offering his hand. "But you can call me Ken."

Shifting her bundle, she awkwardly shook it. "Adalyn," she said. "I'm Gene's granddaughter. What made you decide to stay with us all month long?"

"Well, I have some unused vacation. Boss said I had to use it or I'd lose it this year. Figured this was as good a time as any to learn how to use one of these," he said, lifting his camera. He cast her a playful grin and brought the camera up to his eye. "You mind?"

"Oh," she said, rubbing the back of her neck. "There's better inspiration out there than me." She gestured toward the lake, even as he shot several frames. It was weird, him taking her picture. Wasn't it? Or was she just being paranoid?

"For sure," he said. "This whole park is a photographer's dream." But he was staring without blinking at her.

"Well, enjoy," she said, suddenly eager to get away from him. "I better get to finishing this cabin so your neighbors have a clean place to move into."

"Sure, sure," he said, smiling down at her. He was as tall as Chase was, but more wiry. Near her own age. "See ya 'round."

Adi moved away, the odd exchange running through her mind. For the first time, she wondered if he was a journalist and if he'd just taken a picture to sell. Why else would he have taken her picture like that? But as quick as it came, she dismissed it. The camera was clearly new, and the dude was just…awkward. Maybe he'd thought he was kind of flirting with her or something. West Glacier wasn't exactly teeming with young singles.

That was it. *Quit seeing ghosts behind every tree, Adi.*

—⋙—

Better inspiration out there than me, she'd said.

He'd snapped another picture of her from the other side of the complex, using his telephoto lens. *No, Adalyn. You are wrong. So wrong.*

He focused in on her lips and took another picture. Her body, from shoulder to hip. Frame after frame of her as she walked, in quick succession. Watching them back in his viewscreen, it was almost like a video, but he could pause over each as he wished. Observing how her body moved, inch by inch.

That night, playing it over in his mind again, Kenneth thought he'd handled their initial conversation well. He'd sounded almost...normal. He didn't think she would've been able to hear his heart thundering in his chest, even though it felt like it should be moving beneath his shirt as clearly as a lovesick cartoon character's.

You can call me Ken.

He hoped she would. No one else called him that. It seemed intimate, for her to have a special name for him. Maybe in time they'd come up with some sort of loving nicknames for each other.

He hated that he had lied to her. That he was on vacation. But what choice had he? He'd quit his job two months ago to track her down in Illinois, leaving his apartment in Georgia with nothing but what he could pack in his car. He'd find a new job soon enough. Just as soon as they settled down together, he'd find a job and she would stay home and take care of him.

It pleased him, to see her cleaning. She liked a tidy place. So did he. There had been a part of him that feared she was used to others doing such things for her. He liked a woman ready to do the domestic roles. Cook and clean. Make a home.

He'd really never had a home. His mom had left his dad and him when he was little. His father lived in squalor. Kenneth had taught himself coding and got a job straight out of high school for a tech firm, steadily putting money into savings every month. He'd lived on his own in an apartment that never had more than a chair, a table and a bed. It was easier to keep clean, he'd found.

But here, in Cabin One, surrounded by all that Adalyn had done to make it cozy, he knew she would be all he needed in a wife. He'd give her a strict budget and they'd go shopping, coming home to decorate their little house. Where would that be? Would she want to stay here in Montana, near her grandfather? Or go back to Illinois?

Not that she could go back to Smith & Jessen. No, those fools had set her up to be a contestant on *The One*. They could not be trusted. But maybe she'd miss Molly and want to live closer to her. Or maybe there was someplace else.

He'd take her anywhere. He'd spent months thinking about ways to make her happy. When she was finally his, he'd be sure that she was, every single day.

He leaned back against his pillow and clicked through the pictures again of Adalyn. But then he heard the sound of footsteps in the rocks between his cabin and Gene's, as well as the call of greeting to Adi from the beach.

Kenneth frowned and sat up. It was late. Where was she going? Using the binoculars, he'd found a position in the woods from which he could see into Gene's kitchen. They'd been having supper just an hour before. Now what?

He grabbed his binoculars again and eased out his cabin door. Glancing to the left, he could see Adalyn greeting another man and a short brunette—the two that ran the boat launch next door—and then the guy who had brought her home. He wrapped her in his big arms for a quick, overly familiar hug before sitting down in one of the Adirondacks around the fire. Briefly, Kenneth thought about swinging by the fire, seeing if they'd invite him in. But there were only four chairs. No, he told himself. *No. That will be awkward.*

He'd had his fill of awkward social moments in life. More than a few had destroyed any chance he'd had with a girl. And there was no way that he wanted one of Adalyn's first impressions of him to include such a description. Hadn't he successfully maneuvered through their initial introduction? *Don't screw it up.* Instead, he took a path to the other side of Gene's cabin, leading to the hill above. He wound his way upward, squinting in the gathering darkness, and then found his way back down, closer to their bonfire, where he was able to remain hidden. He took a seat on a boulder and eased aside the thick branches of a fir and birch to focus on the foursome before him.

They were laughing, roasting marshmallows. Debating about peanut butter, for some reason. He saw that the guy with Adalyn resembled the other guy—brothers? And he wore a USNPS jacket with the name ROLLINS in bold letters above the breast pocket, the same name as the boat launch guy next door. He'd seen their names on the sign: *Lake Mc-Donald Boat Launch, operated by Logan and Beatrice Rollins.* Hadn't he taken a picture of it that very afternoon? Not that he needed the picture. He'd filed away the information in his brain. Could still see every curve of each letter of their sign outside the boathouse they'd made into a cozy cabin. Some said he had a photographic memory. Perhaps that's why taking pictures was reassuring, almost mirroring what was in his mind. Proving it was as real as he remembered.

This *other* Rollins rose and offered his jacket to Adalyn when she shivered.

Kenneth's jaw clenched when she allowed him to help her into it, wrapping it around her. She looked adorable and he could see there was some obvious flirtation going on between her and this man. Who was he? How had he found such a ready place in her life? She'd only been here, what?

A few weeks? Unless...*Unless*... Her grandfather lived here. She'd obviously come here before. Maybe all her life. Had this guy too? Was he some old flame?

He dropped his binoculars, staring hard at the man. It mattered not who he'd once been. All Kenneth had to do was keep him from being anything more.

What would keep USNPS Ranger Rollins busy?

Fire immediately came to mind. But then he negated it, deciding he could do nothing that would endanger his Adalyn. He'd need to do some research. Find out what Rollins's responsibilities were.

And then make sure they kept him very, very distracted. And far from Adalyn.

CHAPTER 19

Two days later, Adalyn helped Gramps into his old truck. She was attempting to help him with the seatbelt when he waved her away in agitation. "I'm an old man, not an invalid. I can do it! It just takes me a minute…"

She sighed and went around to the other side of the truck and slid into the driver's seat. She had her seatbelt buckled and had the truck engine revved and glanced at her grandfather. He was still searching around, trying to click it. Gently, she took it from his hand and secured it. "There's no shame in it, Gramps. Not really. You can't see it, can you?"

"It's my neck," he said with some disgust, rubbing it. "Just won't bend like it used to."

"Maybe we can ask the doctor about that too today."

"Add it to the list," he said with a sigh.

They passed their long-term guest, Ken, by the side of the road. He was pointing his camera up to the trees. Capturing an image of a squirrel? A bird?

"He's an oddling, isn't he?" Gramps said.

"I don't know," she said, watching his bouncing image in

the rearview mirror. "He seemed okay to me. Maybe just a little lonely?"

"Well, he's not going to make any friends if he spends all his time behind that camera or those binoculars."

"Oh, think of all the birders who come through here. Maybe Ken is just waiting to find his people. Maybe this is his summer."

"Maybe. I hate to see a young man be lonely. Speaking of lonely young men," he said, turning in his seat to look at her. "Are you easing young Chase's lonely heart?"

She huffed a laugh and shook her head. "You'd have to ask him. And he's with Hannah right now anyway. Up on the Highline."

"Well, all I can say is that he never looks at Hannah like he looks at you," he said.

"So you've said, Gramps. Now just leave it alone, okay? Let God and summer and this place do what they will with us. We'll see where it all leads in time."

"Those are some powerful forces."

"Yes, they are."

They drove the rest of the way to Kalispell in relative silence, pulling up outside a new medical building on the south side of the hospital. They rode the elevator to the third floor, found office 314, and checked in. Five minutes later, they were led into the doctor's office, rather than an exam room. Adi frowned as she sat down next to Gramps. "I thought this was a check-up," she said.

He lifted his hands and gray brows in confusion. "Me too."

The doctor came in, pausing to shake Gramps's hand, then Adi's. It was Doc Victor, an old friend of her grandfather's, his primary care physician for as long as she could remember. He'd even had a few meals with them in summers past, when he was up at the park for the day.

"My office has been trying to reach you for three weeks, Gene," Doc Victor said.

"Yes, yes," Gramps said, waving away his complaint. "They kept telling me you needed to speak to me. I figured it could wait for this appointment."

"I wish you hadn't, Gene." He set a file on his desk, sat down, and then folded his hands atop it. "However, I'm glad your granddaughter could be here too." He gave Adalyn a sad smile. "I'm afraid I have some difficult news for you both. Sometimes it helps to have a family member present to help absorb such things. Do I have your permission to share openly with you, in front of Adalyn, Gene?"

"Sure, sure," Gramps said, gray brows now arched in worry and confusion. "What is it, Doc? The ticker worse than you thought?"

"As you know, your ticker could be a lot better," he said. But he didn't smile. "It was your initial bloodwork that alerted me there might be something more. I dug a little deeper. That's why I ordered that MRI and more blood tests the day before we sprung you from the hospital." He swallowed, making his Adam's apple bob above his crisp, white shirt and bright blue tie. "Gene, there's no easy way to say this. You have cancer. Aggressive bone cancer."

He rose and went to a lightbox on the wall, turned to take a larger file from his desk, checked the name, then slid two x-rays to the clips on either side. They were pictures of Gramps's spine, curved with age, and his pelvis. Doc Victor traced spots. "You can see it, here in the neck. And here, in the pelvic cavity, right above the hip." He tapped other spots down the vertebrae, then glanced at them both, sorrow in his eyes. "It's everywhere, really. You're riddled with it, Gene. Frankly, I don't know how you're not in a ton of pain. How you're upright at all."

Adalyn stared, unblinking, at the x-rays. *It couldn't be. Not this...*

"Stubborn Scot, you know," Gramps said. But his voice sounded weak. He wiped a hand over his mouth, his eyes wide and vacant. "I thought...I thought the pain was just arthritis."

"You have a fair amount of that too," said the doctor with a rueful smile.

Gramps heaved a sigh and turned to Adi at last. Seeing the fear that must be evident in her face, he took her hand in both of his. "There, now, Adi girl. It will be all right."

But she took no consolation from his words. Because right then, she knew that nothing would be all right for Gramps ever again. She looked to Doc Victor to confirm it. *You're riddled with it.*

"This cancer," she said. "Can it be treated? With radiation? Or chemo?"

"I wouldn't recommend it," he said, sorrowfully shaking his head again. "It's gone too far. If we'd discovered it last year, maybe..."

"I wouldn't have taken such measures then, either," Gramps said. "I've lived a good life. A full life. I'd never want to spend my last days sick from medicine that is supposed to somehow make me better. I watched my Alice do that. I won't do the same."

"But Gramps—"

He shook his head at Adi, still holding her hand. "No, Adi. I can't. I won't."

"But *Gramps*," she said again, her voice breaking. Was this happening? Really happening?

"No, Adi," he said again. He looked to the doctor. "How long do I have, old friend?"

Doc Victor winced. "You know no doctor really wants

to answer that question. At best, it's a guess, and I've been wrong more times than I can count over the years."

Gramps kept waiting—making it clear he'd wait out the doctor—until he relented at last. "I'd say you'd two best fill this summer with some fine memories."

Gramps nodded and tried to smile. Was it just her imagination or did he appear ten years older now? "We're already on our way," he said, patting her hand. "I have my girl here again. Nothing could have made it better."

She managed to keep it together until they had driven home to the cabin. She helped Gramps inside, made some sandwiches—which neither of them could do more than pick at—and when he said he was going to "go rest a while," she cleaned up the dishes and walked out the door, heading to the Rollinses'. She knew Chase was gone with Hannah, but she hoped Bea or Logan were around. She needed a friend. Desperately.

As soon as Bea spotted her approaching the dock, she finished tying a knot in a canoe rope and hurried toward her. Tears were already flowing down Adalyn's face and her throat ached. Bea reached up to push the hair from her face and hold her lightly by the shoulders. "Oh, my friend. What? What has happened?"

"It's Gramps," Adi said, voice cracking. "He's...he's got cancer." She shook her head. "It's really bad."

"Oh, Adi," she said, pulling her into a hug. She whispered, "How bad is it?"

"We'll be lucky to have the rest of the...year," she said, choking on the last word.

"I'm sorry. So sorry. Come. Let's go to the cabin. I'll put on some tea. I'll text Chase. See if he can get home tonight."

Logan—on the far side, talking to a family there to rent a

boat—cast them a concerned look. "We'll tell Logie after he gets those guests on the water," Bea said. She pulled out her phone and started dialing Chase.

"No, Bea," Adalyn said. "You don't need to disturb Chase. It can wait. I have you and Logan. I'll be okay."

Bea shot her a look. "He'd kill me if I didn't tell him. He'd want to be here for you, Adi. For Gene too. Both my boys will. You know how they feel about you and Gene. You're practically family. And Chase…Well, Adi, that guy is pretty much over the moon for you. Logan had to practically shove him out the door this morning. He did *not* want to go."

That made her smile through her tears. "He's on the Highline, right?"

"Yeah. He and Hannah were going to spend the night at Logan Pass. But I'd bet he'll convince her to come back or hitch a ride with someone."

Adi nodded. She hoped Bea was right. Because right then, the most comforting thing she could think of was Chase wrapping her up in his arms.

—⁓—

Kenneth had doubled his pace, seeing Adalyn leave the cabin, face crumpling as if she were about to cry. When she reached the neighbors' and fell into Beatrice's arms, weeping, rage flooded his heart. Who had hurt her? Was it that fool?

In what had become his favorite lookout spot in the woods, he had watched Chase Rollins pull out in the early morning hours with the blonde. She had been smiling; he had not. Half of him hoped Chase had taken up with the female ranger and broken things off with Adalyn. But seeing her so broken, so distraught—in tears like when Connor had ended their engagement—half of him was enraged at the thought. He'd sworn to himself that he would never let Adalyn be so hurt again. He had failed.

Failed failed failed failed failed...

Half an hour after she arrived, Logan disappeared into the cabin too. Beatrice left ten minutes later to greet a couple returning to the dock with a canoe, and as he studied her face through the telephoto lens, he saw she had been crying too. He rose and paced a few steps, then returned, biting his thumbnail. What was happening? What had them so upset?

He needed to know. Needed to find out so he could figure out a way to comfort Adalyn. How could he help her if he didn't know what was going on? But how could he get close? Try and listen in?

He lifted his camera and idly took some shots of Beatrice helping the couple with the canoe. It came to him then. He'd say he was stopping by to rent one himself.

Excited, he scurried down the trail, crossed the road and neared the Rollinses' old cabin. He paused near the kitchen window and after a look around to make sure no one would see him, dared to peer inside. Logan was standing near the front door, his arms around Adalyn. She appeared to be crying.

He turned away, nostrils flaring.

He considered knocking on the door. Demanding to see her. But that wouldn't do. It wouldn't do at all. Instead, he moved around the cabin and took the path down the beach to the dock. He forced a smile to his face as he passed the young couple who had just returned and Bea spied him.

"Hello!" he said. "I was just wondering if I might rent a kayak for a while." He lifted his camera. "I'd like to try and catch a few bald eagles on the western shore."

"Oh! Sure, sure," she said, with none of her usual enthusiasm. He'd watched the Rollinses long enough to know this woman seemed to rise with the sun and burn with a spark all day. "How about this one?" She gestured to the blue one.

"That'll be fine," he said. "I don't think we've officially met, but I've seen you around. I'm Ken. I'm staying over at the cabins." He hooked a thumb to his left.

"Oh, yes. You're their month-long renter, right?" she asked. "I'm Bea."

Bea. Not Beatrice, he noted, pleased to know.

"Yep. I'm the lucky man." He settled himself on the side of the dock and set his camera in the water-tight compartment. Then he eased onto the seat and reached for the paddle Beatrice offered him. "Say," he began casually. Or at least he hoped he sounded casual. "I saw Adalyn come over here and she was in tears. Is she all right?"

"Oh, Adi?" Bea asked, eyes widening in surprise. "Yeah. She'll be okay. She just got some hard news."

He nodded. "I'm sorry to hear that. Think there's anything I can do?"

"That's sweet of you, Ken. But we'll take care of her. No need for you to worry."

"I'm glad she has friends like you," he said. Then he turned and paddled away, liking the pull of each stroke against his arm muscles. Maybe he'd rent a kayak again tomorrow. Or go to town and buy his own. Every morning in his cabin, he did two hundred pushups, two hundred sit-ups and a hundred squats. He knew he needed to do more aerobics—Adalyn deserved a fit partner—but he was reluctant to leave the property for long, fearful that he'd miss a critical opportunity to see her, hear her, even talk with her again, if he wasn't nearby. Perhaps if he had a kayak he could keep an eye on the cabins and yet still be doing something. The more he paddled, the better he liked it.

Maybe, just maybe he could convince Adalyn to come out with him some evening. Hadn't he seen Rollins and her arrive with two of the kayaks on the crossbars of his Jeep? Perhaps she would enjoy getting out again. Maybe it would make her forget about whatever had made her so desperately sad. In time, she'd see that he could be her comfort, her rock. She didn't need any of the Rollinses. *Especially that Chase.*

He'd eaten at the diner that morning, choosing a bar stool beside two rangers. As they ate and drank their coffee, their conversation turned to the day's tasks. It came up that Hannah and Chase were heading to the pass, to follow up on a grizzly study or something. After returning to the cabin, he'd done a Google search, found Chase Rollins's Park Service bio and his Facebook page, which he could scroll through without friending him. It didn't take long to figure out the man's passion was grizzlies.

Kenneth lifted his paddle and watched as the water dripped to the surface, sending ripples outward. It came to him then, like a divine word. The way to keep Chase far from Adalyn.

He'd never hunted grizzlies, but a coworker had taken him deer hunting a few times. He knew you had to bring a griz down by shooting it right between the eyes. And what would keep a ranger distracted to the point of ignoring a girl like Adalyn for a while? He shook his head. He could not quite imagine it. But yes, he believed for a man like Chase, it would work. The only questions remaining were when and where.

He knew the how. In his cabin, beneath the mattress, were a loaded Magnum and a high-powered rifle.

He dug his paddle in again, feeling strength pour down his arms into the water and away. Then he dug in on one side, turning the kayak in the opposite direction. Spying Adalyn leaving Bea and Logan's cabin, he pulled out his camera, zoomed in on her and took three shots as she walked.

"Oh yes, my love," he whispered, feeling her obvious pain as his very own. "Someday you shall turn to me. And I will make sure no one ever hurts you again."

—ᴧᴧ—

Adalyn managed to see the afternoon's new arrivals to their cabins—cringing as she opened the door to four old ones, and eagerly telling them about her hopes of refurbishing them by next year. She hated sending guests to the old pods, fearing more terrible reviews on TripAdvisor, but they had no choice. They had to honor the reservations that Gramps had taken over the phone and all the new cabins were full. At least the showers were new and improved...perhaps the guests would take mercy on them and mention that when it came to reviewing the property.

Adi had set up her website to clearly delineate between the old and the new, making it plain that they were in the middle of renovations. Just last night she'd upped the rental rate of the completed cabins to triple the price of the others, so those who got the old ones felt like they were getting a really good deal, at least. She'd posted clear and representative pictures of both, so there were few surprises. She consoled herself with the fact that at least the bedding was new throughout the property and they were currently rodent-free.

When Gramps had seen how nice the new pod looked, he'd blessed spending the money on the mattresses, pads, pillows and bedding for all the rest, figuring that refinishing the floors and changing up the kitchenettes and toilets could come later. "If you decide to stick it out, Adi girl," he said.

Again and again he'd brought it back to her. To her decision. To her choice about staying or letting it go forever. He'd known he was done, that he didn't have the fight left in him to do it himself. Was there some part of him that had known he was sick, really sick, all along?

It had blindsided Adi. But Gramps seemed to be taking it in stride. While she hadn't eaten dinner, he'd wolfed down his own. But when she suggested that they track down her mother to tell her what was going on, he'd flatly refused.

"Mom has to know, Gramps," she'd said, totally surprised at his resistance.

"She's off in Borneo or New Zealand," he said with a wave of his hand. "If she cared a whit about me, wouldn't she check in with me once in a while?"

Adi's cheeks had burned. Had she not been guilty of treating him similarly in the last year? What would have happened if she hadn't come back this summer? If he had died and she never saw him again?

"She'll want to see you, Gramps," she tried again. "She'd want to at least know."

He shrugged and then rose. "We'll see how soon she shows up."

"That's not fair," Adi said. "You're angry with her. I get that. But to live your last months…" Her voice broke and tears flooded her eyes. "To not give her a chance…Is that really how you want to go out? Angry and separated from your only child?"

He'd relented then. Rose and put a gentle hand on her shoulder. "I'll consider it, Adi girl. For now, leave me be. Okay?"

—⁂—

Night came and while Adalyn had washed her face and put on a nightshirt for bed, she couldn't rest. She'd cried so much that afternoon that she felt worn out and hollow. But her mind would not let her give in to sleep. Over and over again she wondered what would have happened had she not come to Montana this summer…if Gramps had died, without her ever seeing him again. He was mad at Mom; she understood it. Would he have died, angry and disappointed with her too?

Chase wouldn't have allowed that to happen, she consoled herself. But what kind of granddaughter relied on her grampa's neighbor to keep track of him?

A totally negligent one, she thought grimly. She cascaded between self-recrimination and silent thanks to God that he had brought her home in time, then to wondering if Gramps would ever allow her to call Mom. What if he didn't? Did she go behind his back and call her anyway? Adalyn didn't care if it would force her parents to consider very costly changes to their round-the-world itinerary. At least they would have the choice. She'd give Gramps another couple weeks to come to that same conclusion, or she'd make the decision for him.

After all, *it's me who will have to live with the decision, not him*, she laughed to herself, in grim fashion. And that thought brought tears she didn't have left streaming back down her face.

Frustrated, she rose, pulled on sweatpants beneath her nightshirt, a thick sweatshirt over her head, and slipped into her Ugg boots. Then she walked down the dark hall and out the kitchen door, easing it shut behind her.

That's when she saw the flash of lights between trees down the road and noticed they were coming her way. A moment later she saw it was Chase's Jeep. When he hadn't returned before nightfall, she'd figured he hadn't gotten Bea's message or couldn't get away. But now, seeing him pull up, she realized how much—how very much—she had wanted him to come. She started walking toward the parking lot. Didn't realize she was practically running until she flung herself into his arms.

He held her tightly. "Hey, hey," he murmured, holding her close, stroking her back, her hair. "Oh, Adi. I'm so sorry. So sorry."

She wept, clinging to his flannel shirt, fully letting loose to the sobs that she'd done her best to strangle all afternoon. She cried so hard and so long that at one point, Chase bent, picked her up and carried her to a bench on the beach, settling her on his lap and letting her cry into his neck, babbling about her grandfather, the diagnosis, his refusal to let her contact Mom in between hiccups and coughs. She even cried about him coming back early.

"You came, Chase," she said, gasping for breath. "I didn't think you were coming. I told myself I didn't need it. But I'm…so glad…you're here." She struggled then to get herself together.

"Hey," he said, cupping her cheek and bending a little away from her to look her in the eye. He was in deep shadow, with nothing but the soft lights of the dock to illuminate them, yet she could see the determined angle of his brow, his jaw. "I would have been here sooner but Hannah and I had to respond to an emergency call. We weren't done until after nightfall and then had to wait for the chief before we could head back."

"What happened?" she asked, hating the hiccup that reminded her that she'd just ugly-cried in front of him. She eased off his lap and onto the bench beside him, holding his hand and leaning her head against his shoulder.

"There was an…incident. On the far side of the lake."

"What sort of incident?"

"Somebody shot a deer this afternoon, but didn't kill it. Near the creek on the other side. It wandered onto the road, wounded. A tourist almost ran over it."

"Did it die?"

"We had to put it down. There was no hope."

Adalyn nodded. She knew how he championed the animals of Glacier—even the deer, marmots and chipmunks. "That's awful."

"But we also found a porcupine had been killed too. They're rare on the west side."

Adalyn frowned. "Some stupid kid? An idiot passing through?"

"I hope he or she is passing through. Because if I get my hands on them…"

She wrapped her hands around his bicep, comforted by the strength of it. "That's a lousy way to finish your day."

"Still, it was better than yours," he said, touching her chin with his knuckle. "I'm really sorry, Adi. Gene…well, I kind of thought Gene would always be with us. Somehow. He's such a force, you know?"

"I know," she said. "I keep thinking I'm so grateful that you came to tell me something was up with him."

Chase nodded. "Clearly, you were meant to be home."

"Thank you," she said simply. "And thank you for coming home tonight."

He wrapped an arm around her and leaned his head against the crown of her head. "I only wish I could've been here sooner, Adi girl. From here on out, I'll do my best to stick as close as I can."

—※—

Kenneth watched as Chase led her back to the cabin, his arm around her the whole time.

He froze as they walked past him, standing stock-still in the deepest shadows of Gene's cabin. By edging around the cabin, one soft footfall at a time, he'd tried to get close enough to hear them. Had watched, holding his breath, waiting—just waiting—for Chase to make a move on his girl. Stroked the cool metal of his pistol in the chest holster, half-praying he would, and this would all end. Because Kenneth knew one thing: He would not stand idly by and see her risk her heart, only to then suffer when it was trampled by another thoughtless male.

Only Chase's restraint—his utter, careful care of Adalyn—had saved him. The way he had held her, like a caring friend or brother or uncle. Kept his arm around her, murmuring to her. Let her cry in his arms. He hadn't interrupted her. Just let her go. That had left Kenneth with a grudging respect that let him live one more night.

But his plan had worked. A few more wounded animals and this ranger would be kept busy for some time. He'd have to escalate his plan, apparently. Map out when and where he would destroy the creatures this one had sworn to protect. Because it was important that he give Adalyn the chance to get to know him better. Then, next time she was distraught, it would be his turn to hold her, comfort her.

CHAPTER 20

When Adalyn left the cabin the next morning to begin cleaning Cabin Five and set to work on the floors of the second pod, she almost stepped on them.

"Oh," she said, bending to pick up the small pottery jar and the tiny bouquet of wildflowers. *Chase*, she thought, turning to set them on the kitchen table, then quietly shut the door behind her, smiling all the while. He had come home for her last night. His caring gesture, the way he'd held her... could this really be happening? Was he falling for her like she was falling for him?

She shook her head, her smile fading. Did she even know what it was to fall in love? Hadn't she failed miserably at it?

Her cell phone buzzed and she pulled it out. From Chase. *Good morning, pretty girl*, the text read. *Sorry to say I have to head up the pass again. Poacher struck again last night.*

Oh, no, she thought, hating that another innocent animal had died as much as Chase being away all day. She thought it might be time for a Relationship Intentions talk. Neither of them wanted to risk their friendship unless they were really game to pursue this. If he wasn't ready to address it, she would. If there was one thing *The One* had taught her—days counted. And she didn't have the capacity to risk her heart any further unless Chase was ready to fully reciprocate.

I'm sorry to hear that, she texted back. *Come see me tonight when you get back?*

You know I will, he texted. Apparently he wasn't far away if he still had cell service.

It made her smile again. The promise and flirtation in his words. She read the phrases three times-over. *Pretty girl. You know I will…*

She'd really have to throw herself into her work today or she might be liable to stare at the lake all day in a dreamlike state. Chase Rollins. *Could it be? Chase and me? After all these years?*

She'd entered the first pod and belatedly glanced up to see Ken snap her picture. He was sitting on Cabin Five's doorstep and had been shooting the lake until she came into view. Her smile faded to a scowl. "Hey," she said, blocking his view with her hand as he continued to take rapid frames. "Stop."

He lowered his camera and frowned. "What? You're as pretty as the sunrise. Can you blame a budding photographer? You have to go with inspiration. Especially when you rounded the corner with such a beautiful smile on your face."

She flushed, realizing she was probably overreacting. Ken was a nerd, not the paparazzi in disguise. Wouldn't the news have broken yesterday if he was? "Sorry," she said, moving to open the cabin's screen door and prop it open with a rock. "I'm just not fond of people taking my picture without permission."

"I'm sorry," he said, following her in. He set his camera on the table. "I should have asked. Here. Let me make it up to you." He began to strip the bed opposite of the one she was working on. "I'll help you clean this cabin in record time."

"Oh, you don't have to do that," she said, now thoroughly embarrassed as they stood up in the center. "You're a guest here!"

"A guest getting a really good deal as I understand it. I heard others say these cabins are going for $300 a night? I'll do what I have to to keep my $199 rate." He bundled up the sheets and set them by the door, then went to the next one.

"There's no need," she said, trying to take the stack of sheets from his hands. "You signed up for a month when you arrived. We're not going to change your rate."

"I'd like to help, Adalyn," he said, stubbornly holding on to the sheets. "It makes me feel useful."

"Well, all right," she said. "If you're sure." Did she not understand that exact need, to be useful? Together, they set to work. "How are you liking your time in the park?"

"I like it very much," he said, creating a hospital corner on his bed worthy of a Marine drill sergeant's. "It's very quiet. And yet..." He stood and cocked his head a bit. "It's kind of noisy in its own way. So full of beauty and life," he paused to gesture around. "It all kind of shouts for attention."

Adi smiled. "That's a lovely way to put it."

You would have thought she had said something miraculous. Ken got an almost beatific look on his face at her words and he grinned from ear to ear as he nodded. "I'm glad you think so," he said.

She got a little shiver of fear, then felt silly about it. *He's so lonely*, she told herself. *So oddly hungry for any encouragement. He's just a lonely, sad, nerdy man, Adi.*

Adalyn turned to reach across the bunk to make it. She felt the hair stick up on the back of her neck and turned, wondering if he was watching her. But he seemed to be intent upon nothing but working on his own. She finished and then went to the bathroom to clean it.

"Want me to work on the kitchen?" he asked, hand on the doorjamb of the bathroom.

"Sure," she said. "Knock yourself out. But you really don't have to." she called, as he moved on.

"Happy to. I have all day to take more pictures," he returned. Then he called, "Say, Adalyn. Why is it you don't like to have your picture taken? Aren't you into selfies, like most girls?"

"I just—I'm just not one of those girls," she said. "I've come to appreciate a measure of privacy. I don't want to share every moment of every day with others. And pictures of me…Well, they feel a little like a piece of me, you know?"

He seemed to accept that. She could hear the creak of the fridge door, the clink of bottles. "Do you want me to dump all this they left behind?" he called.

"Yeah. I'll keep any ketchup or mustard," she said. "Just leave them on the counter."

"Gotcha."

She moved to the hall closet for the broom and dustpan, and saw that he was meticulously scrubbing the counters with a sponge and soapy water from the sink. He finished one tile before moving to the next.

"Oh, I just usually spray those down with Lysol and clean them with a rag. There's a fresh one on the stack over there," she said, gesturing toward the linens.

"Really?" he asked, pausing mid-stroke. Was that a shadow of disappointment that rushed across his face? "Do you mind if I do it my way? It feels more thorough."

His jaw was so tight she could practically see his muscles clenching. "Oh. Sure. I don't care, as long as it gets done."

This time she was sure it was disappointment. As if her methods did not measure up to his standards. Was he a neatnik? One of those odd, OCD guys? Was he worrying that she hadn't cleaned his cabin well enough before he checked in? She'd have to take some extra time with it when she went to do the weekly cleaning in a couple of days. She snuck another look at him, moving from tile to tile. *Or maybe I'll have Mrs. Larson do it*, she thought. *This guy is super weird.*

When the cabin was complete, she went outside, carrying the bundle of dirty linens over her shoulder. "Well, thanks for the help, Ken. That was sweet of you," she said.

"No problem. I can help with the rest," he eagerly offered.

"No, no," she said, raising a hand. "I can't accept any more free help from a guest."

He ran his hand along the strap of his camera, hanging from a shoulder. "What if I charged you a kayak ride with me tonight?"

"Oh," she said, finally figuring it out. He was trying to ask her out. That's what this was all about. "I'm sorry. As lovely as that sounds, I think I have plans tonight." With luck, Chase would be home...

A red tide surged up his neck and began climbing his jaw, his cheeks. Was that rage in his eyes? Were his hands clenching?

She took a startled step backward.

He seemed to remember himself then. His hands slackened and he lifted one to run through his light brown hair. "Oh, no worries. Sorry. I mean...sorry." He bit his lip, looked to the lake and then back at her. "Sure you don't need any more help?"

"I'm sure," she said, forcing a smile. "Now go. Enjoy the park. Take some pictures of birds and animals. They don't care as much as I do."

That made him smile a little, halting the slow rise of his blush. "Your wish is my command," he said, casting her a lopsided grin and bowing like a court lord. "See you around, m'lady."

Yup. Full-on, lonely nerd, she decided. "See you," she said. She turned to go. But she didn't start to breathe normally until she'd rounded the corner of the next pod of cabins, fully out of his lingering gaze.

—⟋⟍⟍—

Kenneth alternately exalted and cursed his first, tentative strides with Adalyn. As he booted up his computer, he ran the things she'd said through his mind. He uploaded the pictures he'd taken of her, scrolling through them again and again, from her beautiful, dreamy smile he'd captured as she rounded the corner to the scowl at the end, just before she lifted a hand to block him. Even the picture of her palm, studying each line on her skin, tracing the love line, which was split in several branches. *Adam,* he thought, tracing the first. *Connor,* he added, tracing the second. Then he hesitated over the third. *Me? Or...*

He grimaced and then turned to the next tab on his computer, a shortcut to his hack into the ranger station. In short order, he figured out his plan had worked. Chase and Hannah had been sent to collect the remains of a disemboweled stag, found near McDonald Creek by some hikers that morning. Kenneth picked up his large hunting knife and ran his fingers along the edge of it, remembering the iron-rich smell of blood, the warmth of it as it had gushed out.

He remembered that Adalyn said she had plans tonight, and the way she had looked at him—as if she were letting him down—made him realize it was with his rival that she had those plans. He tapped his fingers on the wooden table in agitation. What would keep Chase Rollins away for a few days rather than just one?

He had to go bigger. And farther away. Give his boss reason to send Chase and Hannah over to the other side for a good, long while. And leave Adalyn alone.

Well, alone, but not alone, he thought with a slow smile.

—〰—

Adalyn was building stone sculptures on the shore when Chase came home at last. She'd just completed the third when he trudged toward her on the beach, hands in his pockets. Feeling unaccountably shy, she rose and put her own hands in her pockets. "Welcome back," she said.

"It's good to be welcomed," he said, grinning down at her for a long moment. "Those are amazing." He gestured toward her sculptures.

"Thanks," she said, turning toward them. "Want to try your hand at one?"

"Maybe in a bit," he said. "But all day, Adi, I've been thinking about walking and talking with you. Mind if we go to the point?"

She followed his gaze to the point that stretched out into the water, with one lonely, storm-ravaged pine at the end. "Sure," she said.

He offered his hand and she gladly took it, interlacing her fingers with his. She held on to his arm with her other. "I missed you, today."

"I missed you too," he said. "How's Gramps today?"

"Good. I mean, pretty good. He's sleeping in now. It's like…like the doctor's diagnosis has given him permission."

Chase nodded. "All my life, I've never seen him sleep past sun-up. Now?"

"Eight or nine o'clock even," she said. "But that's okay. The rest is probably good for him."

"Undoubtedly. Cancer has to be taking a lot out of him."

"More than we'd even guess, I think. But he seems at peace about it all. More than I am for sure."

They reached the point and Adi leaned against the curve of the tree. He still hadn't let go of her hand. Now he was playing with it. Rubbing her palm before giving her a shy smile. He raised it then to his lips and kissed it slowly, then set it against his chest, holding it there with both of his own.

Adalyn found she was holding her breath.

"Adi, I wanted to walk and talk with you tonight about us," he said. "About this, what's happening between us."

"That's funny," she said. "I was just thinking it might be time for the Big Talk."

"Oh? And what were you thinking about saying?"

"Uh-uh," she warned playfully. "If you were any decent fan of *The One*, you must've caught the footage of me saying it was important to me that a man declare himself first."

"I might have caught that episode," he allowed, lifting her palm to his lips and kissing it again, all the while staring at her. Sparks traveled down her hand, arm, shoulder and up her neck. How did he do that to her? With such a simple, little action?

"Oh. Good," she mumbled, staring at his lips as they moved to her wrist.

He paused and took both her hands in his. "Adalyn, I do have something to declare. I declare I'm an idiot."

She frowned in confusion. "What?"

"I'm an idiot," he said steadily. "It wasn't until I was watching you on that show that I realized how big of an idiot I was." He cocked his head and squinted a little at her. "Because seeing you on there, with other men vying to claim your heart, I realized something, Adi."

"Oh?" she whispered.

"Yeah. I realized that I'd always wanted to be the one who would claim your heart. And when you came back, when I felt how good it was to have you around, I realized I always wanted you around. I'm hoping," he said, pausing to dig his boot toe against a rock, dislodging it. "I'm hoping that I'd be enough to make you want to stay. Regardless of what happens with Gramps and the cabins."

"Chase. Are you saying..."

"I'm saying this." He stepped closer to her, putting one hand on her waist and tugging her closer. "I'm saying *this*." He lifted his other hand to move her hair from her eye and tenderly cup her cheek. "I'm saying *this*." He leaned down slowly, his eyes on hers until his lips hovered over her own. "Do you like what I'm saying, Adi girl?" he whispered.

"Yes," she whispered back. "I-I think I do, Chase."

He needed no further confirmation. He kissed her then, kissed her with all the fervent desire and draw and hope and care that she'd dreamed of, back when they were kids. He kissed her for a long time, drawing her in close to him, his body heat welcome against the chill of the mountain evening. Kissed her like he wanted to keep on kissing her, but then made himself stop. Which she was glad he did. Because she didn't know if she would have ever stopped him.

He pulled her close in his arms, rubbing her back. Then kissing the crown of her head, he sighed. "Do you know how long I've wanted to do that, Adi?"

"Probably not as long as I wanted you to do that," she said.

He pulled back and gave her a look of surprise. "No."

"Yes," she said with a laugh. "I always had a crush on you as a kid. You knew that, Chase. There's no way you could've missed it!"

He laughed under his breath and pulled her close again,

rocking her slowly back and forth. "Yeah. Maybe I knew it. Just as I knew I had a crush on you. But I was never willing to risk our friendship for it."

She nodded. That had been her reason too. "But now it's worth the risk?" she asked, looking up at him.

He stared down at her, his gaze so tender and sincere it took her breath away. The last time she'd seen a man look at her like that...

Abruptly, she broke from him, turned away, rubbing her neck.

"Adi?"

"No, it's fine," she said, lifting a hand. "It's only that— Chase, the last time a man looked at me like the way you're looking at me, he ended up breaking my heart."

He stepped toward her, carefully, as if approaching a skittish deer. Then walked around to face her. She looked away, to the side, well aware she wasn't being fair to him. "Adalyn," he said gruffly. "Look at me."

Slowly, she forced herself to meet his gaze.

He put gentle hands on either side of her face. "Have I ever betrayed you?"

She shook her head a little.

"Have I ever knowingly hurt you?"

She shook her head again.

"Have I ever turned you away?"

"No," she whispered.

"I am not one of those guys," he said, leaning down to put his forehead against hers. "That's what I'm praying now, Adi girl. That other men's mistakes don't impede my progress with you."

"Is that what this is?" she said, his words striking her funny. "Progress?"

"I'd say so," he said, again letting his lips hover over hers.

"Wouldn't you?"

"It's one word for it," she said, unable to resist him any longer. She stood up on tiptoes and kissed him.

After a bit, he lifted her and twirled her around in a circle. "Oh, Adi. Adi. I knew I wanted to kiss you. I didn't know it would make me this crazy-happy."

She smiled with him and kissed his nose before he set her down again and began walking her back to the cabin. "Why now, Chase? Why risk our friendship after all these years?"

He rubbed his neck then reached out to take her hands in his. "Because watching you on that show made me sick to my stomach. When it was on, I thought it was because I was watching you make terrible mistakes with your heart, and watching those fools turn you away. But then I saw you, Adi, in *person*. Once I had you in my arms—once we were in Glacier again, I had to admit it. I felt sick to my stomach watching you with those other guys because I had feelings for you myself."

"Did Logan have anything to do with that?" she asked, putting a hand on his chest and playing with his collar. She knew the brothers—and the way they talked, pushed each other—well enough to guess.

Chase smiled. "You know Logan. He made me tell him and Bea that I had feelings for you." He pulled her closer. "But also confess that I always had. Back in college, he said he would've gone for you himself if he didn't know how crazy I was for you."

"You're crazy for me?" she said, running her fingers through his hair.

"More than you could believe," he whispered, kissing her again. His walkie-talkie buzzed to life then. Grimacing, he reached to his back belt clip to grab it. "Rollins here."

"Chase, we've got a report of another one," Hannah's voice

crackled through.

He frowned.

"It's worse, partner. They took out a sow over near Two Medicine. Left two orphan cubs."

Chase let out a sound of total frustration and ran a hand over his mouth, eyes wide.

"Want to head over tonight?" Hannah asked.

"Yeah," he said. "I'll be there as soon as I can." He turned down the volume button and slid it back to his belt clip, then turned to Adalyn. "I'm so sorry."

"No. I get it. You have to go." She took his hand in both of hers. "I'm just glad," she said, shyly bringing his hand up to kiss one finger after another, "we had this talk."

"Me too," he said, smiling at her. Gosh, how she liked it when he smiled at her. What would it be like to see that smile every day?

She took his hand and they walked back to the cabins. In front of Gramps's cabin, he turned, cupped her cheek and gave her a slow, searching kiss, wrapping a big hand at her lower back, pulling her closer. And then he took a step away, leaving her breathless and wanting more, so much more. But he was waiting for her to go inside, quietly protective.

Reluctantly, she turned and went in, easing shut the screen door and then the wooden door, as to not wake Gramps. Leaning against it, she closed her eyes and grinned. Chase Rollins was crazy about her. Chase Rollins!

Adalyn rubbed her swollen bottom lip, thinking about all the men she had kissed on the show. That had been the oddest part...being so intimate with so many. And Chase had watched all of that. It made her sick to think about. Didn't the thought of him going to the other side of the park with Hannah make Adi feel a little jealous? What had watching her kiss others make him feel? And yet, had that not been part of what made him realize his own feelings?

She sighed and leaned her head back against the door, wondering where he was right now. Back in the boathouse cabin? On the beach? She swallowed and closed her eyes. "Please, God," she whispered. "Please let Chase Rollins be the last guy I ever kiss and get to keep on kissing. I want it to be him." She paused, thinking. "Could it be that he is the one for me? That he has always been the one?"

Chase leaned against Gene's cabin, one hand on the door frame, one hand on his face.

He was both exhilarated and devastated. "What is this, Lord?" he whispered. "What have I done?" And then, "Why didn't I do that before?"

He turned and walked down the pine-needle covered path to the beach and out on to the dock. He knew Hannah was waiting on him. That there was urgent business for him to attend to on the other side of the park. A grizzly sow? Leaving orphaned cubs? But this—this thing with Adi—seemed to demand he think it through now.

It was cold now, as night had thoroughly closed in, but he only dimly felt the chill on his skin. He paced from one end of the dock to the other and back again until Logan showed up on the beach, arms crossed.

"You trying to wear out my new dock?" he asked.

Chase pulled up, surprised. "Nah," he said. "Just thinking."

"Need me to think with you?" his brother asked, coming to stand beside him, arms crossed, looking out to the mirror-glass lake reflecting the stars above. They stood there for a while in easy silence.

"I kissed her," Chase said then.

Logan let out a sound of surprise and delight. But he didn't turn. "*Finally.*"

"That's just it."

That made Logan glance at him. "What?"

Chase heaved a sigh, remembering every tear Adi had cried on that stupid show. "If I'd done that years ago, maybe I could've protected her, Logan. I could have shielded her from all that pain we watched her go through."

Logan thought on that a moment. "You can't go back in time, bro. You just can't. There's no guarantee that if you had kissed her that last summer…what? Six years ago? That it would've made it different. You were college kids then, you a senior, she just a freshman. She still had big city dreams. You knew you'd have to go to the middle of nowhere for a time. It just wasn't right. Now maybe it is?"

"Maybe," Chase said. "I hope so."

Logan took a deep breath. "Can you just take it for what it is, for once? Rather than dissecting it into a hundred pieces?"

Chase nodded, taking that in. That was how they were made up. He was the more analytical brother, the quiet thinker. Logan was the more spontaneous, take-it-as-it-came sort. That's why he'd become a wildlife scientist, content to be alone for hours at a time, tracking, capturing, studying, logging. And why his brother was happiest moving between people-oriented jobs.

"You're doing it right now, huh?" Logan asked, turning to put his hands on Chase's shoulders. "Analyzing why you can't just take it in?"

Chase laughed under his breath. "Maybe."

"Okay, so stay with me on this. How'd it feel to kiss Adi?"

"Amazing," he said. "Better than I thought it would."

"Like you wanted to kiss her more?"

"Only all night."

Logan's white teeth gleamed in the starlight. "Better than any girl you've ever kissed?"

"Uh, *yeah.*"

"Did you make plans to see each other again? I mean, see-see each other?"

"As soon as I get back. I have to go to Two Medicine. That poacher has struck again. Or a copycat. And this time it was a grizzly."

"That's horrible," Logan said. He paused a moment. "But while you're gone, when you think about Adi, why not just concentrate on the fact that you just kissed the girl you've always had a crush on?"

Chase took a deep breath and turned toward the lake, rubbing the back of his neck. "Because what if…what if she doesn't think I just gave her the best kiss she's ever had?" He lifted his hand. "You saw it yourself. She's kissed, what? Maybe ten, twelve guys in the last year? I didn't have that much action in college."

"She held back more than most bachelorettes. That's what Bea tells me, anyway," Logan said.

"But still, Logan. Twelve guys."

His brother's smile had disappeared. Chase thought he was nodding. "I get it. It's not what any man wants to think about. But here's the thing you should get your analytical mind around." He clamped a hand on his shoulder. "There's a high probability that you aren't the best kisser she's experienced."

Chase pulled back, slightly offended, but Logan held on.

"No, stay with me, here," Logan said, holding on to his shoulder. "Truth be told, there was one girl when I was a ski instructor at Mammoth that was about the most beautiful creature who ever gave me the honor of looking my way. And her kiss?" He sucked in his breath and let it out in a low whistle. "Yeah. I'd have to say she had some expertise in that arena. But Bea? When I first got a chance to kiss my beautiful

Beatrice and she kissed me back? That, *that* brother, was the best kiss of my life. Not because it was perfect. But because we were perfect. Well, you know. No couple is perfect. But you see what I'm getting at?"

Chase smiled. "Yeah."

"So I'd say you just better stand out here a minute longer—no, longer—" he said, lifting a warning finger, "thanking God that you might have just had the chance to kiss the girl you always wanted to. And trust him with the rest."

"Gotcha."

Logan gave him two firm pats on the back and turned to walk off the dock. Chase thought for a sec about resuming his pacing, but instead, he did what his younger brother had directed. He stood a moment longer, looking up at the stars, breathed a silent *thank you*, then turned and headed toward the cabin.

CHAPTER 21

"Oh, you've got it bad," Gramps said with a knowing grin, shoving some scrambled eggs in his mouth.

"What?" she asked, letting her fingers fall from the small pottery vase.

He grinned at her and gestured to the vase with his fork. "You keep staring at those flowers as if it was Chase himself at our table."

"I don't know what you're talking about," she tried, even as she smiled. "Okay, yeah," she relented. "I have it bad."

"He's a good kid. A fine young man. You could do worse." He shoved a bite of eggs in his mouth.

"There's a ringing endorsement, Gramps. 'You could do worse'?"

"You know I love those boys almost as much as I love you," he said. He set down his fork and covered her hand with his. "But I've always thought that no one could ever be quite enough for my Adi girl."

She smiled back at him. "That's sweet, Gramps."

He took another bite. "So, did he declare himself last

night on your walk?"

"How'd you know we took a walk?"

"Well, I can't be asleep all the time, right? I have cancer, but I'm not dead yet."

She shook her head, half-amused, half-irritated by his cavalier words. But she figured this was just going to be his way....dealing with a death sentence with a little bit of humor. "Yeah. He declared himself. We both did."

"Well, I'll be," Gramps said, wiping his mouth with a napkin and sitting back in his chair, arms folded. "Took you two long enough."

"Yeah. That's what we both think now, too."

He waved in the air. "Ach. Sometimes we don't take the simplest route. But eventually we find where we're supposed to get to in time."

She nodded. Then, studying the flowers again, she pulled out her phone. *Good morning,* she texted to Chase. *I forgot to say thanks last night.*

Good morning, came the return. *For my fabulous kiss?*

For the flowers you left me yesterday morning, she typed, grinning as she did so. *That was really sweet of you. So much better than roses...*

He didn't reply for a while. All she saw was the scrolling ellipsis, indicating he'd started to respond but then stopped. Then it came through at last. *Adi, I didn't leave you flowers,* it said. *Who do you think did?*

She felt the blood drain from her face. *No. No, no, no.* It couldn't be. Or it was a coincidence. It had to be.

"What?" Gramps asked. "Adi girl, what's happened?"

"Gr-Gramps," she said, rising and pacing. She wrapped her arms around herself. Went to the door and locked it. She knew it was silly. She was overreacting.

"Adi," he said, rising on weak legs but then gripping her

shoulders with surprisingly firm hands, stilling her. Forcing her to look at him. "What is it?"

"Those flowers…" she said, glancing at them. "Do you know who left them for me?"

He frowned. "It wasn't Chase?"

"No." She lifted her phone. "He just told me."

The phone was ringing then. *Chase.*

"Hi," she said, not sure of what else to say.

"Adi," he said, the line cutting out periodically as he continued. "Did you…hear me?"

"No, Chase," she said. "You're cutting out."

"…probably Bea or someone. But…precautions," came his partial words.

"Yes, you're right," she said. "I will. Can you…can you come back soon?"

"…or two days," he said, regret evident in his voice. "It's bad, really bad here. This guy, he…"

She sighed in frustration. But she understood. He was dealing with his own crisis. "Listen, Chase. Do what you need to do. I'll be fine. I promise."

"…his .44?"

"Yes, yes, I'll get it. I'll keep it nearby."

"I'll be home…as I can."

"Thanks, Chase." She forced a laugh. "I'm probably just being paranoid."

"In this case, Adi girl," he said, the line suddenly clear, "I'd rather you take precautions. Just in case. Have you noticed anyone around? Anyone odd?"

She thought back. No one was around, really, other than the Rollinses. Gramps. The rangers and locals in Apgar. People were coming and going at their cabin complex, new people every day.

Except for Kenneth.

But Chase and Gramps didn't need to worry about that. *Gramps's heart…*She looked at him worriedly, watching her talk, face wan. "No, no one," she said. "Listen, I'm going to go over to your brother's and see if maybe Bea left them for me and Gramps. It'd be like her, right?"

"That's true," Chase said, his tight tone easing a bit. "You're right. Go see her. We'll both breathe a little easier if we find out that's true. Then text me, okay?"

"Okay. Thanks, Chase. I'll talk to you soon."

"Take care, Adi."

She clicked the red button, ending their call, and then moved over to the drawer she knew contained the .44.

Ken was just a weirdling. *A lonely nerd*, she thought, returning to her previous thoughts. Only trying to connect in his own, awkward way.

But then, wasn't that exactly the kind of guy who ended up being a stalker?

She stared at the drawer, wanting to resist the fear that threatened to overtake her. Not since she had stood in her apartment, knowing the stalker had been there, had she felt so weak in the knees.

"Go on," Gramps said, "take it out. You should have it with you."

"No," she said, taking a deep breath and moving to the kitchen door and unlocking it. "I'm just going over to Bea's. Chase and I think she might've left the flowers for me."

"I'll go with you," he said.

For the first time, she fully looked at him. And he really did look as ghastly as she felt. "Gramps," she said, moving to grab his elbow even as he faltered. "Here, sit," she said, and he fairly fell into the chair. She went to grab a glass and filled it with water for him. "Breathe, Gramps. Breathe. It's okay."

"If anything happened to you, Adi girl," he began, his lips

trembling. His eyes filled with tears.

She sank into the neighboring seat and held his hand. "I'm okay. It'll be okay. Now all this excitement isn't good for your heart. Come. Let's get you into bed for a rest."

"You'll take the .44 with you?" he asked anxiously, as she helped him stand.

"Yes," she said. "You rest. I'll go see Bea and come straight back."

"All right," he said. "It will be good if we find out it was just that girl all along."

"Yes," she said, helping him to the edge of his bed, then when he seemed to struggle, lifting his legs atop it. "I'm sorry to stress you out so much."

"It can't be half what your beau across the mountains is feeling," he said, giving her a conspiratorial little smile.

"Yeah, right," she said. She pulled a blanket across him, then bent to kiss him. "You rest. I'll be back in two shakes of a lamb's tail."

He smiled and then pulled off his glasses, closed his weary eyes and rubbed them.

She eased out of the room, went to the kitchen, paused at the drawer and then thought, *No. I'm not going to give in to fear.* Wasn't that like letting the stalker win, in a way?

She grabbed the ring of cabin keys, found the main cabin's and locked it behind her. Then, glancing around, she breathed a sigh of relief when she didn't see another person in sight. Still, as she walked, she placed a key between each of her knuckles. She'd read, once, that it was an excellent defense weapon.

In minutes, she was knocking on the boathouse cabin door, glancing over her shoulder, left, then right. Bea answered it.

"Hey, girl!" she enthused, giving her a quick hug. She

pulled her inside. "I hear you have big things to tell me about last night. *Big.* Now prepare to dish."

Adi smiled, finding a reprieve in thinking about Chase's kisses and sweet words rather than a potential stalker. "I will. Soon, I promise. But I need to get back to Gramps. Bea, did you leave me a sweet little pottery vase yesterday, with wild-flowers in it?"

Bea smiled in confusion at her. "Me? No." She nudged her. "Sure it wasn't Chase?" She waggled her eyebrows.

"No, it wasn't," Adi said. "Listen, I need to go check on something. If I'm not back in an hour, come check on me, okay?"

"Adi," she said, following her to the door. "What's up? You don't think…"

"No, no," Adalyn lied, backing away. "It's probably nothing. Thanks. I'll be back soon."

"I'll come with you!" she called.

But then Logan was calling to her from the beach, gesturing for her to come down. It looked like he was trying to juggle three different sets of guests.

"You go! Your hubby needs you," Adalyn said. "I'll be fine." She turned on her heel and strode back to their cabin. But as she reached the door, a van pulled up and out spilled a family of six—parents and four teens. The teenagers looked like they wanted to be anywhere but Glacier. Adalyn forced herself to wait, turning to greet them. After all, Gramps was in no shape to play the kind innkeeper at this point.

The dad smiled and reached out a hand. "Hi, we're the Palmers. We saw your sign. Any chance you have room for us tonight? Maybe a couple of cabins?"

"I'm afraid all we have are our older cabins. They haven't been renovated, but they have new bedding, at least. And we have a new shower complex. If you're willing to rough it…"

"We'll take them," Mr. Palmer said. "For two nights. We were thinking we'd have to drive all the way to Kalispell every day. This will save us."

"O.M.G.," said one of the teen girls, stepping forward to stand beside her parents. "You are Adalyn! It's Adalyn-freak-ing-*Stalling*," she said to her sister.

"Uh…" Adi began.

"No way!" said the other girl. "She totally is! You are, right?"

The first was taking Adi's picture with her phone. "It's her!"

Adalyn frowned. "I think you have me confused with someone else."

"Uhh, I don't think so," said the first, looking confused. "I'm a part of One Nation. Do you know that everybody in the whole world has been looking for you?"

Her parents frowned in confusion. "Girls," Mrs. Palmer said. "You two are being kind of rude to this kind woman. How about—"

But the girls would not be dissuaded.

"This was the *lake*!" cried the second. "The lake where she took that picture she posted on Instagram!" For the first time, the teens seemed to think that this particular part of nature wasn't bad at all.

"What are you doing here?" asked the first.

"Has Connor called you?" asked the second. "He totally has, right? I thought he was completely lame when he cut things off. He *has* to regret it."

"Listen," Adalyn said. It was clear she couldn't lie her way out of this. She had been identified. She reached out a hand toward the first girl, who seemed poised to post a picture. "I really need your help, girls. If you keep the secret that you saw me here until September, I will tell you three things that nobody else knows about *The One*. An insider scoop. Your friends will think you're amazing, finding it out. But," she said, holding up a finger. "I really, really need you to not tell anyone where you saw me until this fall, when you get back to school. Because this," she said, waving around, "is my refuge. From the paparazzi. And a place to heal my heart. If it gets out that I'm here, well, it would be awful. Can you help me keep my secret?"

The girls stared at her, considering her words. Her offer of insider secrets was clearly tantalizing, but was it enough to dissuade them from posting a photo-sure-to-go-viral?

"I will take a picture with both of you," she said. "If you keep it under wraps until mid-September. What do you say?"

"They will do as you asked, Ms. Stalling," the dad said, crossing his arms.

"Yes, they will," the mother said, shooting both a menacing glance.

"But, *Mom*," said the first girl. She lifted a hand toward Adi. "You don't get it! This…this is the biggest thing that's ever happened to me in my *entire* life."

"Mine too!" cried the second.

"Still," Mr. Palmer said. "She has asked you to keep a confidence. And you know what the right thing to do is, don't you?"

Both heaved a sigh and nodded. The first then looked Adi in the eye. "But you promise? You'll give us the scoop tonight?"

"I promise," she said. "Want me to show you to your cabins? You can dump your stuff. They're empty now."

"That'd be great," Mr. Palmer said.

Adalyn led the way to the third pod of cabins and opened Cabins 14 and 15 for them, as the girls whispered excitedly between themselves. Even the boys leaned in to listen. As promised, she posed for a picture with both girls before departing. Could she really trust them to keep her secret?

As she turned away, she decided she had no choice. It had only been a matter of time before this happened. At least she'd get to try out this strategy, so she'd be more prepared when it happened again.

She was walking back to the main cabin, crossing through the first pod, when she slowed. Cabin 1. Kenneth's. Hadn't she been heading his way when she left Bea? She'd just stop, talk to him, see if she got any sort of creepy vibe again. If she did, she'd get Logan to see him out tonight. Make some excuse about a water main or something.

Before she could talk herself out of it, she knocked on the door. "Ken?" she called. She knocked again. "Ken?"

He was probably gone for the day. He'd been gone all day yesterday. Just out taking more pictures, she thought. Biting her lip, she wondered about going in, checking out his stuff. Making sure there weren't any clues that he was her stalker. *There's no way,* she told herself. His license plate clearly said Georgia, not Illinois. *You're being an idiot, Adi. The guy's lonely, not a menace!*

Still, she found herself keying in the code to unlock the door—another improvement she'd made on the new pod of cabins. How many keys had been lost or taken with guests in years past? All keys Gramps had to replace? The door beeped and the light turned green. She heard the lock snap. Tentatively, she opened the door. "Ken?" she called. Seizing on an excuse, she added, "Housekeeping!"

Adalyn peeked in. Everything was in meticulous order. The bed made. No food out on the counters. The toilet seat down. A jacket hung on the hook by the door. On the table sat a laptop computer beside a couple books on photography, birding. Glancing over her shoulder and then through the window to make sure no one was coming, she eased over to the table. She hesitated, knowing she was about to totally invade his privacy on a whole other level. *But I gotta know.* She opened the computer and watched it light up. Fifteen or more Word docs were on the screen. She began to scan each one. They were reports from the park service. Ranger reports. Animal reports. *Chase's* reports. On the dead animals, found over the last three days. Of potential plans to apprehend the perpetrator.

Her heart hammered in her chest.

What on earth was Ken doing with these?

With a trembling hand, she opened the next tab. There were hundreds of pictures. The very first one made her heart stop. The second turned her stomach.

Because inside this file was picture after picture after picture of her.

CHAPTER 22

"I really wish you hadn't come in here, Adalyn," said a low, pained voice behind her.

She whirled around. He was closing the door. Locking it.

"Ken. Oh, I...I just was stopping by to see if you needed some...uh, supplies."

He took the jacket from the hook and walked over to her. "Here, put this on," he said, seemingly lost in his own thoughts.

"What? No," she said, shaking her head. "I'm not cold." She tried to step past him, but he reached out and grabbed her arm with an iron grip. "Put it on," he said. Then he seemed to remember himself. "It might be cold, where we're going," he said, his tone now like a caring boyfriend's.

"I can't go anywhere," she said. "I have to stay here and take care of Gramps, Ken. Now, if you'll let me go, I—"

"Listen to me," he said, wrenching her closer to him, grabbing hold of her other forearm then. "We have to go, and we have to go now. I saw what happened out there. Saw those girls. Your secret is out, Adalyn. I'm going to take you someplace safe." He dragged her toward the bathroom. "Wait inside while I pack, okay? Please do not scream or draw attention to us, Adalyn. Do you understand me?" He shook her a little, face reddening when she didn't immediately answer. "Do you understand me?" he asked, leaning closer.

"Y-yes," she said. "I understand." At that point, getting away from him—even as far as the bathroom—would be better. He was hurting her and didn't even seem to notice it.

"Good," he said, reaching up to smooth her hair back in place as she stepped inside. "You have to know that I will do whatever it takes to keep you safe, Adalyn. I've spent months thinking of nothing else. I've dedicated my entire life to this cause. After all you've been through..." He shook his head. Were those tears in his eyes?

Madness, she thought. *This is what it's like to face madness.*

He closed the door softly behind her. She looked around, knowing already that there was no window, only a vent. If she screamed, what would he do? She thought about the Palmers, just arrived at the cabins. Those four kids. And Gramps...She put a hand on her head and looked left and right, trying to figure a way out. If he saw her, being hauled away screaming, would his heart give out right then and there?

No, no, no, she thought. *You have to figure another way out of this. A smart way.*

She thought back to an interview with a kidnapping victim who had been held for months in a cellar-prison. It was only in convincing her captor that she was with him, that she loved him, that he eased his guard and she could make her escape. Could that be her way out too?

She stared at herself in the mirror. *Oh, Adi. Why did you not take that gun?*

—⁂—

Over in a back office at Two Medicine Lodge, Chase tried to concentrate as they completed their examination of the dead mother bear. Her cubs had been found and captured. But this beautiful creature wouldn't be around to nurture them. To show them how to forage beneath rotted logs for insects, or among the huckleberry branches for fruit, or how to corner a fish in the shallows of a river...

Still, he kept thinking of Adi. He checked his watch for the hundredth time. Hannah glanced up at him, her blue eyes still piercing through her plastic lab goggles. "Am I keeping you from something urgent?" she asked.

"No," he said, even though he felt like he was being slowly ripped in two. Half of him wanted to stay here, see if they could find some clue as to who this murdering predator might be. Half of him wanted to race for his Jeep and get over the pass, back to Adi. It had almost been an hour. In a few minutes, he would step outside and call her again. Find out what she'd heard from Bea. Surely she'd tell him all was well. *False alarm*, she'd say. *See you when I see you.*

But even as he helped Hannah lift one of the bear's paws and scrape blood from beneath her claws, his mind kept screaming *Adi.*

Adi, Adi girl, please be taking close care...

—◊◊◊—

Minutes later, Ken opened the bathroom door and grabbed hold of her arm. "I have everything ready. You take those two bags and I'll take these. We'll go straight to my car. Do not call out to anyone, you understand? *Anyone.*" He pushed his vest aside and she saw the holster and the pistol tucked inside. "I do not want this to end in violence. I'm a peaceable sort, Adalyn. You'll see. But today...well, it might take extreme measures to extricate you. To get you some-place safe. Understood?"

She nodded numbly. "Yes."

"If anyone speaks to you, you wave and say something to put them off, okay? Make them think you'll see them in a bit. Just tell them that we're heading out on a date. Got it?"

"Yes," she said, seizing on this. If she could tell Bea they were going on a date, she'd sound the alarm. But what if she didn't see them? What if she was down at the docks? Adalyn thought about running. Would he really shoot her? When he claimed to care for her? But then she thought about that unhinged look he had in his eyes, right before he stashed her in the bathroom. His blushing rage when she turned down his offer to go kayaking.

He looked around. "I hate to leave a mess for your grand-father," he said. "But he has Mrs. Larson, right? She'll see to it. And when we get to Canada, you can call him. Tell him you're well. Safe." He reached out and took her hand. Brought it to his lips and kissed it. "I know you'll worry about him."

It took everything in Adi not to recoil.

"You'll see, Adalyn. I'm not a monster. I'm your savior. I'm here to rescue you." He cast her that lopsided grin. When she didn't return it, it swiftly turned into a frown. "Adalyn…"

"I understand," she said hurriedly. Right now, she only wanted to get him away from Gramps and the other guests of the cabin complex. She'd figure out how to escape him when no one else was in danger. After all, this was all her fault. If she hadn't gone on that show, if she hadn't managed to pick up a stalker, then no one else would be dealing with a de-lusional man with a gun. She thought back to the stack of photos in that computer file. And the file on Chase. *Chase…*

"Come on," Ken said, gesturing toward the two duffel bags.

"What about clothes for me?" she asked. "If we're going to be gone for a long time, I'll need clothes. If I can just stop in the cabin for a minute—"

"Adalyn," he said, touching her chin. Again, she struggled not to shrink away. "My love, don't you know I've already thought of that? Those two bags are yours."

———

They'd finally hit a stopping point in their exam, and Chase peeled off his paper jumpsuit and strode outside, searching for a signal. Finding a connection, he quickly dialed Adi.

No one answered.

He immediately dialed Gene's cabin. The old man still had a land line.

Still, no answer.

Then he dialed Bea and Logan, choosing the boat launch phone, knowing someone would be there. Bea picked up.

"Bea," he said, interrupting her chirpy, formal boat launch greeting. "It's Chase. Have you seen Adi?"

"Yeah," she said. "She came over this morning. Asked if I'd left her flowers. I was—"

"Did you leave those flowers for her, Bea?"

"No."

"What'd she do then?"

"She said she had to check on something. Told me if she wasn't back in an hour, to come and check on her."

"How long has it been?"

"Just about an hour now."

"Can I speak to Logan?"

"Chase," she said, her voice lowering in concern. "What's up?"

"Logan! Please, Bea! Let me talk to him."

She apparently turned and handed the phone to his brother. Chase had never talked to her that way. But his sense of urgency was growing...*Adi!*

"Chase?" Logan asked, coming on the line.

"I'm worried something's wrong," he said. "Adi's stalker might be there with you all. Can you grab your gun and go check on her?"

"I'm on it," he said, already on the move.

"I'm staying on the phone with you. I need...I need to know she's okay."

"Got it."

Chase paced while he listened to his brother run for the boathouse, find his revolver, then run over to the cabins. Listened to him knock on the door. Gramps coming to answer it, after forever. Then a woman's faint call, in the distance.

"It's Bea," Logan said in the phone. Again he was huffing, running, apparently.

Chase heard their muffled conversation. Could only hear a few words.

Adi. Ken. In a car. He's taking her!

"Logan!" he cried. "Use your phone and call 911! Have law enforcement close every exit to the park! Tell them Ken is trying to kidnap Adi! Now let me talk to Bea again."

He took a deep breath, not wanting to scare his sister-in-law more than she already was. "Beatrice, tell me what Ken looks like. Height. Weight. What he's driving."

After she told him he hung up, called dispatch and repeated the order. "This is a code red," he said. "Close every exit to the park."

Stacy, the dispatcher, was already typing. He heard the loud clicking of her ancient keyboard in the background.

Walt Boyce, a law enforcement ranger, overheard Chase and came closer. He waved over Sam Johnson, another ranger, to listen in.

"There is a suspected kidnapping taking place right now," Chase said to Stacy, glad that he could inform Walt and Sam at the same time. "Suspect is named Kenneth. He's six foot, sandy-brown hair, 180 pounds, mid- to late-20s. Driving a blue sedan with Georgia plates. Victim is a brunette female, twenty-four, a hundred-and-thirty pounds, 5'8". It's Adalyn Stalling."

The female dispatcher paused. "Our Adi?" There wasn't a member of the park service who didn't know Adalyn or her grandfather.

"Our Adi," he said grimly. "Do it. Do it, fast, Stacy."

"On it," she said, typing furiously. Then she said, "Code has been released."

"Good. I'm going to try and secure an air lift." Walt nodded and turned away to speak in the radio worn strapped to his shoulder. "Be there as soon as I can."

"Roger that. We'll find her, Chase. He couldn't have gone far." He hoped she was right.

But as the helicopter swept into the air twenty minutes later and Chase looked out at the vastness of Glacier Park, he knew that if Ken was smart, there were a thousand different directions he could head. Particularly if he ditched his car.

Please, he prayed silently, tightening his grip on the rifle in his hands as he stared out at the velvety acres of pine trees, *don't let him ditch the car.*

—⁓—

"Hop out," Ken said, after he had turned onto a dirt road Adi had never been on, eventually pulling up next to an old Ford truck that rivaled her grandfather's in age.

"What are we doing here?" she said.

"We're switching to this truck," he said. "Your friends back at the cabins," he said, hooking his thumb backward as he stood outside the cab. "They saw you with me. If they're worried, they'll be looking for this car."

She hesitated, realizing this was a tangible juncture. Was it here that she made a run for it? Because if they were in an unidentified vehicle…a vehicle no one was looking for…

"Hey," he said, coming around the sedan. He took her hand and pulled her close.

She fought to not squirm away.

He lifted her chin. "Don't worry, sweetheart. I've got this figured out," he said. "It doesn't matter that Bea saw us. Don't you see?" he said with a smile. "I've thought of everything. You're safe. You'll always be safe with me."

She knew he was waiting for her to respond. "Th-thank you," she managed.

"Anything for you, Adalyn. Now come." He led her to the truck cab and opened the door for her. Shut it behind her. Then he tossed their bags in the bed and climbed in beside her. "It's not the best ride, but I figured if an old truck was good enough for your grandfather, it was good enough for me too. And it will help us blend in when we reach Canada."

"Yes," she forced herself to say. "Good thinking."

"That's your man," he said, tapping his temple. "Always thinking. Always thinking, thinking, thinking." He turned the truck around in a U-turn and instead of turning right, which would have taken them back to the highway, he turned left. "Thinking, thinking," he continued to whisper. "Thinking, thinking…"

She frowned. "Wh-where are we going?"

He smiled, seeming to remember himself. "I've mapped it all out. We'll drive until sundown. Camp out until morning. I've figured out a way to get into Canada," he said proudly. "All via logging roads, once we clear the park border."

"Oh?"

"Yes. From what I can tell, there is a good ten miles that is only patrolled by border agents on horseback, maybe once a week, if that. We'll cover that last stretch on foot. And then we'll be home free. It will take us a good fifty miles of hiking, but then we'll reach a town. It's not much, but I can pretty much guarantee that they don't have cable or an Internet signal strong enough to ever have seen an episode of *The One*. We'll be safe there. We'll have time there, just for us. We can get to know each other better."

"Sure," she said, hiding a shiver over *get to know each other better*. "It's a good plan, Ken."

Her words made him grin like he'd just won the lottery.

What, Lord?, she prayed. *What am I supposed to do?*

CHAPTER 23

What now? Chase wondered, still in the helicopter. The blue sedan had not been spotted on any of the main roads, nor along the highway to Kalispell—the quickest exit. The chopper banked at the valley's door when they saw the highway roadblocks erected by highway patrol. In short order, they found out from Stacy that all exits were monitored.

"Kalispell police chopper is in flight now and will monitor the West side," she said.

"They can't leave without someone seeing them, Chase," Hannah said, touching his arm.

He nodded. But then why had they not been found?

"Let's check the road to Bowman," he called to Walt and the pilot.

"Roger that," said the pilot.

Chase turned to eye the other three rangers in the helicopter with him—Hannah, Sam, and Michael. Walt was up front with the pilot. Sam and Walt were law enforcement rangers, present at Two Medicine to try and figure out who was killing the animals. They were trained for this kind of thing. But Michael and Hannah were wildlife biologists. Chase pulled off his ear protection, and they did too, when he gestured for them to do so.

"You guys don't have to do this," he called over the roar of the chopper blades and wind. "We can circle back and drop you off in Apgar."

Hannah lifted her chin. "This dude has your girl," she said. "We're going to help you get her back."

He smiled, grateful. She really was a great partner. Setting aside whatever candle she'd lit for him in order to do what was right. Michael nodded. "I'm in too," he said. "Let's find Adi and bring her home to Gene."

Gene. Adi's grandfather had to be beside himself. Was he all right? Chase pulled out his phone, found a fleeting signal and tried dialing Bea.

"Bea?" he asked, when she answered. "We're up in the chopper, looking for Adi. Will you go be with Gene until we find her?"

"Already here, bro," she said. "Gene and I are just hanging out. When you find Adi, tell her Gramps is just fine."

"Thanks, Bea," he said, feeling a new rush of love for his sister-in-law.

"Logan's out at the park entrance," Bea said.

And then he lost the signal. But it seemed to strengthen him, knowing Adi's grandfather was cared for. Knowing his brother was helping, any which way he could. *Do you feel that, Adi girl? Do you feel that? We're coming for you. We're going to find you.*

And when he had his hands on the man who had dared to take her...He grimaced and looked away, before any of his teammates might see the rage on his face.

If he had hurt her...

If he had laid a hand upon her...

Well, the man had better pray that Walt, Sam, Michael, or Hannah could stop him. Because never in his life had he wanted to beat another man. Beat him until he begged him to stop. The rage building in his chest surprised him. He could actually see himself beating Kenneth to a bloody mess.

He leaned his head back against the seat, feeling his gut clench in fear and fury. Why would God allow him and Adi to separate all these years, only to find each other now? Allow her to go on that show? Pick up a stalker? A man who now threatened to separate him and Adi forever?

Dimly, he recognized that "allow" was not the best term. Adi and he had chosen their paths. Chosen other people to date. Even as far as Adi had "dated" so many others. Free will, and all, had its cost.

His heart switched from rage to panic to resolve. *We'll find her. We have to find her.*

But as he stared down the long, bumpy gravel road line toward Bowman and saw no vehicle on the road—other than an old, beat-up Ford truck—he wavered.

Where are you, Adi girl? Where could you have gone?

—∿—

Adi heard the chopper roaring up behind them, even before Kenneth seemed to register its presence. As it passed them, he leaned forward—just a bit, so as not to be seen—to gaze upward. When it continued on, didn't bank to come around, he smiled.

"See there?" he said, gesturing upward. "Your man is a genius," he said. "They're looking for a sedan. Not this old truck."

"You are," she said. *A sick, evil genius,* she added silently. *Now. How to outsmart one such as you?*

He checked his odometer. "Fifty more miles, Adalyn. Fifty more miles and we're on our way to freedom." He reached for her hand and she allowed him to take it, kiss it. His lips were cold, wet. But had she not managed to fake it with a few bachelors on *The One* to spare their feelings? In much the same way, she had assumed the same stance. Now, as if she were on camera, she strived to find a way to preserve this man's dignity in a critical hour. Inherently, she understood this was vital.

Because if Kenneth felt that he had been disrespected, if he felt his stance as protector and savior was undermined, she wasn't sure what would happen.

They drove on, bumping painfully along, the truck's shocks gone a good ten years before. *How long until we reach the border?* she thought. Surely they were reaching the end of their fifty-mile drive.

All she knew was that once they came to a stop, she would need to make a run for it.

—⁓—

"Rollins, we found the sedan," came Stacy's voice from dispatch.

"Roger, that," he said excitedly. "Where?"

"Off Four-Mile Drive. Looks like they took another vehicle from there."

Chase sucked in his breath.

"Any idea what kind of vehicle?" Walt asked, on the same radio frequency.

"Treads tell us it was a truck," she said.

A truck...They'd passed a truck on their way to Bowman, hadn't they? One of only three vehicles they'd passed. And only a few miles or so behind them.

Walt and he shared a long look. They were thinking the same thing. Recognized the possibility.

"Let's go back," Chase said into his helmet microphone. "Make sure that's just an old truck…"

"Roger that," Walt said. Then to the pilot, "Rodriquez."

"Yes, sir?"

"Let's head back to that old Ford we spotted earlier. Set down on the road in front of it, if necessary, to stop it. That driver may very well have our girl."

The pilot hesitated. "Sure we shouldn't wait for Kalispell police?"

"Let me say it this way," Chase said into his microphone. "That driver may very well have *my* girl and we're closer."

The pilot didn't hesitate longer. He banked in a steep curve.

—◊◊◊—

Kenneth cursed as he saw the helicopter heading straight back toward them, just twenty miles short of the border.

At first, they both thought that the chopper was simply returning from their reconnaissance mission and it would likely sweep by. But as they got closer, the chopper flew lower—so low that it was barely twenty feet above the ground, hurtling toward them down the road. It was coming for them.

Kenneth swerved to the side of the road and slammed to a stop.

"Out," he cried, reaching for her and pulling out his pistol at the same time—not allowing her to escape out her own door and make a run for the helicopter. The chopper was slowly lowering to a landing spot on the road in front of them. Adalyn stared at it, mesmerized. Help was here! They were going to rescue her and—

Ken grabbed her hand and bodily hauled her across the bench seat, practically dragging her out and into his arms. "C'mon!" he cried, abandoning all his carefully packed bags, clearly thinking only of their escape. Adalyn glanced at his gun. What choice did she have?

They ran into the steep, deeply shadowed valley to the left of the road, Ken dragging Adi behind him. As the helicopter landed on the road, a shower of fine gravel swept through the air and down upon them. They ducked, feeling it rain down. Then Kenneth yanked her forward and they ran down the steep hill. Beneath them, a creek wound its way westward.

She fought to figure out where she was, even as Kenneth pulled her from tree to tree. If they'd been heading north, and the helicopter had landed on the road to the north of them, she figured they were moving northwest. Ken wasn't losing track of his ultimate goal. Nor of her, never allowing her to get a foot farther than his reach.

She was chagrined by his attentiveness, and struggled to catch her breath at each, lurching stop. It was odd, this. Running from those who might save you. But inherently she knew that if she gave Kenneth any inkling that she wasn't totally with him, he might turn on her. He was unstable. Possibly unstable enough to shoot her and then kill himself, having failed at this goal to make her his own. Even then, he turned mad, blue eyes her way. He gripped her wrist.

"This way," he whispered, nodding toward a shadowy hollow.

Seeing no other option, she nodded. Together, they ran.

CHAPTER 24

Chase leaned back, holding his tranquilizer rifle across his chest, wondering if he'd really seen what he just thought he'd seen. Had Adi really gone along with him? Why wasn't she fighting to break free?

He'd had them both in the view of his scope. As had Walt, who brandished a far more fearsome weapon than he. It was good they were armed—he saw the pistol in Kenneth's hand. "What do you make of it?" he dared to ask the older man.

"She's going along with it," Walt said. "The cow afraid to break from a bull who's lost his wits in the middle of mating season. She'll find the right time, right place, to make a run for it. She just hasn't found it yet."

In spite of himself, Chase laughed under his breath. He thought back through different wildlife scenarios he'd witnessed. Females, in the crossfire of males. The smartest did not intervene. He knew that Adi's deeply-felt feminist roots would balk at the thought, but he could not toss out Walt's analogy. *So, she's just rolling with him to keep herself—and maybe us—safe*, he surmised. The trick, then, would be to find a place in which he could divide Ken from Adi.

He looked down the valley in which the two scurried along, from tree to tree. Time was short. Daylight was fading. And if Kenneth succeeded in disappearing into the dark, Chase knew they may not find them again on this side of the Canadian border. And on the other side, it would become infinitely more complicated.

Hannah turned a corner and eyed him. He waved her and Michael closer. "We have to find a way to divide them," he said lowly. "But if we do," he warned, "this guy might become unhinged."

"Understood," Hannah said. "I'll roll toward the south."

"And I'll veer north," said Walt.

"I'll take the west flank," said Sam, sliding the strap of his rifle strap more firmly about him.

"Michael, you go with Hannah, okay?"

"No, Chase, I've got it—" she began.

He knew it wasn't kosher. Not the current way of the PC. But he didn't care. Even if Hannah was a dude, he'd want to make sure he was safe too. It was his responsibility to take care of his partner, and she only carried a tranquilizer gun. "Hannah, just go with it, all right?" he asked, voice high and tight.

She shrugged and Michael prepared to follow her out on the southern flank.

Walt turned back to Chase and paused, running his hand along his rifle again. "So, do we consider this guy a lethal danger?"

Chase paused over his words. Was Kenneth a deadly menace? Or like a mad beast, needing to be brought down? But then he thought of Adi, and his last glimpse of the man's grip on her wrist. The thought that it was this man, who had been in her apartment in Chicago. The man who had tracked her all the way here, to Glacier. Set up his cabin, right in front of them for the past week. All in order to be close to her.

"Do what you need to. The priority is Adalyn's safety. If you can bring him in by winging him, great. If it takes more..."

Sam leaned in, offering his fist to bump Chase's. "Roger that," he said.

"Roger that," the rest repeated, moving off into the woods.

Chase's heart beat in triple-time. What if he'd just sent his teammates off to pursue his girlfriend, at the risk of their own lives? But then he checked himself. Wouldn't he do the same, regardless of who had had been kidnapped? He traced back through his decisions, feeling more secure by the second. This was as much about his responsibility as a ranger as it was about being Adi's boyfriend.

Boyfriend, he thought. *Is that what I am?* The title seemed trivial. Inadequate for what he felt for her. Impossibly inadequate. He wanted her back in his arms. Now.

—⁓—

Ken hauled her against him in the shadow of a giant ponderosa. They were both heaving for breath.

"Kenneth!" shouted Chase behind him. "Give this up! We have you surrounded!"

"Go away!" Ken shouted. "Leave us be!"

"Neither of us want Adalyn hurt. Send her out, okay? Then you and I can talk about how we can resolve all this."

Ken glanced down at her. He frowned.

He'd seen it. Adi had let her face register relief at the sound of Chase's voice.

He pulled her closer, his hands around her forearms again. "He does not love you like I do," he growled, shaking her a little. "Can't you see that?"

She looked up at him, not knowing what to say.

He shook her again. "Adalyn, don't you see? You make the wrong choices, again and again. First Adam. Then Connor. Now this guy." He reached into his back pocket and pulled out a plastic zip tie. Swiftly, he tied her hands together.

"No, Ken. You don't need to do this," she said.

"I do," he said. "Because you are obviously not in your right mind."

His words made her want to laugh in his face. But she knew that if she gave into that, he'd only become further enraged.

"Ken, what if you let me go?" she said. "What if we went back to West Glacier and talked this out?"

He shook his head, disgust twisting his mouth. "Have you learned nothing?" he said, leaning close to her face. "I will do anything to get you to safety. And I will be the man beside you forever. Not some ranger," he added in disgust. "And if you try to run from me, Adalyn, if you go to him, I will shoot him."

Adalyn swallowed hard. He was trembling with rage now.

"Don't you see?" he said, letting go of one of her arms to pull the pistol back out from his holster. "It's for your own good. I'd kill him so he can never break your heart like those others did. *That's* how much I love you."

"Ken," she said, slowly shaking her head. "That is not love. That is insanity." Before she could think twice, she wrenched loose of his grip and reached for his gun. It toppled out of his hand and into the thick brush behind them.

Adi thought about searching for it, but she knew that pausing would only allow him to grab hold of her again. She didn't think he would shoot her in the back. But even if he did, wasn't that better than if he shot at Chase? Someone around them—if they were indeed surrounded—would have a shot at him if she was safely away.

But she had to get away...

"Adalyn!" he screamed. She could hear him sweeping aside summer-dry branches looking for his pistol. "Get back here!"

She continued tearing down the steep bank, tripped over a hidden log, rolled, got to her feet and ran again.

There was more shouting behind her. Chase? Hannah? But all she could think of was escaping. Gaining enough distance from Ken so that the others could take him down. She heard the crack of a gun and instinctively dived to the forest floor again—in case the bullet was heading her way.

—⚬—

Chase was slowly approaching the ponderosa when he saw Adi and Ken scuffle, the gun tumble from Ken's hand and Adi begin running down the hillside. He brought up his tranquilizer gun to his shoulder, watching as Ken searched for his pistol.

"Stop!" he cried. "It's over, Ken! Put down your gun!"

"Put down your gun!" Hannah repeated from the other side, as Ken rose, half-crouched, with pistol in hand again. "We have you surrounded!"

"Drop it and put your hands on your head!" Walt said, easing into Chase's line of vision, gun at his shoulder.

Ken, eyes wide, looked from them to Adi, still running down the hill, then sneered in rage.

"For Adalyn!" he cried, bringing the pistol up to point at Chase.

Walt, Hannah and he all fired at once. Walt's bullet pierced the man's thigh, making him shudder at the impact, then stumble backward. Hannah and Chase both shot him with tranquilizing darts. It was twice the dosage that they had calculated they needed to bring him down…maybe enough to kill him. Kenneth wavered, took a stumbling step, then fell flat to his face.

Chase ran past him—leaving it to his teammates to see to him—continuing down the hill.

"Adalyn?" he called. "Adi! It's me! You're safe!"

Her head popped up from a patch of green ferns, pine needles and weeds in her hair, dirt smudged across her cheek. But never, ever had Chase thought she'd looked more beautiful. He reached her at last and helped her to her feet.

"Adi, are you hurt?" he asked.

"Oh, Chase," she said, leaning in to him. She glanced over his shoulder. "Ken?"

"He's down. The others are taking him into custody. It's over, Adi." He grimaced as he saw the plastic tie holding her wrists so tightly together her fingers were turning blue. He reached for his pocket knife and swiftly cut it apart.

Once she was free, she flung her arms around him and held him tight. "Chase," she said. "Oh, thank God. Thank God you are all right."

"Thank God *you* are all right," he said. "You gave me quite the scare."

"What about Gramps? I had to get Ken away from him before…"

"I understand," he said. And before she could ask, he reached for his radio and connected to dispatch. "This is Rollins, do you read me?"

"I read you, Rollins," Stacy said.

"We have Adi. She's safe. And the suspect is in custody," he said, watching as the others lifted the unconscious man and began carrying him up the hill. "Let Kalispell Regional and the police know we're bringing in an injured prisoner."

"Roger that."

"Stace? Tell Gene his girl is okay too, all right?"

"Right away," said the dispatcher.

Adi hugged him again and he kissed the top of her head. Then he lifted a hand to pull out the weeds and pine needles. "You up for the hike back up? Or do you need me to carry you?"

"No," she said. "I can walk. But hold my hand, would you? Don't let me go, Chase."

"I won't," he said, taking her trembling hand in his own. *Never again*, he added silently.

CHAPTER 25

It proved to be a long night, but Chase was true to his word. Through it all, he never left her side, other than to go and get her tea or something to eat. Not that she could eat much. They had reached the hospital with Ken—who nearly died from the combined doses of tranquilizer in his bloodstream and the bullet wound to his leg—but appeared to be stable when twilight finally gave way to night. The police took initial statements from her and asked her to come in the next day too. They assured her that Ken would be watched at all times; even now, he was shackled to the bed rail.

"He's not going anywhere," said the detective, thumbs tucked in his belt. "You can rest easy tonight, Miss Stalling. You have my word on it."

She'd nodded gratefully and allowed Chase to lead her out. They were heading home, where she knew that Gramps, Bea and Logan were eagerly awaiting them. Hannah and Walt were waiting outside, and together, the four of them drove back to the park. Chase sat in the back with her, one arm around her shoulders, her hand in his and resting on his thigh. For a long time, Adalyn struggled to come up with the right words to say. "Th-thanks for coming after me," she said to them all at last. "I don't know…I don't know how I would've escaped him if you hadn't found us."

"You would've found a way," Chase said, giving her hand a squeeze.

"Maybe," she said.

"You were tough back there," Hannah said over her shoulder as she drove. "Making a run for it."

"I just…I just couldn't stand it. The thought of one of you hurt because of me. And you all…" Her voice cracked. She coughed and gathered herself again. "You all put your lives at risk. Michael and Sam too. For me."

"For one of our own," Walt said. He smiled at her. "Can you imagine the misery that Gene would have put us through if something had happened to his granddaughter on our watch?"

That made her smile. "Still. I'm grateful. Thank you."

"Any time," Hannah said. "Especially if it means I can stop a poacher to boot."

Adi took a deep breath and looked outside to the dark, silhouetted forest. Ken had killed all those innocent animals to distract Chase. Keep him away from her. How many more might he have killed if the Palmers hadn't broken her cover? If the threat of the media raining down upon them wasn't imminent? She groaned and covered her face.

"What?" Chase whispered.

"The media," she said. "They're going to be all over this. I disappear for a time and when next they hear of me, it's this news? They're going to be relentless."

"But they'll have to get through me," he said. "I'm taking a leave of absence, Adi. Whatever comes, we'll face it together. And maybe, just maybe, the faster you answer all their questions, the faster it will all blow over?"

"Maybe," she said. Right now, even the thought of it made her bone-weary. But the fact that he had taken a leave of absence and was ready to do anything it took to help get her through this, made her smile a little again. She covered his hand with hers. "Thank you," she whispered.

"Of course," he whispered back. Then he pulled her closer to kiss her temple.

"You know you're going to just make it worse, right?" she asked.

"Me? How?"

"You. When people find out I've fallen hard for a big, handsome ranger…Well, they're just going to be all the more curious to know all the details. I'm talking all the details. Seriously, you had better get ready."

He considered that a moment. "I think America just wants to know you're okay, Adi. That you've found love."

"Is that what this is?" she whispered. "Love?"

"Well, I don't know what you think about me, Adi, but it didn't take this kidnapping for me to know I'm head-over-heels in love with you."

She smiled.

"Are you in love with me?" he asked.

"So far gone it's not even funny," she said, lifting her lips to his for a quick, tender kiss, well aware that their friends in the front were doing their best to give them some privacy.

"Won't this thing—this thing between you and me—help satisfy their curiosity?"

She rolled her eyes and grinned. "You, mister, really have no idea what you're in for."

"Regardless, as long as I get to do it with you, I'll consider it a win."

"I'll remind you that you said that," she said.

Given their remote location, it took until the following afternoon for the news crews to get to Glacier. To keep stress at a minimum for Gramps, she'd agreed to a press conference at the Lake McDonald Lodge at five, following up with individual interviews from five-thirty to eight. A publicist at Smith & Jessen had arranged it all.

"You'll be with NBC at five-thirty," Ivy said on the phone. "ABC at six, and CBS at six-thirty. *Wall Street Journal* at seven and *USA Today* at seven-thirty. That will cover all the biggies. *The Today Show* would like you on tomorrow morning at five-thirty. They'll create a temporary studio space at the lodge today."

Adalyn sighed and rubbed her eyes. "Can you put them off until seven-thirty?"

"Since they're getting an exclusive TV interview with both you and Chase? Absolutely. I'll see to it. Then if you can answer questions via email from some other journalists, we'll have covered the main bases. Oh, and Jeremy Ferris from *The One* called too."

"What'd he want?"

"He wants you back on the show, of course. To sit down with you for an interview. They'll air it during the next season of the show."

"Tell him—tell him I'll think about it."

"Will do."

"Thanks, Ivy. For everything."

"Absolutely. Give me a shout if I can do anything else for you from here. You have something simple to wear tonight? No plaid or gingham, right? That never plays well with the cameras."

"Right," Adalyn said, stifling a laugh. What did the woman think she wore here? Lumberjack clothes? Although she had to admit, she'd thought about borrowing Chase's green plaid to wear over a tee and jeans. There was something deliciously intimate in thinking about being all wrapped up in his shirt...

The first interviews made Adalyn tremble and perspire, remembering the trauma of what had occurred the day before. But Chase had sat next to her—off-camera—his warm hand on her knee through it all, and she had absorbed his silent encouragement like a tattered sponge.

She was partway through the final TV interview when the anchor delved into what she had been doing here at the park since she arrived. As she spoke of her renovation efforts, the desire to hold on to a place that had been in her family's possession for decades, it struck her. She could use this opportunity to gain public support for her efforts! Not only would she ensure that the renovated cabins would be booked solid for the summer...public opinion might very well convince the park officials that she should be given the chance.

Even as she was wrapping the interview, she was thinking what Ivy might do with this particular interview, already mentally making arrangements to reach out to *Montana Living, Tiny House Today*, and various home-improvement web sites and magazines.

"What is going on in that beautiful mind?" Chase asked, as CBS cleared out and the *Wall Street Journal's* team moved in. "I can practically see the wheels turning."

"I am mentally securing the future of A Cabin by the Lake," she whispered back.

He sat back in his chair, arms crossed and stared at her in wonder. "You've just gone through one of the most terrifying days of your life and your mind is on marketing?"

"Hey, something good has to come out of all this hoopla, right?" she said, as a journalist arrived and introduced herself and her photographer.

"I suppose it does," Chase said. And his wondrous grin made her smile all the more.

Chase had slept on Gene's family room couch both nights, refusing to be farther from Adi in case she needed anything. But he went over to the boathouse cabin to shower before their morning interview. As arranged, they canoed over to the lodge together, deciding some time alone on the water would do them both good before they were on camera.

"So, your first big interview," she said to him as he took her hand and they began walking to the beach. "You ready?"

He took a deep breath and blew out his cheeks. "Watching you yesterday helped."

"You know they're going to want to know a lot about us, right?"

He gave her a slow smile. "That's fine. Nothin' secret in how I feel about you, Adi girl." He pulled her to a stop and lifted a hand to her cheek. "I'm in deep, girl. My heart is yours. I knew it before that guy kidnapped you. But after…" He lifted his head to look to the lake, shook it as if he were trying to shake free of the memory, then dug a toe of his boot into the rocks. He returned his gaze to her. "After he took you Adi, I thought…Well, I thought if anything happened to you, I might die myself. The thought of being apart from you…" He shook his head again and the pain in his hazel eyes made her own heart lurch. "Well, it just about does me in. I don't want to be apart from you, Adi. Ever again."

"Ever is a long time," she said quietly.

"Yes. Yes, it is." He paused. "Look, this isn't how I planned it. Heck, I really haven't planned it at all. But I just know, know deep in my bones, Adalyn Stalling, that I love you. With everything in me. I want you to marry me, if you'll have me." He huffed a laugh. "I don't have a ring from a fancy jeweler to give you and I know this is really fast. But I..."

He slowly lowered himself to one knee and pulled her closer, so her hand was over his heart. "Will you marry me, Adi? I'll always cherish and adore you. Will you be my wife?"

She stared down at him, at this face that she suddenly couldn't ever remember *not* loving. He loved her. He really loved her.

Still, she hesitated. The last time a man had gotten down on bent knee and proposed, she had gleefully accepted. And then his rejection had nearly destroyed her.

But this man—this wonderful man who had long been her friend—was not some rendition of a television show's manufactured groom-in-waiting. He was hers. Wholly hers.

And yet the *risk*. It made her heart falter.

"Adi," he said quietly. "Mark my words. I will never leave you. I am yours. I think I've always been yours."

And it was those words that convinced her. She nodded happily, tears coming to her eyes. "Yes, Chase. You are mine, just as I am yours. And I would love nothing more than being your wife."

His face alit in surprise. "Really?"

"Really," she said, but he was already on his feet, sweeping her up into his arms and hooting with joy. She laughed and smiled down at him. They were engaged. She and Chase were going to get married.

The *Today Show* hosts and One Nation were going to go wild.

CHAPTER 26

As expected, people did go wild over the news that Adalyn Stalling was no longer America's biggest loser at love. Everyone seemed hungry for a happily-ever-after story and was eager to learn more. Together, Adalyn and Chase weathered the media storm over the weeks that followed, electing to go on hikes and kayaking together on their days off, rather than anywhere public.

After a busy day among the cabins, they paddled out on the lake to enjoy a pristine, late August night. Twilight lasted a long time in Montana, but the full moon was due to rise as dark truly descended. All day they'd talked about getting out on the water to watch it. After they'd settled Gramps for the night, they'd practically run for the docks.

"Being engaged is so different this time," she said, dipping her paddle in tandem with Chase.

"How so?" he asked.

"I'm more settled." She studied his dark profile as he drifted close.

He set his paddle across the front to rest, then gripped

the edge of her kayak and pulled them side-by-side.

"You make me feel settled, Chase,"

"Just as long as you're settled, but not *settling*."

She smiled. "No way. With you? Settling? I feel like I won the lottery. No, I mean with Connor, after the proposal, I was unsettled all the time. There was constant upheaval. For a while we blamed it on the external chaos. But it was really internal upheaval, between the two of us."

She turned toward him. "You and I…We've had our share of external upheaval, but never internal." She paused and set down her paddle too and looked out at the lake. "When we were engaged, Connor and I were just getting to know each other, really, without a camera crew around. On the show, you're always presenting your best self, you know? Now that I look back on it, I think we both sensed something was wrong. He was just faster to realize it."

Chase took her hand. "I think it wasn't that he was faster. I think it was that you were more loyal. More willing to keep trying to find a way." He lifted her hand to his lips and tenderly kissed it. "That loyalty trait? That desire to find a way to make it work? I think it will serve us well in our marriage."

"I hope so," she said.

"I know so, Adi girl."

They were silent then, drifting on the water until they came to a standstill. The reflection of a sky full of stars made Adi feel like they were surrounded by a sea of light. They could make out the mountains' silhouette, with a rising moon behind their collective bank. But for the moment, between the mountain guard and the warm glow of the cabins far enough in the distance, nothing intruded on their star gazing. Adi looked up to the Milky Way—never more visible than when she was in Glacier—and countless constellations that Gramps had helped her, Chase and Logan learn.

"There's the Big Dipper," she said, finding it at last. "With this many stars, it's hard to pick out! In Chicago, it's easy."

"I prefer to call it *Ursa Major*," Chase intoned.

"Of course you do," she said. "'The Greater Bear,' right? How did they see a bear in that?"

"It's the back and tail," he said easily.

"Oh, right," she said, not seeing the rest of the bear at all. "I guess those ancient astronomers had a better imagination than I do."

"There's Orion," he said, spotting the three-star belt.

"Yep. I still like the 'W' that Cassiopeia makes," she said, finding that one too.

"Why?"

"I don't know," she said, smiling. "I guess whenever I could spot it, it reminded me of our summers together with Gramps out on the dock or by the bonfire."

"Maybe it was God, reminding you of me. Calling you home."

"Maybe," she smiled.

A breeze came up, ruining the reflection of the stars in the water. "Ooo, feel that?" she said, rubbing her arms. "I think that's a touch of fall."

"I don't know about you, but that's fine by me," Chase said, kissing her hand again. "I can't wait for fall."

"Me neither." Their wedding was set for October. By then, Kenneth would surely be on his way to prison or a mental health facility for criminals, and their presentation for the renewal of the cabin concession would be done. No, she couldn't wait for October, but the best reason was that she was going to become Chase's wife. Forever.

They drifted in the breeze, occasionally turned to the east, waiting as the glow of the moon behind the mountains became steadily brighter, even as twilight finally faded to the west. The orb crested the mountains and climbed until it at last cleared the Divide and rose, as if free.

"Well, that never gets old," Adalyn said.

"It certainly doesn't," he said.

"I don't know why I feel like moonrises should take longer than sunsets."

"Maybe it's the hour?"

"Maybe. In ways, I wish they both took longer. They're so…mesmerizing."

"A good way to start or end the day, taking the time to observe it."

"The best. Although I have to say I'm partial to moonrises over getting up in time to see a sunrise."

They sat there for a while longer, relishing the shimmering reflection in the water that now streamed between the moon and them, like a heavenly link.

"You ready to head back?" he asked, feeling her shiver.

"I guess so," she said reluctantly. They separated and began paddling back toward the dock, and Adalyn thought back on the whirlwind of the weeks behind her. They had settled into a comfortable rhythm at the cabins. Each day, she greeted everyone who arrived, mostly to get it over with if they were fans that would recognize her. About a third seemed to look at her with faint recognition, a third were fans—some even wanting pictures—and a third had no idea she was anyone but the Cabin by the Lake's manager.

With Chase's help, they had made their way through the renovations of the remaining cabin pods, and given the media attention that followed her kidnapping and rescue—as well as their impending nuptials—they had easily filled every one, every night. It might have happened anyway, given the park's popularity and visitors' surprise that you had to make reservations way ahead of time to secure a room or a campsite, but Adi liked to think that something good came out of all of that trauma and drama.

"I hope we get another ten years," Adalyn said, as Chase held her kayak at the side of the dock and she climbed out.

"Me too," he said, knowing exactly what she meant. They'd talked it over again and again. "But if we don't, we have a plan, right?"

"Yes." The plan was to find a house in Columbia Falls to share with Gramps. Chase would end his leave of absence and resume his job as a park ranger; she would freelance for Smith & Jessen. Rhett had already approved that plan for seven months of the year; he'd likely be open to the other five. He dearly wanted her on *The One* account.

Chase pulled her into his arms and pushed the hair from her eyes. "Yes, you say, but I can hear the 'but' in that yes."

"But I really, really want to be here, on the lake. This is home. Right?"

"Adi girl," he said, dipping his head until his lips hovered over hers. "I think anywhere I am with you will feel like home to me. We have to trust God to lead us to that best place, together." He kissed her, softly, and then pulled back. "But God brought you back here. You've made amazing changes to the place. Why would God—and the park officials—not smile?"

"We'll see."

He took her hand and she followed him down the dock and onto the beach. He was right, of course. It was likely that she'd receive permission to continue the business—Gramps was handing it over to her—but she wanted to protect her heart. When a girl had been through what she had, she supposed it just was how it would always be. *Or maybe, maybe,* she thought, looking at her handsome fiancé as he stopped beside the cabin door and turned to her, *Chase's love will help heal this gap in my confidence.* Hadn't he already helped close it a good bit?

A week later, they were in Kalispell for a doctor's appointment. Doc Victor was pleasantly surprised at his latest lab work, and praised him for gaining some weight.

"Looks like you might be with us a bit longer, old friend," he'd said, patting him on the shoulder.

"Well, I have to see my granddaughter marry the kid next door, you know," he said, winking at Adalyn.

"Something to look forward to is always a good thing for a body." The doctor turned to Adi. "Maybe you can give this old dog something else to look forward to after the wedding?"

"Absolutely," she said. "I need him to show me how to winterize and care for the cabins. And next summer, to help me with the 'summer folk,' as he calls them. Returning guests love him." She paused. "That's if we get the renewal on our concession."

"Oh, we'll get it, Adi girl," Gramps said. "They'd be fools to refuse you."

"We'll see," she said. They were supposed to hear any day now, and she was on pins and needles.

After the appointment, they went to Norm's News for burgers and shakes, then to the thrift store to see if any new historical photographs had been brought in. Adalyn still had about ten cabins that needed a few. She'd just found a gem featuring workmen hovering precariously on the edge of the brand-new Hungry Horse dam when her cell phone rang.

"Hi, this is Adalyn," she answered, not recognizing the number.

Gramps and Chase continued to sift through the photographs in the bin in front of them.

"Adalyn, this is Neil Young," a deep voice said.

Adi reached out to grip Chase's arm and he turned to her, alarm on his face. She nodded, eyes wide, and then he knew. It was The Call.

"The board spent the day reviewing your proposal yesterday, Adalyn. I have to say, that between your presentation of what you want to do with the site and what you've already accomplished, there was little debate. We're granting you ten years."

Adi stifled a yelp and grinned, smiling and nodding at Chase and then Gramps. Then she tried to temper her excitement a bit to sound more professional. "Oh, Mr. Young, that is such good news. My grandfather, Chase and I will make you glad of that decision, I promise you."

They chitchatted a bit more before hanging up. Once done, Adi flung herself into Chase's arms. He hooted and lifted her up, turning her in a circle and then set her down so she could give Gramps a proper hug. "Can you believe it, Gramps? It's ours. For another ten years!"

"Oh, I can believe it, Adi girl," he said, hugging her tight. "You're a wonder. For more reasons than one."

"I couldn't agree more," Chase said, putting an arm around both of them.

EPILOGUE

After the media hype receded, when the summer-folk had all gone home and the lodges closed their doors for the season, as the tamaracks faded to a deep gold against the pine-green of their neighbors, Adi and Chase wed.

It was a small affair, with only their closest friends and family members invited to the point on the lake to witness them exchange their vows. There had been no invitations sent, no flowers ordered, no trips to a bridal salon—anything that might tip off the media. Adi hadn't wanted photographers with telescopic lenses or hovering helicopters to ruin this day. It was enough to deal with her mother and father— newly arrived from Singapore—and their collective angst over Gramps's diagnosis and all that Adi had gone through. Given their remote locations, they had only recently pieced together the aftermath from *The One*, culminating in her recent kidnapping.

But it was Gramps that kept her focused through it all. He had insisted on walking her down the "aisle"—a path to the point where Chase awaited her, by the old, curved pine.

And Dad had acquiesced, daring not to deny him anything, given his fragile health. Now he and Mom were likely ahead at the point too, along with Bea, Logan, Hannah, Mrs. Larson, and a handful of rangers.

Gramps was looking frail these days, but there was a sparkle in his eye that afternoon that made Adi smile all the broader. He looked good in his old, gray suit, even if it was a bit baggy.

"It's a good day, a fine day, Adi girl," he said, holding her hand in both of his. "You have made this old man very, very happy to see it come to pass."

"And I'm very, very happy you're here too, Gramps," she said.

"You look pretty as a picture," he said.

"Do you really think so?" she asked, looking down at her mail-ordered gown and white Keds.

"Prettiest girl I've seen in white," he said. Then, catching himself, added, "Besides your mother and grandmother of course."

"Of course," she said, taking his arm.

As they walked, she spied the first stone sculpture, a tower on her left, by the shore. And then an arch to her right. And then another tower. How long had Chase been out here this morning, working on them? Each one was like a bouquet tossed to her from her grandmother, a woman who had been married to her grandfather for sixty-some years. She smiled at Chase as he came into view, the lake behind him, gloriously still. Dressed in a charcoal-gray suit, he stood with his shoulders straight, hands clasped before him, legs slightly spread apart. Logan was to his left, Bea to his right, holding a small bouquet of late summer flowers, just as Adi was.

He grinned back at her and all she could see was him. Everyone else—her friends, her family—faded to black and white while Chase seemed to become deeply saturated with color.

He was a good man. A good and caring man. She had chosen well at last.

When they reached him, Gramps gave him a firm handshake and then pulled him close. "Take care of my girl, young man."

"Always and forever, sir," Chase said, grinning down at her.

Gramps patted him roughly on the shoulder, kissed Adi's cheek, then went to stand beside the others who formed a small circle around them. Adi took Chase's hands. "I like the sculptures," she whispered.

"Just some temporary miracles to make you smile," he whispered back. Together, they turned to the pastor who patiently waited on them.

And as Adi and Chase repeated the ancient vows, formally binding their lives together like their hearts had already been bound, she knew that this particular miracle—of finding true love at long last—was not temporary at all.

ACKNOWLEDGMENTS

Many, many thanks to Karen Barnett, author and former park ranger, who answered many of my questions on national-park life and ranger duties. My brother, Ryan Grosswiler, answered rifle and helicopter questions. Also to my editor, beta-readers and proofers: C.J. Darlington, Andrew and Debbie Spadzinski, Shaina Hawkins, Staci Murden, Melanie Stroud, Sharon Miles, Mindy Houng, Julie Graves, Mandi Warrick, Narelle Mollet, Betsy Hildebrand, Jaime Heller, Priyanka Desai, Annie Wilkinson, Alicia Miller, Julie Grant, Amanda Lamb and Margaret Nelson. I'm always startled by the fact that so many eyes can spot so many *different* errors—proving there is no such thing as an error-free work—you helped me make this a better book with your frank responses and encouragements. Thank you, thank you.

Dear Friend,

Once Upon a Montana Summer is the first in a series of stand-alone romances that will release in the coming years. I plan to write future titles that will be set in Scotland, Italy, California, the Caribbean—basically, anywhere I think is fabulous and romantic! If you'd like to know when I release a new novel, be sure to subscribe to my enewsletter at LisaTawnBergren.com. And if you enjoyed this book, please consider recommending it to others on Amazon, Barnes & Noble, Bookbub, goodreads and/or on social media. Nothing helps an author more than spreading the word about books you love!

Thanks for spending some of your precious reading time with me. I value you and your investment.

Every good thing,

Lisa

Also by Lisa T. Bergren

Breathe
Sing
Claim

Glamorous Illusions
Glittering Promises
Grave Consequences

Waterfall
Cascade
Torrent
Bourne & Tributary
Deluge

Remnants: Season of Wonder
Season of Fire
Season of Glory

Keturah
Verity (April 2019)
Selah (February 2020)